LENIN'S BRAIN

LENIN'S BRAIN

TILMAN SPENGLER

TRANSLATED BY

SHAUN WHITESIDE

FARRAR STRAUS GIROUX / NEW YORK

LIBRARY OF CONGRESS CATALOGING-IN-PUBLICATION DATA
Spengler, Tilman.
[Lenins Hirn. English]
Lenin's brain / Tilman Spengler ; translated by Shaun Whiteside.
p.   cm.
I. Title.
PT2681.P46L4613 1993 833'.914—dc20 93-17744 CIP

LENIN'S BRAIN

ONE

The assistant was alone when he stepped up to his teacher's corpse, it is said. The professor lay naked on the marble slab, which curved slightly inward toward the center. Between his calves, on which black dots had formed, there ran a little gully. As always, the dissection room smelled sickly-sweet, of formalin. A bright overhead light shone down on the little body, eyes peacefully closed. Those who had known him—and the assistant's first encounter with him had been more than twenty years ago—described the professor as dynamic and jovial, occasionally short-tempered. Now he just looked soft and vulnerable.

A nurse had laid out the instruments on the white wooden table beside the marble slab: scalpel and trephine, spatula and saw, hammer and chisel. The assistant pulled the rubber gloves over his long fingers, slowly stroked the front of his lab coat, and picked up the scalpel. With a few incisions he severed the scalp. As he carefully removed it from the top of the skull, the silence in the room was broken by a sharp, taut rasp, which sounded like a sausage being peeled. The assistant drew the scalp back behind his teacher's ears.

An hour later he had bored the requisite holes in the top of the skull, enlarged the openings with the hammer and chisel, and, applying a wire saw to the area between the holes, had mechanically sawed his way through the bones. As he removed the top of the skull, beads of sweat stood out on his forehead.

The professor's cerebral membrane glistened a reddish brown. The assistant, as he had been taught to do, severed the nerves and vessels, grabbed the brain with both hands, lifted it out, and placed it in the glass container holding the formaldehyde solution. Then he replaced the top of his professor's skull, pulled back the scalp, and sewed everything neatly back together.

Once again, Oskar Vogt looked soft and vulnerable. The assistant carried the brain into a side room. On his way he passed a bulletin board displaying news from the anatomy department. There was an announcement of his teacher's death. The thirty-first of July 1959, it read, had seen the end of a life of research that had begun on the sixth of April 1870.

T W O

As always when he had a terrible hangover, Max Landsberg thought about Fiebiger, the great Albert Fiebiger, who had trained him: perspective, color, proportions, transparency, architectonics. Fiebiger, known to his colleagues in Berlin, Marburg, and Leipzig as the Canaletto of the brain because he had painted such unsurpassed portraits of the convolutions and the frontal lobe, the vermis and the temporal bone. And his exquisite coloration: the tonalities, the gloomy color of brawn, the reddish-gray streaks, the white of the tissue in the frontal lobe, a rich, somewhat dull white, not to mention that unmistakable dark violet, or the subtle pink that he used to depict the thin-walled arteries. No, Fiebiger—and even those who envied him had to grant him this—Albert Fiebiger had earned every single leaf of the laurel crown that his pupils had awarded him the previous day, on the occasion of his sixtieth birthday.

For the past seven years, Fiebiger's birthday celebrations had coincided with that date in June 1888 on which Wilhelm II had ascended the throne as Emperor of Germany and King of Prussia. A mark of destiny, Landsberg claimed, as if a comet's tail had left in its wake an exclamation mark on a date that linked the genius of government with the genius of the paintbrush.

As always when he had a terrible hangover, Max Landsberg mixed his metaphors.

Fiebiger was, of course, able to sleep in after a night like that. He, the great success, who received the great men of the scientific world in his studio in Rothenburg, was not a mere practitioner; he was an artistic adviser. Privy Councillor and Professor Flechsig, whose book *The Brain and the Soul* Fiebiger had illustrated, had even mentioned this in his preface, while Professor Zweifel, also of Leipzig, not only had allowed him to record scientific matters but had also commissioned him to paint an allegorical portrait, depicting the professor as a knight in shining armor impaling a monster resembling a salamander; around its neck it wore a yellow ribbon, emblazoned with the word *Ignorantia*. This picture was later, in fact, transferred to a brightly colored stained-glass window. It adorned Zweifel's study in the tower of his villa in the Kling-engasse, and was also available as a full-color picture postcard.

As always when he had a terrible hangover, Max Landsberg felt that the breakfast waiter was not giving him the attention due a guest who orders a glass of sparkling wine first thing in the morning.

Comparing himself to his famous teacher, he, Landsberg, could boast only his talent as a rapid chronicler of events. Nobody—and no less a figure than the surgeon Fedor Krause had assured him of this—could sketch an operation as swiftly without in the process disturbing the course of events. Spaltholz of Jena—Landsberg had captured his virtuoso excision of an abscess of the temporal lobe —had been similarly enthusiastic. Another grateful party was Se-lenka of Munich, who operated so slowly that Landsberg had been able to complete a souvenir painting of his godchild, the sixteen-year-old Amanda von Alvensleben, at the same time. He placed the portrait an inch to the left under a bone flap the size of a plum. Thus Amanda was gazing up with wide-open eyes—a shade of brown that Landsberg had exaggerated ever so slightly, giving it a reddish hue—like an adoring cherub, into a pale and gaping skull with a moustache. The painter had originally intended to place a lily between her slim hands, crossed over her breast, but then Selenka had suddenly started chiseling and sawing away so quickly that Landsberg was obliged to take refuge in routine, and gave her, instead of a flower, a brain spatula.

The waiter brought the bill. Landsberg picked up his apron and the little satchel in which he kept his painting equipment. His hands were at rest now, his sketchpad wedged between his chest and his upper arm; beneath his soft artist's hat his brow flushed with excitement. "A new expedition," Landsberg said to the cab-drivers who crossed his path, to the paperboys who were already selling the noon editions, to the housekeepers running their errands. But no one paid any attention to him.

He had borrowed the word "expedition" from young Dr. Vogt. It seemed to him to convey precisely the feeling that stirred in him as he fought down the nausea brought on by the pungent, sickly smell in the operating theater, as he regained his composure, as he felt the pen in his hand, willing and disciplined, obediently carrying out his every command. "Expedition": It was not only the challenge to keep one's nerve at the moment when sharp blades penetrated soft matter; it was also the eagerness to learn new things, to be present, just as painters had once accompanied explorers on their travels.

At the gates of the clinic in west Berlin, Landsberg bumped into Vogt and felt an urge to tell him his idea. "A journey, not into the world," he cried, "but through the cataracts and the convolutions, past the abysses of evil and genius."

"Don't slack off," Vogt said, holding the heavy door open for him.

A demonstration was announced: Slobodskoy, recommended by the great Bechterev, wanted to show his German colleagues how an operation on the cerebral cortex could eliminate the symptoms of epilepsy. This demonstration ought to have taken place weeks ago, but the original patient intended for it had died unexpectedly, and the search for a suitable replacement had proved unusually difficult. It was not until a Berlin jury had condemned forty-three-year-old Otto Tischke to death for the robbery and murder of the barmaid Frieda Ruhpieper that the doctors' hopes were raised again. Tischke, it was learned during the trial, suffered from epilepsy of the affections, a condition which the court did not consider to be a mitigating circumstance since witnesses reported that he had been "as cold as a fish" when carrying out the deed.

"I don't give a damn whether I go now or later," Tischke had answered when they offered him improved prison conditions in return for a postponement of the execution if he would make his body, and later, if appropriate, his corpse, available for purposes of scientific research.

Vogt greeted his colleagues outside the operating theater. Bielschowsky, Brodmann, and Schweninger had arrived together and were talking about the patients they had previously examined for mental defects. Schweninger, physician to Bismarck, Krupp, and Cosima Wagner, was leading the discussion.

"A clear case of mumbling epilepsy. Did you notice how he was constantly chattering to himself?"

"And with a surprisingly intact speech pattern, although with a considerable tendency toward compulsive joking."

"My diagnosis exactly. When I asked him how he was, he kept saying: 'Damned good.' "

"Compulsive joking, you see?"

"Perhaps with a tendency to schizophrenia?"

"It's certainly a possibility. When I said, 'I don't know if it's struck you . . .' he said, 'I've been struck often enough.' "

"Forel would infer *épilepsie marmottante*, a form of alcoholic epilepsy."

"I don't suppose Forel's arrived?"

The group looked at Vogt, who had invited the famous neurologist from Switzerland. The previous spring Vogt had been his guest in Zürich-Burghölzli, and had extended the customary return invitation three months later.

"I hope he hasn't forgotten our appointment," said Vogt. "Last year in Zürich he completely forgot that he'd invited me. And he'd also forgotten the cerebral defect that occurs when the corpus callosum is absent. And when I told him, he tried to correct me."

August Forel had not forgotten; he had slept in. He had not slept in like an ordinary mortal, however, but had nodded off again after his morning coffee, which he took, as always, at four on the dot. He had even had, as he immediately confided in his diary, a wonderful and faintly exciting dream, at the center of which was Crown Princess Luise of Saxony. A few weeks earlier, to the delight of the court in Dresden, she had run off with her private tutor. In a scientific report, Forel was to declare her "uninhibitedly instinctual," a judgment that was to play an important part in the certification proceedings then under way, and which would throw the line of dynastic succession into confusion. This report should in fact have been completed in the early hours of the day, when Forel's intellectual concentration was at its peak; the lawyers and the Crown Judiciary in Dresden were awaiting with the greatest excitement the scientific basis for a political decision that had been taken long before.

Forel's dream brought the legal process to a temporary halt. He had, he recalled, been eating—and perhaps picking?—morels with the princess. Either way, they had both put their hands on a ladder, and the princess had laughed and had jokingly said that she wasn't afraid of blemished fruit. At this point the dream became all too clear to Forel, and he woke up. Fantasies of omnipotence, he had thought, sighing, and then he had gone back to sleep and found himself in a sleigh with the princess, traveling through a countryside in which snowmen plucked the carrots out of their faces and waved them at the pair. The movement of the sleigh, in fact, was more like that of a coach on soft cobblestones, with an agreeable shaking motion, constant but gentle.

When Forel opened his eyes he realized that this movement had been produced by his secretary, who was gently shaking his right shoulder.

"The operation is scheduled for eight-thirty."

It took Forel only a few seconds to distinguish dream from reality.

"Leave out my gray suit and a hat to go with it."

Afraid that his late arrival might jeopardize an experiment that required the most intense concentration, Forel entered the operating theater by a side door. To his relief, the only person there was Max Landsberg, who was coloring in three studies, on a sketchpad, of the remarkably flat nose of the Russian guest surgeon.

"Is it all over?" asked Forel anxiously.

"It hasn't even started yet," said Landsberg, without looking up from his pad. He had turned to a new page and was trying to recall the wings of Amanda von Alvensleben's nose.

"A lovely picture of Crown Princess Luise," said Forel, unable to shake off his dream. Between his bushy beard and moustache his lips parted as he smiled, or rather, thought Landsberg, who had been unable to stand moustaches and beards ever since his portrait classes at the Kunstakademie in Munich: He's lifting his snout and dropping his chin-rug. To his regret, he had burst out laughing when Forel had mentioned the name of the crown princess. Not an amused or, worse, a superior snigger, but a great guffaw from the depths of his belly. The Swiss gentleman took a few steps closer, sniffed like an officious supervisor at Landsberg's breath, which still reeked of sparkling wine, and, with remarkable offhandedness, laid an invitation to his lecture on the influence of alcoholism on racial devaluation and racial improvement next to the artist's sketchpad. The lecture was to take place at a gathering of the Knights Templar, to be held the same evening in a meetinghouse in north Berlin. Admission, the invitation stressed, was free.

Landsberg took his revenge by drawing Forel as Diogenes in a beer barrel, not only mercilessly transforming the already sparse hair on the back of Forel's head into a completely blank surface but also suggesting a syphilitic bulge in the skull, which he emphasized with a red pencil. Then he concentrated once again on the wings of Amanda von Alvensleben's nose.

Meanwhile, Forel had joined the group around Vogt in the vestibule. He was relieved to find that he was not the last, but only the second-to-last of their number. Slobodskoy was still speaking to the patient, and Paul Flechsig was nowhere to be seen.

Vogt described the situation in the minutes with barely disguised malice: "The trepanation of the patient"—he corrected himself—"of the well-prepared patient was delayed while the assembled colleagues waited for Professor Flechsig to arrive."

"The expert's responsibility in the difficult matter of the emotional life," August Forel began abruptly, shrugging his shoulders as if to shake off grasshoppers on either side, "can be assumed only by the boldest of men. Consider the power that is placed in our hands, and consider how close we are to the abyss of error!"

"Only if we get into such a position," whispered Brodmann into the right ear of his colleague Vogt.

"It will happen," said Forel, who had extraordinarily good hearing.

Flechsig had delayed his arrival not because being a bit late has always been a way to assert one's status, but because he was simply unsure whether his sense of honor would allow him to meet Vogt in public, so to speak, even if only within the context of a scientific demonstration. Everyone knew, in the end, that Vogt had quite clearly and openly attacked him because of his, Vogt claimed, "both profound and profoundly disillusioned understanding of the efficacy of the myelogenetic method." It was Flechsig himself who had encouraged the young Vogt to work on fibrous systems and the medullary development of infant brains. And then this Brutus had had the gall to bring into disrepute the research strategy of the very man who had encouraged him.

"A stab in the back," said Flechsig's loyal pupils.

"In the medulla oblongata, to be precise," his colleagues joked.

The argument had only intensified, shrilly and dramatically, a few weeks earlier. Flechsig informed his colleagues on the faculty that he was not prepared to confer lecturer status on his former pupil. He had also indicated that he would protest most vehemently if any of those colleagues were to take the necessary steps to grant Vogt the *venia legendi*. This applied not only to Leipzig or Berlin but to all the renowned medical faculties within the Reich.

In reply, Vogt had immediately attacked Flechsig. Not only scientifically—the related works and annotated contributions to the debate were already in existence—no, Vogt went straight for his social honor. Flechsig was a "pathological thief of intellectual property," Vogt had said before witnesses. And added that he was in a position to supply the relevant proof at any time. "I simply see more quickly, more clearly, and more contextually than other people" was one of the statements he made that went the rounds with a speed otherwise reserved for rumors concerning academic appointments.

In other circles people would have challenged one another to pistols at dawn for much less, but the two adversaries felt that such rituals were beneath them.

"The progress of medical knowledge will vindicate me," said Flechsig. "Academic parvenus need to be taught manners. For their own sake and for the sake of science."

"He may still head committees," Vogt announced, "but first of all, his sight is failing, and second, there will come a time when science is governed by powers that value creative will and creative courage more highly than appeals to past merits."

Flechsig turned up at this point, of course. The burning curiosity of the specialist had triumphed over any tactical considerations. Perhaps the Russian would indeed accomplish something. Admittedly Flechsig didn't think it very likely, he had attended too many similar operations for that; but the diabolical thing about science was that old certainties always turned out to be fragile, and if a victory was to take place today, then one would be an eyewitness, miles ahead of all those people who would only be able to read of the event in a "provisional note" in a medical journal. And apart from anything else, this was his very own hunting ground; a Flechsig couldn't be put down so easily. At worst the thing would be a failure. And that wouldn't be his fault.

Flechsig greeted his colleagues with the quickest of bows and without a word of apology.

Otto Tischke already lay strapped to the operating table when the gentlemen assembled around him. Beneath the bright lights of the lamps little pearls of sweat gleamed on his shaved head. With a pen Slobodskoy had marked the points where the drill was to be applied, and drawn the lines along which the saw would run.

"Robust constitution," Schweninger said appreciatively at the sight of the patient's biceps and abdomen.

Slobodskoy stepped up to a blackboard and explained in a few sentences how he intended to proceed with his operation. Then silence fell. When Landsberg heard that sound which always called to mind the woodwork classes he had been forced to attend as a child, he reached for his pen.

"I saw the collapse before the hyperventilation set in," Vogt declared two hours later. "The circulation could not bear the shock, the blood pressure dropped, voilà . . ."

They had sat down to a late breakfast of herring, venison pâté, a few crabs, nothing extravagant. Out of consideration for Forel they drank lemonade. The only people missing from the group that had attended the failed demonstration were Flechsig, who had stormed off without a word, Slobodskoy, who wanted to be alone, out of anger or despair at his failure, and of course Otto Tischke, whose corpse was being prepared in the anatomy department.

"Who does the brain actually belong to?"

"The next of kin, which in this case is the court."

"I'd very much like to examine it," said Vogt. "From the psychopathological point of view, as is well known, the brain contains formations which in certain circumstances encourage a developmental process leading to criminality, and in other circumstances an analogous dynamic process leading to genius. Both forms are extremely interesting when it comes to analyzing the correspondences between the life of matter and the life of the mind. Particularly at a time like ours, when there is a general shortage of elite brains available for scientific research—at a time, and we all know to what I refer, that has seen a considerable increase in imbecility."

The gentlemen nodded thoughtfully and picked up their lemonades.

THREE

The slim woman, her blond hair plaited into a diadem, was lying on an ottoman with a brocade cover ending in a wine-colored fringe. At its foot stood two fashionable boots, their medium-sized heels facing one another. The woman's breathing was heavy, almost a wheeze, and her eyes were closed.

One of the two men in the semidarkness of the room walked up to her. He raised his right hand and lowered it over one of her bare, outstretched forearms without touching her.

"You feel quite peaceful," he said slowly and emphatically, "quite peaceful and relaxed. I shall now count to ten, and then you will feel nothing but blissful peace."

He began to count, his hand gliding up and down over her arm. "Now you can feel nothing."

The patient opened her eyes. "Just you stroking me. It's like a pleasant breeze wafting across my chest."

Vogt turned around abruptly. "We will have to make a note of that." He straightened up and dictated: "After the first hypnotic intervention, remarkably high level of affective resistance." Then he bent once more over the woman on the ottoman. "I shall now count backwards from ten, and order you to go to sleep immediately."

The patient folded her arms across her chest. She was now breathing regularly.

An hour later Vogt had corrected and signed his notes on the session. His assistant had already left to deliver tested remedies for insomnia to two or three addresses. The only reminders of the slim, blond woman were the notes and her perfume, which vaguely reminded Vogt of a city, perhaps Paris, or London, or even Berlin. He walked to the window and looked into the street. Solemnly dressed pedestrians were walking calmly to the Kursaal. That evening and the following two evenings, concerts were being given in Alexandersbad by a visiting Russian pianist who had already caused something of a stir in Nuremberg and Meiningen.

"In the fast passages, like the ones between the Eighteenth and Twenty-second Variations, he played a very clean, even almost bony *martellato*," said Amanda von Alvensleben, taking out her hatpin. "During those parts I was able to stop thinking about his forehead, which was just as negligible as his chin. I didn't like the slower parts quite as much. My piano teacher would have said, 'He's being a bit too cloying there.' I felt he was creeping up on the new chords with false *rubati*, at least some of the time. I don't know if that's a good way of doing justice to Bach. I couldn't see very well because the lady in the row in front of me was wearing a sort of tulle frigate on her head, but it sounded as if he was using a lot of left-hand pedal. It may just have been the acoustics. But for a spa concert, I thought it was an eminently notable performance. Now I can almost imagine I smell the asters I arranged for you this afternoon. As if all one's senses were sensitive simultaneously, and as active as bloodhounds. It really is a shame that your nerves didn't allow you to attend this entertainment. But what a shame, what a shame about those false *rubati*."

"Please don't be so technical," Margarethe Krupp asked. She was lying in her bed like a fairy-tale character who doesn't exactly know the ending of her story yet, but knows that it isn't going to be happy. "Technical matters only make my nerves all the worse. Tell me instead what the atmosphere was like, whom you met, who asked after me. And please close the curtains a little more tightly."

Amanda von Alvensleben got up and walked to the window. "Night darkens the room," she said casually. "No, the light will certainly not irritate you tomorrow. After the concert the Cronbergs invited me to dine with them in the Grosses Restaurant tomorrow—if that suits you. I met Councillor Haniel, he still seems very reserved. Most of the people we know from last year, Frau von Cronberg told me, are still taking the cure, and are not leaving for post-treatment until the weekend." She carefully opened her handbag and felt around for a little praline. She silently removed the wrapping, and a few seconds later her tongue pressed the chocolate into her palate.

"Your liking for sweets is a bad habit," said Margarethe Krupp. "And it is decidedly foolish of you to try and keep it a secret from me."

"Some people claimed they could even smell chrysanthemums," Amanda continued, without responding to this objection, "I'm fascinated by these matters of the sensual life. On the way home a lieutenant tried to court me, from a Baden regiment to judge by his uniform. But I paid no attention to him."

Frau Krupp struck her blankets with the palm of her hand. "It's high time my brother was here. I expect that lieutenant was the same one who left a bouquet for you downstairs. Such impertinence! And a visiting card! Amanda, I think you might show a little more dignity, not to mention reticence. Particularly in a spa town like Alexandersbad. I can't bear the idea of people talking about my companion." Frau Krupp's voice now had something of that bony *martellato* which Amanda had mentioned in her account of the concert. "And nobody gives so much as a thought to my nose—my nerves, I mean."

Amanda von Alvensleben pushed the carafe of water closer to the bed and looked around for the little bottle of smelling salts. She could barely make out anything but silhouettes in the room, where the only light came from a shaded candle.

"You know I could never intentionally subject you to such torments," she said softly, "but idiocies on the part of young officers on their summer holidays are not within my jurisdiction—within the jurisdiction of our War Ministry, perhaps. But at the moment they're more concerned with all the continents you can think of than with what happens in Alexandersbad. Frau von Cronberg also informed me, by the way, that a new doctor has just taken up office this season, a specialist from Berlin, clearly an eminent authority on nervous ailments. Privy Councillor Haniel is already being treated by him, Frau von Cronberg said, and so is Frau Wiendorff, who caused such a sensation here last year with her operetta arias and—"

"I can't bear gossip!" Frau Krupp interrupted.

"I was really only going to talk about her singing. Anyway, Professor Binswanger holds his young colleague in the highest esteem. He studied hypnosis with Forel. Forel from Zürich, who they say is as brilliant as he is forgetful."

"And does he have a name, this new miracle doctor?"

"Frau von Cronberg told me his name, but I shall have to try and remember. Something very short—Vogt, I think."

"My temples have been troubling me so all day, I may have to call him tomorrow. Good night, my dear. Please make sure the door is firmly closed when you leave my room. Last night there was such a brouhaha in the corridor, as if a whole battalion had been marching past. I had to take two grams of bromide to get back to sleep. It was very late by the time they took effect. And do check that the maids really are alone in their rooms. I didn't like the way the bath attendant was looking at our Elsa, and I liked even less the way Elsa looked back at him."

A quarter of an hour later Amanda von Alvensleben had performed her tasks. Elsa and Frauke were giggling in their room when she wished them good night, but there was no sign of bath attendants, or of any other men.

At the front desk, Amanda was handed her admirer's flowers in a smoked crystal vase. They were eleven long-stemmed carnations of a pink that reminded Amanda disagreeably of inflamed mucous membranes. She took Lieutenant Most's handwritten request to see her by the Stollwerck advertisement at eleven o'clock the next morning, and threw it in the wastepaper basket under her writing desk. Next to the wastepaper basket she placed the crystal vase with the carnations.

The night air streaming through the open window smelled sharp, strong, and terribly penetrating. Amanda took off her boots, skirt, and blouse. Her black shantung silk dressing gown rustled as she put it on. In the top drawer of her writing desk she found the sheet of paper that she had only half filled that morning. She glanced at the tip of her silver fountain pen, jabbed it into the bottle of violet ink, and covered the paper to its nethermost edge. She didn't stop until the pen began to scratch.

A draft swelled the checkered curtains, sending them into crazed motion. Amanda von Alvensleben leaned back and hummed a tune that she remembered only because of its lyrics: "Such is the value of a hospitable roof . . ." She lay down on the bed and contentedly breathed in the smell of the freshly washed sheets. Then she reached into her bedside-table drawer and pulled out a little red lacquer box adorned with a Japanese character. With her thumb and little finger she picked out the opium pill, briefly rubbed it around her mouth like a lipstick, and bit into it.

Vogt sat at a heavy oak desk and looked with satisfaction at the beautiful young woman whom the maid had ushered into the consultation room. He rose and pointed to the lilac velvet-covered chair where patients sat in a light most favorable to the doctor.

"I am here on behalf of a friend," Amanda von Alvensleben began. "She insists that her name should not be mentioned at this point, as she has not yet agreed a consultation with her husband . . ."

"You can rely on my discretion."

"Please do not construe it as suspicion on my part if I concede to my friend's request. She wants me to ask about the general odds of the hypnotic method effecting a cure for complaints that sometimes take the form of severe headaches, and sometimes of anxious states of emotional tension."

Vogt scribbled the key words on a calendar. Then he looked expectantly at Amanda, but she said nothing.

"You are not exactly making things easy for me, my dear lady, and my answer will have to be every bit as general as your description. First of all, then: I would suggest to your friend that she undergo a thorough organic examination, to discover whether her headaches might derive from causes other than her emotional condition. Second: In my opinion and the opinion of my colleagues Hilger and Ringier, hypnosis is suitable as a therapy for a whole range of symptoms—from insomnia and states of weakness, certain addiction-related illnesses, hysteria, epilepsy, and compulsive disorders, to melancholia. I am unable to judge which of these applies to your friend."

Amanda looked up from her notebook. "You speak almost as though you knew my friend," she said drily.

"Which is certainly not the case, for if she knew me I'm sure she would have had the confidence to contact me personally. Which would, however, have deprived me of the great pleasure of meeting you. I must also add that according to statistics, male patients are easier to hypnotize than females. But that may have something to do with the fact that a woman is subject to stronger defense mechanisms in the presence of an unfamiliar doctor. Personally, may I say, I have encountered this problem only very rarely." Vogt threw Amanda a glance intended to express both irony and impudence. "Another uncertain factor lies in the patient's age. According to received opinion, the ages between one and twenty are the most receptive to hypnosis. The subsequent twenty years, on the other hand, display a greater inclination to resistance. We might also speak in terms of increasing skepticism, were it not the case that in the last years of life the likelihood of success increases once again."

"Perhaps patients become more trusting as they approach death?" suggested Amanda.

"I would prefer to put it this way: In old age their imagination does not have such rigid boundaries. The doctor's work is naturally easiest with creative people and members of the lower classes." Vogt looked thoughtfully at his letter opener for a moment, and then back into Amanda's brown eyes.

"Let me guess," cried Amanda, "artists because they believe everything, and the lower classes because they have to believe everything."

Vogt laughed. "You have an enviable gift for simplification. Enchanting! My professional colleagues might put it rather differently, however. And as we are now talking almost as if we were colleagues, would you like to know how we classify the depths of hypnosis?"

"There's something that interests me much more: Would the patient be alone with you during the treatment?"

"I could take that as an insult, but I shall assume that you are asking out of solicitous curiosity. No, if it matters to her she can bring along a person whom she trusts. In the case of your friend, should it come to a course of hypnosis, I should feel extremely honored if you, my dear lady, would personally undertake that role."

Amanda stood up and smoothed her skirt. "I have robbed you of much of your valuable time without giving you any concrete hope of a case for treatment. Thank you very much indeed for the insights that you have given me."

She held out her right hand to Vogt. The doctor seized it and made as if to kiss it.

"Are you interested in bumblebees?" he asked suddenly when she had already reached the door.

"Bumblebees?"

"You know, stone bumblebees, field bumblebees, and what have you."

"Why would I be interested in bumblebees?"

"A sudden inspiration of mine. I have studied bumblebees since I was a child. If you feel the inclination, I could show you my bumblebee collection. Or we could consider the creatures together, in the countryside."

"I shall be in touch the minute I—how did you put it?—feel the inclination. Farewell!"

Margarethe Krupp and Amanda von Alvensleben were lunching on the terrace. The heavy awnings cast shadows.

"Veal cutlets, I love veal cutlets," cried Frau Krupp when the waiter had brought them their food. "Veal cutlets are splendid!"

Amanda resumed her story: "And right at the end he asked me if I was interested in bumblebees."

"Bumblebees?"

"I was rather surprised as well. Clearly bumblebees are his passion. He studies them, and he collects them."

"I don't see anything so extraordinary about that. Bertha collects butterflies, and my husband, if I have understood correctly, collects sea horses. Classification, Fritz once said, means learning nature's vocabulary."

The waiter brought dessert.

"Raspberry ice cream, I love raspberry ice cream," cried Frau Krupp. "Raspberry ice cream is really something special."

The two ladies picked up their little silver spoons.

"And there's something of the bumblebee about the man himself," Amanda continued. "In his appearance first of all. It has to be said, his face is somewhat overgrown, with a black velvet beard sprouting everywhere a beard can possibly grow. But I don't just mean outwardly. Although there is something sturdy and burly in his build. No, I'm thinking of the stubborn energy that he communicated to me, that sense of harnessed implacability."

Frau Krupp's expression betrayed implacability of the purest kind. "Amanda, you seem to have had extraordinarily intense dealings with this young doctor."

Amanda smiled. "I'm only trying to describe to you where I think his strength as a hypnotist lies. I consider it my duty, if I may put it this way, as your medical scout."

"And would you, in this role, recommend him to me?"

"My governess always told me that bumblebees were a manifestation of the soul. It was a superstition where she came from.

I was suddenly reminded of it. It had something or other to do with witchcraft. If a woman in the village died and the neighbors or the vicar thought she was a witch, they would say a bumblebee had risen from her body. And then they covered the corpse so that the bumblebee couldn't find its way back in."

"Does that mean that this Dr. Vogt puts you in mind of some sort of warlock?"

"Certainly of somebody who has a good understanding of souls."

"So you would advise me to entrust myself to him?"

"Only if the pressure of your suffering, as Dr. Vogt would put it, deems this to be necessary."

As if by some secret agreement, two waiters had appeared behind the two ladies. They pulled out the chairs just as the skirts left them.

"Ask Dr. Vogt whether an appointment for a consultation here tomorrow afternoon would suit him," said Margarethe Krupp on the top step. "The governess has been instructed to accompany Bertha and Martha on an outing with a team of donkeys. We shall leave the rest of the day to take its course. Of course I should have liked to speak to Fritz about this matter, but the state of my nerves leaves me no choice, any more than Fritz, to all appearances, has a choice between his obligations to the company and his obligations to the family."

Elsa, the maid in charge of laundry and sewing, was standing by the ironing board when Amanda entered the room. To the hiss of the iron she sang a song that she had been taught by Knipp, the bath attendant:

> *Balancez, dance away,*
> *Rieke dances all the day.*
> *Stepping on each other's toes,*
> *That is how the pleasure grows.*

And she swayed her hips like a swingboat.

"Elsa, please get the silk train for the gray skirt ready. And the bright green petticoat."

Elsa turned around in surprise and curtsied. "When will Madame require them?"

"Late this afternoon."

Elsa curtsied again. "But of course. I've already prepared the new corset and put it in your room."

Before Amanda had closed the door she heard Elsa again snorting with laughter. Then the maid continued:

> *That's where Rieke waits for me,*
> *That is where the pleasures be,*
> *Rieke, Riekchen, Riek-a-kay,*
> *And a bit of whay-hay-hay . . .*

Amanda shut the door with a loud slam. Why she should have reacted this way was not clear even to Amanda herself.

Vogt used his late-afternoon tea break to scan a painstaking report by the American brain researcher Samuel P. Hunter, which he had been sent from Berlin along with a letter from the Prussian cultural authorities. Hunter had, as his colleagues had gathered at a number of conferences, examined the question of the growth or shrinkage of the interior of the human skull in the context of cultural history. Hunter was racking his brains over the fact that these changes, statistically recorded with such precision, did not run parallel with the intellectual history of world civilization.

Admittedly the interiors of the skulls of the Egyptians, as bones from various sites attested, had significantly declined over the millennia. This comforted some academics, because the development was apparent in real historical terms, given that Egyptian civilization had passed its peak. It was also clear—the files of several generations of Paris milliners left no doubt about it—that the circumference of the heads of Parisians and thus their cranial cavities had grown since the French Revolution. Here, too, conclusions could be drawn about a correspondence between anatomy and cultural progress. But how was it possible to explain the greater volumes found among the Chinese, New Guinea bushwomen, and even the population of North Hessen?

In many previous works Hunter had clearly demonstrated that his methodology was beyond reproach. He had not, of course, fallen into the elementary error of using the absolute weights of brains to support his theories. In those terms, the elephant and the whale were far superior to Homo sapiens. Nor had he been guilty of proceeding from Aristotle's hypothesis concerning the relationship between brain and body weight. For that suggested that the thought capacities of the common sparrow, not to mention the various kinds of apes, were far superior to those of the European woman, who came out ahead of the mole and even further ahead of the European man.

Vogt read with increasing irritation, two red patches darkening rapidly above his beard. He threw the offprint into the wastepaper basket and once more scanned the accompanying letter from the Berlin authorities.

"Red wine!" he shouted suddenly. "Brodmann, bring the red wine! Let us drink to the burial of our project and to the erection of another cathedral of brain research. The interior of the skull! That's what they want to promote now, the gentlemen in Berlin. Presumably edicts have already been issued to the military authorities to record the sizes of all the Prussian spiked helmets, strictly divided according to social class and national origin, of course."

Brodmann took a bottle of red wine that had already been opened and pulled out the cork with his teeth. "Could there be anything, anything drearier? Our life's work ruined by the skull's interior!" he said, after he had spat out the cork.

Two glasses later Vogt screwed the letter into a ball, which he solemnly placed on his head. Brodmann picked up the cork and took aim at the paper ball.

"Forgive me for simply marching in," said Amanda von Alvensleben when she walked into the room. "The door was ajar and I heard your voices. I know that appearances contradict me, but I had no intention either of disturbing you or even of eavesdropping. And you are criminally unprotected, gentlemen. The porter's lodge has an emptiness that the word 'yawning' is inadequate to describe. My friend has asked me to give you this letter, Dr. Vogt, and— if this is not impertinent—to bring back a reply immediately."

Vogt got up so quickly that his thighs bumped into the edge of the table. The red wine began to thrash wildly in the glasses.

"My dear lady, I am overcome," he said after he had kissed Amanda's glove, "overcome first of all because of the miserable reception accorded you by our staff, and secondly because of the impression that we must be making upon you." He made a gesture that might have taken into account the loose knot of his tie, the wine bottle, or the crumpled piece of paper that had unfolded maliciously so that the letterhead was visible.

"My colleague Brodmann and I"—Brodmann hastened to bow deeply—"may look at present as though we were inclined to in-dulge in early-evening alcoholic excesses, but appearances de-ceive."

"I would not necessarily classify a bottle of Bordeaux, two-thirds empty, as an alcoholic excess," said Amanda. "Forgive me, I'm talking as a medical laywoman. My late father used to enjoy cham-pagne at this time of day. White if there was something to cele-brate, and red if there was bad news."

"Your father, in his choice of colors, captured our mood exactly." Vogt tidied up his tie and shirtfront. Then he picked up his letter opener, carefully placed the envelope on the writing pad, and precisely applied the blade to the extreme right-hand edge.

"Margarethe Krupp, _née_ Baroness von Ende, requests a consul-tation from Dr. Vogt," he read. Vogt made a bow that was meant both for the letter and for Amanda. "Please be so kind as to arrange a time and place."

Amanda picked up her bag. "Your choice of words shows no sign of weakness." She wrote the name of the hotel, the requested time, and the room number on her visiting card.

Vogt and Frau Krupp's first meeting occurred much earlier than arranged, just an hour after Amanda's visit to the spa doctor's office, thanks to the letter the industrialist's wife had received in the evening mail.

"She gave such a piercing shriek," said Elsa, the maid, "and then Madame was suddenly lying flat on her back."

He had been called at most two minutes, or possibly even one minute, later, the hotel doctor said, and the good lady was lying on the carpet, a crumpled letter in her hand, motionless, certainly, but with her eyes open. Fräulein von Alvensleben had then sent for the spa doctor, Dr. Vogt. The hotel doctor had provisionally diagnosed a nervous breakdown. As was well known, nerves were as sensitive as glass vials. Frau Krupp, as the press had reported, had spent a lot of time traveling by train and coach over the last few days, and it was clear that certain mechanical vibrations had invaded her mental state. Dr. Vogt had countered this diagnosis, however . . .

As far as primary care was concerned, the two doctors agreed; Vogt ordered Elsa to unlace her mistress's corset while he felt for her pulse and called for sal volatile. Then Frau Krupp was laid on a nearby sofa and covered with a light blanket to prevent a chill.

"I think she needs peace and quiet now," said the hotel doctor.

"A performer needs applause," Vogt contradicted him, "or else the performance loses its meaning." He sent the other people from the room.

"In half an hour he understood me better than Fritz ever has in all the years of our marriage," Frau Krupp said to Amanda von Alvensleben before she went to bed. "Tomorrow evening I shall have him hypnotize me. One must risk something new and unusual from time to time. Of course, I am not quite free of anxiety, but on the other hand I feel an urge to be independent. And anyway, you will be by my side the entire time."

F O U R

Returning from his consultation, Oskar Vogt carefully washed his hands, as he had grown accustomed to doing regardless of whether he had been treating the body or the mind. Then he threw the white bath towel with which he had dried himself into the wicker hamper, took off his top hat, grasped the knot of his tie, and looked intently at his face in the bathroom mirror.

"Krupp," he said to the reflection, pronouncing the name as he had in childhood, before the teacher in Husum—and later his fellow students—had eradicated his strong North German accent. "Krupp," he repeated, "Krupp, Krupp, and thrice Krupp."

He took off his monocle, allowed the contours of his face in the mirror to swim away for a moment, replaced his monocle, and stared into the intense grayish blue of his eyes.

"Steely gray," he cried, lapsing once more into his native accent, "steely gray, or maybe steely blue, or best of all, steely bluish gray." His sharp North German *s* rose like a kite.

He finished inspecting the color of his eyes with a brief twitch of the head. Then he took a few paces back, but kept his eyes fixed on the mirror. When his back touched the wardrobe door he stopped and ran his hand over his head, continuing in a straight line across the top of the wardrobe. It was not a tall wardrobe.

"You are now twenty-six years of age," Vogt announced to the mirror. "As your medical adviser I must insist that you abandon all hopes of any increase in your height. But even Rumpelstiltskin accomplished great things." He recalled the chorus of a song that had been popular in Berlin two or three years before. Vogt beat out the rhythm on the cupboard wall.

> *Wardrobes and tallboys,*
> *What the hell, let's make some noise,*
> *You're my sweet Ge-no-ve-va,*
> *But I've got a* je ne sais quoi . . .

The first time he had heard the song he had been with his teacher, Flechsig, at a faculty party in the Hasenheide. At every repetition of the chorus, Flechsig had slapped himself on the thighs and then slapped Vogt on the head. The second or third time, his cigar had jumped from his thin lips, like a ripe fruit from its pod. Flechsig had snorted, ruffled Vogt's hair again, and said, apropos of nothing at all, "Every burly man is a bit of a Don Juan, and I can see that holds for you." And teacher and pupil had laughed.

F I V E

The sun, high up in the sky, cast silhouettes of the tips of pine trees on the lonely forest path. The two strollers were walking some distance apart, thus displaying a degree of formality but also a strong mutual interest. The man was carrying the jacket of his light-colored suit over his shoulder, the woman's white umbrella was unopened. She turned her head toward her companion.

". . . and another tremendous example was the celebrated Hansen's hypnosis experiment," said Vogt, cheerfully beheading a solitary thistle with his walking stick. "That was sometime toward the end of the eighties in one of the most elegant theaters in St. Petersburg. One of Bechterev's people told me about it. Imagine if you will: For weeks the city has been celebrating the famous Hansen, who promises to introduce society to mesmerism or magnetism or whatever they called it. There are posters everywhere, in the salons no one is talking about anything else, little blabbermouths are making self-important and cryptic observations, in short, the city is in a fever, which is the ideal starting point for any hypnotist worth his salt—"

"Just a moment, please," Amanda von Alvensleben interrupted him. "Could we walk at a more comfortable pace, and would you explain to me who Herr Bechterev is? He keeps popping up in your stories and I have never dared to ask you, but in the meantime he seems to be accompanying us like the star of Bethlehem or, to be more in keeping with our natural surroundings, we are following him as Siegfried followed the forest bird."

Vogt stopped and clutched his straw hat. "Bechterev," he said solemnly, "is one of the truly great men in my field. A natural researcher, endlessly ambitious, a man of unstinting hard work and the most precise powers of observation. Bechterev can see things, scientifically speaking—he sees things before other people do."

Amanda unbuttoned her gloves. "Back to St. Petersburg," she asked, "back to the famous Hansen."

Vogt put his straw hat back on. "The theater is full to the very last seat. The ladies are exquisitely attired, the gentlemen similarly turned out. Then a band plays, the master of ceremonies takes the stage, and in wild French he announces the evening's attractions. Polite applause, and from the wings comes the famous Hansen. He talks a little about the mysterious powers of the mind, of somnambulists, constantly stressing the importance of the rapport between the magnetist and his charges, and finally invites willing gentlemen from the audience onto the stage."

Vogt walked a few steps alongside Amanda, made a hint of a bow, and bent his right arm as if asking her to dance. "The stage was filled with medical doctors. All from the very best strata of society and, what is much more important, all very keen to see the experiment fail. They want to unmask the man as a charlatan, they want to make sure that this demonstration will not make hypnosis socially or scientifically respectable. And then the disaster really happens."

Amanda clutched Vogt's elbow. "Allow me to try and guess: The hypnotist sent himself into a deep sleep."

Vogt laughed so heartily that he lost sight of the path and walked into an ants' nest. "Not a bad resolution, and the result might even have been more fortunate. But in fact what happened was this: The medical men simply behaved in a contrary fashion! They stared at the crystal ball held solemnly in front of them and stayed just as wide-awake and refractory as they had been at the beginning. Hard luck! And as a consequence, until very recently, hypnotism has not been practiced in Russia since, and suggestion has been seen as quackery. It was not until Bechterev that the procedure became respectable again."

Amanda released the doctor's arm. "Allow me to remove an ant from the back of your knee." She plucked the insect from his trousers. "I don't like hearing about failures of the will," she said, resuming the conversation. "I'm sure you would have done much better. Let's sit down on that stripped tree trunk over there. You can hold the wood ants in check, protect me from the tree sap, and tell me, in the meantime, how one can be more successful than this Hansen."

Vogt pressed a carefully ironed handkerchief to his forehead, but then thought better of it and spread it out for them to sit on. "You must liberate the intellectual susceptibilities of the person to be hypnotized from their habitual bonds, and produce a kind of aura."

"With a crystal ball?"

"The object is relatively unimportant. For myself, I prefer to work with a pendulum."

Amanda reached into the neck of her batiste blouse and pulled out the lock on her string of pearls. She opened the little diamond clasp at her neck and held the pearls out to the doctor, as though handing him a drink of water fresh from the well.

"A pendulum for you!"

"The patient," noted Vogt a few hours later on a rough sheet of paper of which, as always, he used only the left-hand side, "although at first quite clearly wide-awake, monopolized the conversation, and later the structure of the entire interaction. Relations of dominance broke down alarmingly quickly, or rather they were reversed."

Amanda von Alvensleben also captured on paper what she

wanted to remember of that afternoon; she found "displeasing" the theory that bumblebees, and bees in general, were color-blind. Perhaps science lacked insight into this particular matter, because surely whoever it was who designed the colors of flowers and shrubs would have given the question some thought. On the other hand, it was hard to deny the charm of the notion that the whole kaleidoscope was, so to speak, pointless, and created solely for the sake of its beauty. That the rutting of the bumblebee took place in the clouds she found illuminating from the poetic rather than the practical point of view. Language such as the mating rod or the copulatory opening, she wrote, struck her as very industrial, and also fitted ill with Vogt's claim—which, because it was late summer, at least in the Fichtelgebirge, was impossible to verify—that the male was on his back, as if in a hammock, when performing an act indispensable to the propagation of the species.

Vogt, she noted a few paragraphs later, could be classified as neither gentle nor coarse. In the acts of "unlacing" and "unbuttoning," "skirt lifting" and "stripping," a certain "endearing clumsiness" had become apparent, urgent rather than relaxed. It was only on the way home that she had become properly irritated by the doctor's insistent claim that he could already see Oxhead Mountain. They had not, for purely topographical reasons, had the merest glimpse of the Oxhead throughout the whole of the walk. But Vogt had remained so insistent that she herself came close to admitting that she could finally see the mountain as well. In addition, Lieutenant Most had made himself conspicuous once more by leaving a box of chocolates at the front desk. Frau Krupp, Amanda wrote in a postscript, was just dressing for her appointment with the doctor.

"I wish that Fritz, my husband, also had a medical adviser whom he could come to trust as quickly as I do you," said Margarethe Krupp, after she had risen from the couch. "Fritz, it sometimes seems to me, needs counsel so much more than I. Depression seems to be a hereditary condition in this family. It also afflicted his father. There was some story about a steam hammer, but I can't remember it exactly. Perhaps his grandfather had suffered from the same thing. Although the steam hammer does seem to be part of a more recent memory. Otherwise Fritz would not talk so much about the episode."

Vogt scribbled the word "steam hammer" on the green felt sheet that protected the tabletop from inkblots. "Could you describe more precisely what this steam hammer business is all about? A business misfortune, perhaps? Have you garnered the impression from your husband's stories that the object in question is in motion or at rest?"

"He has never so much as let me in on the secret of what a steam hammer is. Clearly it is something very powerful and mechanical. Please do not press me for details. As far as I'm concerned, technical details are men's affairs, from which I strive to keep myself as far removed as possible. The very term 'steam hammer' sounds to me like something coarse and violent."

"And you cannot—forgive my insistence, but it is my professional duty—you cannot recall whether the 'steam' or the 'hammer' was granted the greater importance?"

Margarethe Krupp's left thumb sought her waistband. "What is most important is Fritz—more so, surely, than my evaluation, or even my interpretation, of his statements."

"It would be more than an honor if I could persuade your husband to consult me. Regardless of the way in which he himself is inclined to interpret his mental afflictions. But my desire for further professional training unfortunately obliges me to move to Paris for a few months at the end of this spa season. The sole reason for my taking the job as a spa doctor was in order to be able to finance this plan. I shall be quite open with you: My ambitions are strictly scientific in nature, but the financial means for their realization are extremely limited."

"Tell that to my husband, he's always eager to hear about scientific risk taking."

Vogt bowed.

"I shall write to you from The Hill. Are you married, by the way?"

"All that will have to wait."

"Then take care in Paris." Frau Krupp turned away and pointed to her companion, who was setting aside a magazine. "Come, Amanda, I'm afraid we're rather late."

Vogt bowed to the two ladies and lowered the curved bronze door handle.

S I X

In the photographs dating from the time when she first met Oskar Vogt, Cécile Mugnier wore her hair piled up, *à la japonaise*, as had been the fashion favored by local coiffeurs a few years earlier. Cécile deviated from the fashion in leaving her ears uncovered, which made her broad face appear more exposed and also more fleshy, in comparison, at least, with Vogt's. By growing an ever fuller beard, he was trying to compensate for the inexorable loss of hair from his forehead. She wore flat heels, he high heels, and yet the top of his head reached no farther than the base of her prominent nose.

Some nights, when the rain fell softly against her windowpanes, when cab doors were sharply slammed in the street, when discreet coughing could be heard in the next room, Cécile was overcome by a melancholy that she was unable to diagnose using any of the methods familiar to her from her student days. For more than ten years, "neurasthenia" had been a fashionable word, although it conveyed less than "mental anguish," which was the phrase they used when talking to patients, for whom medical terms still had a whiff of magic. On the other hand, during those moments of "acoustic intimacy," she, Cécile, found herself merely "unbearably hulking," and complained that she felt "clumsy, but at the same time shivery and fragile." Sometimes this emotional state was simply due to the fact that she was a stranger to the capital, and she would focus on something peculiarly trivial, such as her accent, the broad and heavy dialect she had brought with her from Savoy, which meant that at the butcher's and the grocer's, she automatically had to pay a few sous more for a *saucisson* or a bundle of vegetables.

In letters to her friends in Annecy she also mentioned being ridiculed by her fellow students in the Paris faculty, all of them male, who "watched her closely" as she dissected a testicle, who accused her of being "uncouth," who made her feel that she was neither particularly pretty nor, as the lawyer's son, de Varmais, had discovered, a "terrific catch."

Of course she was not a terrific catch to eyes such as these; her relatively famous and rich aunt had cut her out of her will upon being informed that Cécile, rather than taking the veil in a decent convent, preferred to remain true to her "contrary intentions" and pursue the study of medicine. And of course she did not reflect any of the ideals of the day—or of any time that she knew of— as far as physical beauty was concerned. Her shoulders—there was no need to beat around the bush—were simply too wide, her hands too large, and even the most expensive velvet band could not disguise the thickness of her ankles. And in any case Cécile Mugnier could only afford velvet bands that had for years adorned ankles other than her own. In group photographs she hid her hands in the pockets of her lab coat.

Why she fell in love with Vogt was a puzzle to his friends and acquaintances. His motives were less difficult to decipher. "He always had in mind something like the Curies, the woman as a congenial complement to the man," as one of them put it. "Given the slow way she spoke French, she was the only woman he could understand," another explained. "He seduced her by feigning a lumbago," a third was sure, "the French call it *torticolis*, which sounds much more poetic. He claimed he couldn't go to the opera because a sudden pain had left him unable to move, a pain that overpowered him just as she turned up at his house to correct some scientific work, quite unsuspecting, of course; he used that opportunity to pull the trick—which may well have been new at the time—of presenting himself as a patient who needed to be helped out of his clothes to have certain parts of his back muscles rubbed—all quite therapeutically, of course. You can imagine the rest."

A few weeks later, however, they did visit the opera together. Meyerbeer's *L'Africaine* was playing, and they were both very bored. Vogt only perked up when Vasco sang in his sleep of his love for Inès, but he barely understood what the rest of it was about, and also thought the artistic extravagance grossly exaggerated. In the intermission after the second act, Oskar and Cécile admitted, to their mutual relief, that they weren't really that keen on musical theater, and went and found a café opposite the Louvre. After dinner they discussed their future.

They would collaborate scientifically, that much was certain, working quite closely together in areas that no one else had dared to examine. Questions of the interaction between mind and body, for example, could be approached from completely different angles. Strictly materialistic ones, of course, seeing the emotions as a set of nerve endings. Practically speaking, the brain was no better understood than a factory whose products were familiar, but of which we know only a few chimneys, and perhaps one or two power stations—they were exaggerating now, to get at the core of the matter. But what opportunities there would be in research and later in medicine when the whole plant was revealed, down to the smallest workbench, so to speak, or, to extend the metaphor, all the way through to the labs in the research and development departments. The opportunities to activate something here, close down something there, to understand and influence the various processes so as to bring them to a higher level, these opportunities were simply immense. One had only to think of the most recent experiments carried out by the Russians, and what they had managed to achieve by excising a couple of nerves—dogs wagged or stopped wagging their tails, rabbits showed themselves willing to copulate or stubbornly resistant to it, cocks lost their aggression, and chimpanzees became more aggressive. Certainly, it was all very crude as yet, still miles away from the fine-tuning of human emotions, but the path lay open before them.

In any case, Cécile first had to finish her dissertation in Paris. Vogt would be able to advise her in one way or another, not in clinical or experimental matters, but in "putting ideas together." She would also keep in contact with the "eminent specialists" at the Salpêtrière. Perhaps she would also be able to begin to learn Russian. He, Vogt, on the other hand, would concern himself with the expansion of his social network in Berlin; his chosen area would be what science calls "society" as opposed to "community," which would in the future—along with research—become her most important field.

When the gas lamps were slowly dimmed in the café, and the number of whores far exceeded the number of potential customers, Vogt wanted to leave. But Cécile held him back. That had been a lovely image, the vision of the factory and its various components, she said, and she had had the idea, to put it vaguely, of the "sociologization of emotional shifts, passions, and creativity."

Vogt seized upon the key word "creativity." One of the preconditions of creative power, he explained, was its scarcity. All areas of the brain were capable of thought, whether the brains in question were clever or less than brilliant, just as the passions were sometimes dull and sometimes extremely acute. But in order to understand its highest achievements, one must examine that rarity: the "unique specimen." It might be possible to avoid all the "sociology" that Cécile had mentioned if one devoted oneself exclusively to an examination of the "elite brain." That was a royal road to knowledge. Other people would classify, measure, and catalog the average components of the normally working brain. But this work, meritorious though it might be, would only serve as a backdrop, or, to put it another way, a springboard. The one who would finally emerge successful would be the man who had studied the capacities of genius. Genius in any field, in science, technology, politics, business, of course, and naturally in the fine arts as well —wherever one looked, genius was rare, even among serious criminals—"even in the circus," he added, rather surprisingly.

It was raining the next morning when Vogt set out to buy a hat for Cécile in the sixth arrondissement. The shop had been recommended to him by the wife of Professor Déjerine. A friendly salesgirl confused him with questions about color and shape and the kind of veil required. But what concerned Vogt most was whether he had correctly estimated the size of his future bride's head.

The gift was a great success.

SEVEN

At the beginning of their correspondence, the writing paper Margarethe Krupp used to communicate with Oskar Vogt still bore an embossed and blocked silver K on the top right-hand side of the heavy sheet, interlocked with a slim, less gleaming M. Margarethe added the address, "The Hill," herself. In subsequent years she used cards indicating the sender's location in blue letters that conformed to the prevailing graphic tastes of the day, spelling out "The Hill" and, a line below, in smaller print, "Near Essen on the Ruhr," and later simply "The Hill" and "Province of Rheinpreussen."

Margarethe wrote whatever came into her head and her pen, sometimes making the letters rise sharply, and sometimes spreading them out across the page, sometimes adding a little hook to the little u in the German style, and always sketching out the M as a mountain range. She used the paper sparingly, and her letters were never any shorter than the sheets of paper allowed; often she filled them completely, right across the margins, which she had at first left blank, and then she would write over words she had just written, as if the beginning of her missive had already been delivered.

At the beginning of February 1897, Vogt had offered to put his medical services at the disposal of other members of the family. On February 15 Margarethe wrote back:

Dear Dr. Vogt,
Having just received your letter, I am hastening to thank you most sincerely for it, and quite particularly for your kind offer to devote medical care to my elder sister, who suffers from a nervous complaint. In the event of an emergency, I should in any case probably have been forward enough to consult you of my own accord, and God knows whether I shall ever have to do so in the short or in the long term, but in the case of my elder sister I fortunately have no need to trouble you, quite apart from the fact that she would hardly heed my advice. Such is her own feeling about her nervous breakdown that she has, on her own initiative, consulted the sanatorium of medical officer Professor Hertz, who recently passed away in Bonn, which she had heard about from other patients who had been treated there. Apart from the fact that we enjoy a friendship with a branch of the family of the institution's late proprietor, and have consequently come into contact with the current director. My sister, as far as is possible considering her condition, has recovered a great deal and feels well, as she is now talking about the months that she wants to spend there. On the other hand, I, as I have said, am far from certain that I shall not have to trouble you again about Irene: Since she has spent almost eight years at home, I had to call there today and found her once again in the same nervous state as she was in at Christmas. Except that she is much more physically fit than she was before. After going on a calming walk with her in splendid weather, I put her to bed and advised my brother-in-law that she should be kept in bed, apart from a walk at lunchtime, until I can look in on her again tomorrow

evening. I hope this forced rest will do her good, and that I shall find her much better tomorrow. So I hope, for the next week or so, to be able to send another of my sisters, who is very thoughtful and calm, to see her, as I am only available for a few hours over the next ten days. I can see that Irene needs a guiding hand in the immediate future in order to come to terms with her new situation, which, simple as it is, will "completely overwhelm" her, as she has put it herself a number of times with a painfully anxious expression. If this attempt to familiarize her with her own household in the company of her sister and to grow accustomed to it (for there is no question of her *running* it, and that would not even be necessary) should fail, I shall probably consult you, but in the meantime there is little to be done medically. My dear, dear doctor, thank you very much again. My dear mother, thank heavens, is now feeling better, so that I am not for the time being concerned about her, although the possibility remains that there may yet be worse to come in the future.

With my sincere devotion,
Margarethe Krupp

Formulations such as "having just received" or "hastening to," references to the constant pressures on her time, were often scattered throughout the letters Margarethe Krupp wrote to her "mental adviser." By her own account, she was surrounded by incarnations of some nervous condition. This found expression in the "cases" of people close to her, or for whose protection she felt responsible, but was also apparent in quite ordinary accounts of everyday events, which seemed always to involve a hectic sequence of departures and arrivals, the pressure to keep to railway timetables, and sudden changes of location.

Having just received his letter, she sent Vogt "a few words written in haste" to tell him that her Christmas presents to him, a microtome for his research and a bread-slicing machine, would not be waiting for him at The Hill. "As they will probably not be ready, there would be a lot of unnecessary traveling about, and unpacking them here would pose a fresh set of problems, so I shall request that they be sent to you and the bill be sent to us." Her husband, Fritz, had traveled to Kiel again, she wrote, and would not be returning home via Berlin for a number of days. But he shared her opinion, and she had no wish to delay matters unnecessarily with a written inquiry. For Margarethe Krupp, life was a gigantic organization plan:

> On the twenty-fourth we shall be giving out our presents. But if you are here on the twenty-third, you will be able to attend the distribution of presents to poor children, which is always delightful. Selfish as I am, I shall also be pleased if you can come to the party so that you can stop over to see Irene as well. She is still fine, but I think it would be a comfort to her, and perhaps it would do no harm if you were to have a word with the doctor! Everything else we can talk about, but please tell us in good time what train you will be arriving on.

And once again she was, "Very sincerely, in haste," devotedly Vogt's.

E I G H T

D espite a deep-rooted antipathy toward public displays of generosity, Vogt could see no possibility of declining Margarethe Krupp's invitation to the "distribution of presents to poor children." His patient, the mistress of The Hill, clearly enjoyed her role as benefactress, the courteous bows of the crop-haired boys, the low curtsies of the girls in their neat white pinafores. She also talked to the children, a little too loudly, perhaps, trying to mask her insecurity by laying exaggerated stress on her words: "Your father's dead? How dreadful! But he will be pleased with you in heaven," she said to one of the three kings from the East who was in a fever of excitement over her arrival. "And you have four brothers and sisters? How sweet!"

Margarethe, Vogt had been quick to realize, wished to appear not so much a saint as a loving mother figure, the personification of the generous heart. But even her gestures were clumsy: When she passed her hand along the tops of heads, she didn't so much stroke as ruffle. When the same hand touched blouses or shirts, it didn't so much caress as straighten. "She has," Vogt mused, "a clear desire for feeling, but she lacks the disposition for it."

Perhaps he was so ungracious only because the hall, decked out with Christmas decorations for the deserving poor, was wretchedly cold. The doctor tried not to show it, but he was freezing, and looked enviously at his hostess and Amanda von Alvensleben, who had wrapped themselves in fashionably inconspicuous but visibly well-lined coats. On the tree—"a pine from Oxhead Mountain," Amanda had whispered as they entered the hall—all the white candles had been lit, but Vogt was sitting too far away to enjoy their warmth. And the occasion threatened to go on much longer than the program suggested. At the very beginning, the pastor, a kind but, as Vogt noted, "intellectually feeble, confabulating man," had got muddled in his sermon. He had lost his way between a quotation from St. Paul and its exegesis, slipping into an interpretation that was meant for funerals, and was unable to find his way back again.

During the nativity play, too, there had been a series of gaffes. None of the three kings from the East, for example, seemed to be able to quell his stage fright. The simple lines, easy enough for Westphalians to pronounce, which Herr Klapheck, the school rector, had given the young dignitaries to take with them on their journey to Bethlehem:

> *See the heav'nly star*
> *It guides our journey far,*
> *It lights us through the morn*
> *To the place where He is born.*

—this simple quatrain had induced an incomprehensible state of nervous agitation. As a consequence, King Balthasar, pearls of sweat ploughing white furrows in his dark face—the freezing Vogt was furious to notice this—was concentrating so hard on the rhyme that he said "bar" instead of "far." Melchior was to follow him with the next couplet, but after this confusion he at first said nothing at all, and then came out with "torn" instead of "born."

In short, there seemed to be no more prospect of a dignified occasion than there was of a short one, for the actors were trying—given the presence of their noble guests—to achieve a perfection that could have been produced only by repeating a great many sections, and hence starting them from the beginning. Vogt had, of course, hoped that he would be able to sit in a corner somewhere away from the public eye and devote himself to the unresolved problems for which he had had insufficient time that day. But he was sitting right in the middle of the front row, with Frau Krupp on his left and Amanda on his right; the latter had, on top of the sheet bearing the words to the Christmas carols, which she held in her lap, opened a book which she was reading with great concentration.

After the shepherds had left the stage to attend to their sheep, there was a short patriotic interlude. The Virgin Mary walked up to the two portraits of the Hohenzollerns and declaimed:

> That's the Kaiser, of this pair,
> And that's his granddad over there.

The actress, who was perhaps thirteen or fourteen years old, had long, almost white blond hair that fell to her waist and the golden belt around it. Her face was of such a transparent pallor that the veins in her temples stood out like delicate branches of coral. As she walked backwards toward a third painting—*Heroes of the Battle of Sedan*—she tripped over a wooden lamb that one of the shepherds had left behind on his retreat from Bethlehem. The Virgin Mary lost her balance and fell, hitting the back of her head.

Vogt had seen this disaster coming, but he sat motionless in his chair for a few seconds. He was paralyzed by an image, a vision that had come to him when the girl began to stumble. A few days earlier, a colleague from the United States had told him of a terrible mishap. He had received a brain, his correspondent wrote, a valuable specimen the like of which had never come his way before, the brain of a poet who, more than any other, had "sung the voice of the nation." All the more appalling, then, was the accident that had occurred when the valuable material was being unpacked. While untying the precious cargo, his assistant had suddenly slipped on an oily substance on the laboratory floor and then, carrying the parcel in front of his stomach, had gone sprawling. Now this assistant was a very heavy man, so the result was an unholy mess of shards of glass, string, wrapping paper, and brain tissue, and the whole preparation was ruined.

It was with this memory in mind that Vogt rushed onto the stage to examine the girl. But she had already gotten up again, and merely looked at him with shame, as if awaiting a scolding or some punishment for unseemly behavior. Vogt looked into her eyes, and then gave her blond head a kindly stroke, felt the beginnings of a bump, and returned to his seat. A few minutes later the actress walked—very carefully, this time—in front of *Heroes of the Battle of Sedan* and declaimed in verse the story leading up to the outbreak of the Franco-Prussian War. Amanda became absorbed in her book once more and did not look at the stage until the epic touched on Kaiser Wilhelm's state of mind upon receipt of the Ems telegram:

> *Kaiser Wilhelm was quite merry*
> *And his royal thoughts were very*
> *Far from any worldly thing.*
> *Radiating peace and calm*
> *He quaffed from his posset warm*
> *As a hero and a king . . .*

The homage to Their Majesties finished with a dedication to the Krupp family. After the lines

> *Praised be this house—this House on High!*
> *Its loftiness should give us pause.*
> *It nurtures us, high on its Hill,*
> *And is as kind as Santa Claus . . .*

Amanda reopened her book.

By now the children in the hall also lacked the attention required for the declamation of poetry. Some of them began—either from physical strain or perhaps only because they urgently needed to go to the toilet—to fidget around on their wooden stools; others were already, full of anticipation, scratching their thighs where they would later itch from the woollen stockings which Margarethe Krupp would soon distribute solemnly.

When the gingerbread was finally handed out, there was great relief all around.

A few hours before the guests assembled for the Christmas Eve party, Friedrich Alfred Krupp and Vogt went for a walk. Krupp had only arrived from Berlin that morning, and had, as was his wont, stood on the scales, jotted down in his notebook the number displayed, and then decided to take a walk to the rhododendron bushes with the doctor.

"The reason I envy you," he confided in Vogt before a short climb deprived him of the breath to carry on speaking, "is that you work in a profession in which you are able to express your creative passions: research, analysis, reflection on what the world holds deep within . . . well, you know . . ."

The leaves of the rhododendrons had curled up against the dry cold. A few crows hopped in geometric patterns beneath the bushes and then flew away with a rustle of wings.

"For some time I have been considering the project of devoting myself entirely to marine biology in Capri," Krupp continued. "My previous efforts in this line have been blessed by modest successes, but naturally have suffered from time pressures imposed by my other obligations. But I consider it even more of a deficiency that I lack an overall scientific vision." He stopped, took off his glasses, and breathed with a carp-like mouth upon the lenses. "You see, I amass details that I can classify, but I lack the power to embark on a broader plan."

Vogt waited until Krupp had pulled the gold earpieces back behind his ears. "I, on the other hand," he began cautiously, "have always drawn intellectual inspiration from the achievements of the business world. In structuring my future work, I shall adopt the same fundamental principles that have had such a tremendous effect within German industry—centralization and the division of labor. I am thinking, for example, of setting up a central neurological institute in which, hand in hand with specialized physiological and psychological research, the anatomy of the brain will be systematically examined. Division of labor," he repeated immediately in response to a quizzical glance from Krupp, "by that I mean the breakdown of various research procedures according to the researcher's qualifications. Let us, for example, take the problem of the pictorial representation of anatomical discoveries—"

"I am also interested in that in my work," Krupp interrupted him. "I have never yet seen a satisfactory depiction of a single one of the marine worms that I have discovered. Neither in shape nor in color. You must leave me the addresses of your specialists before you return to Paris. That is a burning problem for us all, one on which the sweat of noble men is being poured, if you understand my meaning."

Their penetrating discussion of the advantages and disadvantages of various watercolors, crayons, and brushes, the use of Japanese-made paper and the prohibitive expense of color printing, so engrossed the two gentlemen that they had reached the door before Krupp was able to broach another topic that fascinated him. He drew the doctor aside.

"My wife seems to feel in the very best of health under your treatment, at least where her nerves are concerned. I should be indebted to you if you would keep me constantly informed as to how things progress."

Vogt made a silent bow.

"I should also be very grateful to you," Krupp added, "if you would exert a calming influence on her over the next few days. She is often very moody during the holiday season. Even this morning, when I arrived from Berlin, we had a little squabble. I found her in the nursery and she actually said, 'Imagine that, your father's here. Do you remember him?' I had to put up with that in front of my own children."

"And how did you react?" asked Vogt.

"I threw her a very telling glance, and didn't give her another thought after that. But such scenes affect my mood for days afterwards. I urgently need careful treatment after all the tensions of the past weeks and months. Even now I'm afraid, once again, that I won't get to sleep tonight."

"Perhaps I might recommend a remedy for that—"

"She accuses me of neglecting her and says, as she puts it, that my constant absences mean that I am not a good father. So I try to stay in touch with her as much as possible. I'm constantly writing her letters or sending her telegrams. Then she accuses me of not respecting her work."

A light rain had set in, but Krupp ignored it. "Marga's family as a whole, leaving aside my brother-in-law, Felix, are not in the best shape where their nerves are concerned. You will already know about this. But I don't care about the family at this point. I just don't want my wife—as long as I am here—to start any rows."

Vogt bowed once again and then followed Krupp into the house. When the maids had relieved them of their coats, the master of the house took Vogt's arm. "And if Marga should mention my planned trip to Capri in conversation, she should be dissuaded from taking a critical stance."

The servant told them that tea was ready.

"You should talk to him about his weight problem as well," said Margarethe hastily when—the tea things were being cleared away—she found Vogt alone for a moment by the fireside. "Of course, anyone who dines so frequently in hotels or clubs simply must be leading an unhealthy life. If, as he should, he would stay here at The Hill, he would not find it so difficult to keep to a diet." ·

The rain had grown heavier, and a cold wind was beating against the poorly sealed window out of which Vogt was gazing into the darkness. The imminent distribution of the children's presents, and the subsequent big dinner, did not particularly lift his spirits. He walked over to the dressing table, poured water over his hands, and carefully brushed the hair at the back of his head. On the other hand, he mused, as the hard bristles triggered an agreeable shudder, it would be worth making even greater sacrifices to have Frau Krupp *and* her husband as patients. He stroked his starched shirtfront and fingered the cuff links that Cécile had given him. Her parcel had come with a long letter, which he would read later, before he went to bed.

When Amanda knocked and, without waiting for an answer, walked into the room, Vogt was tying his bow tie.

"Migraine," cried Amanda cheerfully, "she has a migraine, and he has the feeling that he's going to have a migraine. And both of them, independently, would like the good doctor to give them a powder to ward off this terrible monster. I have promised to undertake the delicate role of the courier, so that the already endangered course of the Christmas festivities does not run utterly off the rails."

"A violent attack?"

"More of an indisposition, I would say. They were having an argument in their dressing room about whether he should travel to Capri after the holiday. His doctors have most insistently recommended it, he said, whereupon she, already in something of a descant range, threatened to get an independent opinion. An opinion from whom? Why, Doctor Vogt, of course. Not even that was enough to calm the situation. Then she came round to her standard theme: Fritz, where are you sleeping tonight? At this point he grew a little more pale and dough-faced, but then said defiantly, although he was stammering somewhat, that he planned, as usual, to spend the night in his private room. Voilà! Doors were slammed, doors opened again, people were calling for powders. And now it's time for the healer's art."

Vogt picked up his black leather briefcase, which had been placed on the wardrobe, and set off.

After dinner the gentlemen moved to the drawing room for port and cigars. Another Christmas tree glowed there. The conversation was halting at first. Fragmentary observations, incomplete sentences, about liver pâté and carp, about the '86 vintage and the difficulty of finding a decent Christmas cake "like the ones we had as children," rose to the ceiling like limp smoke rings.

"Do you really believe in all these theories about enfeeblement?" Vogt's host asked him suddenly. "I mean, this whole business, you know, the waning of power from generation to generation, the blood losing its creative will, and a rise in suspicious elements, a tendency toward waywardness in general and in particular, moral decay and so on . . ."

Admiral von Hollmann straightened the crease of his pants along his broad knees. "The eternal cycle of mutual devouring," he said before Vogt could utter a word, and his voice rattled shrilly on, as if continuing his reflections on the meal they had just enjoyed, "is as cruel as the process of natural selection. The inferior must yield, and the strong prevail, but, gentlemen, if we look one another honestly in the eye, how much longer"—the admiral tipped a slug of port into his glass—"how much longer will we Germans be able to assert our superiority? I can tell you confidentially, thanks to the figures I have at my disposal. First of all"—and his broad right hand encircled his left thumb—"left-handedness is conspicuously on the increase. You may smile, but for me, as a soldier, this is a cause for suspicion. I am no historian, but I know from military history that even in classical Greece, in Sparta, left-handers were exterminated because they had to use the wrong hand, their weak hand, when they reached for their swords as the phalanx marched into battle. Since that time, left-handedness, from a military-cultural perspective, so to speak, has ceased to be a significant problem. Anyone wishing to assert his superiority had to do so with his right hand. This had to do with military schools, training requirements, the supply of uniform weaponry, and many other things besides. Military struggle, I meant to say, has for thousands of years been successful only when the soldiers have been right-handed. There are exceptions, of course"—the admiral waved aside the palm tree next to his chair as though it were about to interrupt him—"where are there none? But that in no way affects the matter at hand." He drank vigorously from his crystal glass.

"Which is precisely why I just used the word 'selection.' Nowadays it poses a great threat to us. Among the recruits who come to our barracks, left-handedness is on the rise. They try to hide it, but we're wise to their little game."

"And red hair, too, by the way," interrupted Pastor Denkhoff, who, distracted by the admiral's rosy face, had understood only in the most general fashion that the topic revolved around changes unrecorded in the baptismal register.

Vogt raised his glass toward the vicar, and the cleric smiled back gratefully.

"A second indisputable observation: the motive instinct." The admiral briefly grasped the index finger of his left hand. "In the past, for centuries, physical movement was regimented by certain organizational principles. Movements were subject to regulations adapted to the body, and could thus occur in the desired sequence. In the act of digging, for example, distinctions were made in the sequence of movements"—the admiral picked up the coffee spoon bearing the monogram of the master of the house, and gave Krupp an apologetic look as if he were about to use the precious item for the purposes of trench digging—"distinctions were made between the following movements: hoist, shove, and throw." The admiral stood up and bent his knees, demonstrating with his massive body what he had only intended to hint at with the little silver spoon between his meaty hands. "This discipline saved men's lives. All in the past," he sighed, as his center of gravity reinstalled itself in its seat. "Nowadays discipline is sacrificed in favor of so-called 'freedom of movement'—utterly wasted. I shall mention but a single example"—von Hollmann raised his hands as if to quiet an orchestra—"I shall mention only one example, but as far as I am concerned, it is one out of thousands: What drives the young people of Berlin? What drives"—his voice grew a few degrees shriller—"the youth of our capital? These young people, and I have seen this with my own eyes"—he slapped the palms of his hands against his thighs dramatically—"they move on roller skates!"

The admiral found himself looking at a row of eyebrows raised in astonishment, some of them raised in scorn.

"Laugh at me if you will," he continued, "but you will laugh no more when I tell you that this supposedly free business of gliding on rollers fastened beneath the sole of the shoe is the expression, if I may say so, of a pervertedly lustful physical feeling, a deviation from the true purpose of the body. Gymnastics—that is where I see the will to discipline; but this sliding around on wheels, for demonstrative purposes, of course, on the Kurfürstendamm, in the center of our civilization—that means, in a way, help me, somebody . . ." The admiral turned his shoulder to one side, but there was the vicar, and he had never been to Berlin.

While the admiral's conversation turned to a series of new points in his catalog of generally observable degenerative phenomena, Krupp picked up a brightly painted soldier-shaped nutcracker from the Erzgebirge and placed an almond between its teeth.

"Curvature of the spine," cried von Hollmann, "and whooping cough are spreading like wildfire throughout large sections of Lower Silesia, and among women"—his voice dropped dramatically—"I shall say only that it has provoked a wave of womb fury."

"Hear, hear," mumbled the vicar, although he was not quite sure what to make of these last words.

Krupp suddenly brought his fist down on the nutcracker's round helmet, and handed Vogt a cracked almond.

"It is presumably to our own inestimable advantage," began the doctor, in response to his host's inquiring expression, "that we finally have reliable statistics about the overall state of the national health of the Reich. But as to the specific question of the increasing or decreasing power of our civilization, it appears to me that, in anticipation, one might say, of future research, our investigations have been restricted to a few exemplary cases." He quickly put the almond into his mouth and swallowed it whole. "Allow me, as precisely as I can, to explain briefly what I mean by 'exemplary cases.' As far as the German Reich is concerned, I shall be bold enough to assume that, on the one hand, the number of physical and mental afflictions is increasing, but that at the same time the total sum of, if I may put it this way, heroic achievements—in the

fields of science, the art of invention, the military, for example—
has risen considerably. Merely glancing around me here"—Vogt
bowed to Krupp, to the admiral, and, after only a very short moment of hesitation, to the vicar as well—"a glance such as this
would only back up my assumption. There may be no denying
that there is, in general, a very discrete correlation between the
growth of genius and the decline of certain general abilities. As in
a brain cell, genius—seen from the point of view of the nation as
a whole—develops its vital centers at the expense of other apti-
tudes. Everything has its price."

Krupp quit feeding the nutcracker for a moment. "If I look
around," he said, "at my own family and that of my wife, all I can
see, at first glance, is an increase in the extent of the damage done.
What I mean is"—and he struck the nutcracker on its head once
again—"that their sensitivity has increased, but what they lack is
the strength required for a stab at innovation, that absolute determination of the will that distinguished our forefathers."

"But that would only be one more reason, if you will forgive
me, to rise to the challenge of undertaking a precise—precise, that
is, in neuroanatomical terms—a precise investigation into the centers of creativity and genius. This research would be geared toward
maintaining, if not enhancing, their potential. I attempted to give
some indication of this during our walk."

Admiral von Hollmann laid his hand on the bulging upholstery
of the arm of his chair and rose to his feet. "I wish you the best
of luck, young man, a very important area and, if I may say so, a
very precise goal. Now I should like to discuss a few matters
concerning armament policy, of national importance, with our host.
But I shall keep a sharp eye on your ideas." Crouching, he remained motionless for a moment, as if he were considering whether
he had chosen the correct figure of speech, and then he stood up
with surprising agility, grumbled something about important documents that he needed to get from his room, and made his way
to the door. Vogt and the vicar took this as a sign to leave as well,
and Krupp made only muted objections.

*　　*　　*

In his room, Vogt took a flat, elegantly milled silver flask from his suitcase, sat at his dark writing desk, and poured brandy into the water glass that stood beside the inkwell. His nose circled above the light brown liquid; he took a little sip and then drew Cécile's letter from his coat pocket. For more than two weeks he had had no news from her, although he himself had written to Paris almost every day.

Cécile told him of a "veil of melancholy" that had slowly lifted from her again. The very fact that she was now able to pick up pen and paper and actually write a letter to the end, take it to the post office and send it off was indeed, and not merely for medical reasons, a very positive sign. This time the inexplicable gloom had overcome her on one of those "still, clear" winter days—a Sunday morning, she remembered exactly, and the emotion had been sparked by the sight of an old lady, sitting all alone on a bench in the park, drinking lemonade from a little bright green bottle. This old yet lively little woman with her gray shawl had at the same time looked so childishly greedy and so old and vulnerable as she pressed her mouth to the opening of the bottle; and those two impressions of unconcealed desire had, in their "contradictory simultaneity," suddenly paralyzed in Cécile any further emotional stimuli. Perhaps it had been an extreme form of pity, but whatever it was, she had started sobbing so violently that she had only just been capable of escaping in a cab and getting home to the rue St. Maur.

As the initial stimulus—as he, Oskar, would call it—this banal episode was certainly of marginal significance but even as she recorded it—and she had begun to do so immediately—she noticed how small and tightly constricted her handwriting had become. Then, in order to trigger a kind of emotional countershock, she had immediately gone to the relevant academic books, but even then she noticed that she had to lie down on her bed to read, she felt so "leaden." Meanwhile that blond sun, reflected in her neighbors' window, had been shining into her bedroom "almost like a particularly wounding sneer."

But she had no wish to overdramatize her experiences, which

she was now able to express; indeed they might merely have been moments of exalted longing. After all, they hadn't seen one another for several weeks, six and a half to be precise. This attack could even be attributed to the "melancholy of great moments," a phenomenon accompanying or ensuing from the violent pulsations of a particularly intense emotion, and she herself would not hesitate to entrust the concept of ecstasy to such ordinary objects as pen and paper.

But since she had perceptibly recovered, both mentally and physically, she had once more become seriously absorbed in the literature that dealt with such situations. In Lombroso—and she would send him the references—she had been struck by a quite unequivocal connection between mental illness and genius. Certainly, what one might think of Lombroso and the whole phenomenology of his followers was not a matter for discussion here; but, on the other hand, it would also be unseemly simply to ignore "the findings of the subjective." All that she herself wanted to say was that her own moments of "supreme and most abandoned sensitivity" had left her just as paralyzed, just as motionless—"rigid," in fact—as that state of melancholy, described by Lombroso, from which she had just escaped. But *one* feeling was a "very short-term" fixation—on happiness, for example—while the *other*, negative feeling was marked by an "overwhelming sense of considerable duration." She was also, incidentally, full of longing, full of impatience for his next visit, and full of sorrow at having had to celebrate the holiday season without him "for this last time." But she had no wish to burden his heart with cares that she herself had resolved to bear gracefully.

Vogt carefully folded the letter and slipped it back into its lined envelope. He got up and fetched from the bathroom the shaving mirror that he had brought from Berlin. He looked thoughtfully into his face, tried to grimace, and then tilted the round surface so that it caught the light from the table lamp and cast a fake full moon on the ceiling.

There was still a second letter that the doctor had saved for those moments during the holiday when he felt "that he possessed very little of himself." This was a turn of phrase that he had borrowed from Cécile because it struck him as being both clinically and poetically precise. This second letter was not from Cécile, and the doctor prepared himself for his reading matter as he might have prepared for an unexpected romantic adventure. In the bathroom he washed his hands, brushed his hair, gargled with mouthwash, and dabbed eau de cologne on his beard. Then he exchanged his formal jacket for his silk brocade dressing gown and lit a candle.

"My dear, dear friend," he read, and swirled the brandy around in his glass while his correspondent went into great detail about the weather she was enjoying in Görlitz at the time of her writing. He grew more attentive when he came to the following passage beneath the first fold in the extremely thin paper:

> In four weeks our long separation will at last be over, and I shall be able to gossip with *mon petit* in person, rather than in writing. How I am looking forward to it! . . . My husband, Hilmar, is at present attending a philology convention, which reminds me most vividly of the Munich conference. Everything hereabouts will be associated, forever and ever, with experiences from the time we spent together. How will it all end?

With the palm of his left hand Vogt lifted his beard, which still smelled slightly of sandalwood, to his nose. He skipped the accounts of domestic misfortunes. The subsequent paragraph had been, insofar as one could judge from the handwriting, written in the same state of mind as the account of neglected window cleaning.

> I am somewhat *chaude* in view of the forthcoming season of goodwill and love to all men, and as I haven't been getting much of that just lately, I've been attending to the job myself, which can't be doing my health much good. Farewell, *mon ami*! All my very best wishes, and think of your *petite amie* as often as she thinks of you . . .

Then came a series of bold flourishes and, at the bottom of the page, a valedictory *Ta Petite*. Vogt cast his eyes with pleasure over the sentences in the last paragraph a few times. Finally he stood up and walked to the dark window. In the faint coating of condensation on the glass he drew a very elaborate initial, then rubbed it out with the sleeve of his dressing gown.

When he returned to his writing desk he placed the letters in two differently marked folders, and from the drawer he took the sheet of rough paper on which he had begun to write early that morning.

"I have met," he read in his own handwriting, "a few cultured hysterics blessed with the rare gift of introspection, and also with a love of the truth concordant with their social standing. I placed them under partial hypnosis, to which I should like to apply the term 'partially systematic waking state' "—Vogt found himself in the middle of a sighing yawn at this point— "and came to the conclusion that the origins and nature of hysteria are, in the final analysis, determined by mental problems which merely acquire a particularly dramatic dimension within this pathological framework. The emotion is expressed—only as a pure emotion—as rage, fear, or joy . . ." He had drawn a wavy line underneath the last three terms and noted in the margin: "Beware! Check the order!" "But one constant feature is the pathological intensification of something that is in fact natural. Just as genius, from the pathological point of view, can be seen as a kind of distortion of—fundamentally—normal states."

He had then jotted down the key words: "intensified breathing, a striking degree of perspiration, and unsteady muscle reflexes," but now, after the two letters, these key points meant no more to him than coins of a foreign currency that might have assumed a particular importance on some holiday or other.

He blew out the candle, extinguished the table lamp, and set about washing in the bathroom.

For his return journey to Berlin, the following afternoon after the church service, the two hosts supplied him with a well-stocked

picnic basket full of Christmas delicacies. Krupp and—a few minutes before his departure—Frau Krupp gave him letters. Their
daughters were also driven to the station. Amanda von Alvensleben
caused great merriment by throwing the doctor a few pinecones
through his open carriage window, in a gesture of farewell.

NINE

Every Monday morning the dogs were delivered by a man whose attire had an old-fashioned elegance but whose suit and face, on closer inspection, glistened with grease. The creatures, pulled along behind him in a wooden handcart, were tethered by their feet, and their muzzles, in which the greasy man had stuffed balled-up rags, were tied with cords.

Sometimes the delivery man brought strays, animals no longer identifiable by breed, their red, inflamed skin showing through their mangy fur, with ragged ears and an expression suggesting that bloodlust had long since yielded to resignation.

On other days nobler creatures jostled in the cart; nothing overbred, no greyhounds or Pomeranians, but sturdy, confident creatures radiating a sense of having been well cared for, and of having a respectable pedigree.

Sometimes the animal trader pressed the doorbell at 16 Magdeburger Strasse, in the Tiergarten district of Berlin, only to deliver a sack which seemed, in some mysterious way, filled with weary life.

The delivery man never stayed long. As he left the house, he waited until the door had closed behind him before putting on his bowler hat.

Sometimes he was to be seen in Erna's Corner, a tavern of not especially good repute in the Magdeburger Platz. He always stood sideways at the bar, beneath the price list and the mirror, in whose grease-mired glass he could observe the shadowy comings and goings in the street. The neighbors knew him by sight and avoided him. The landlord called him Monsewer, and that became his name.

The dogs that Monsewer delivered to No. 16 were received by the animal keeper, Weppermann, and taken to the cellar in a cage. On some rare occasions, in a partitioned area near the ventilation shaft, monkeys crouched, staring with anxious or stupid expressions—long-tailed monkeys or chimpanzees. When such encounters occurred, the dogs barked furiously, the monkeys screeched at the top of their lungs or growled deeply, rattling the bars of their little cages. The only silent creatures were the rabbits in the adjoining cellar, and to Weppermann's astonishment the cats were quiet, too, once the sack had been taken away.

In summer the corpses of the animals were kept in the coal cellar, in washable crates that the knacker was urged to wash and return. In winter a temporary storage area was set up in a passageway. Down there, it was very cold both in summer and in winter, and the troublesome smells a number of neighbors would later report to the police were a very rare occurrence. Neither was there any substance to the objections raised on behalf of so-called humanitarian initiatives by various animal protection leagues. These alleged torments were, as the lawyer asserted, minimal in comparison with the scientific knowledge that could be gleaned from the behavior of the animals following very minor operations on their nerve tracts or certain parts of their brain tissue.

However, care had to be taken that the patients who came to Magdeburger Strasse with their emotional problems were not adversely influenced by the cries of the animals. Vogt had realized the project that he had outlined to Krupp on their brief stroll to the rhododendron bushes. A research institute had been set up, but in order to secure its upkeep, the wealthy afflicted had to be found and treated using the most up-to-date medical methods.

This commercial side of things, so important if the pure research work was to flourish, was protected by a dense, discreet network of referrals and mutual dependencies, which Vogt had been able to build up in an extremely short time. His successes had received an added boost since the start of his practical career coincided with the advance of a syndrome that the feuilletonists called American nervousness. Illness as a fashion? As a line of business, more precisely, in which the most diverse medical processes competed with one another like the various different displays in a big department store: sleeping and waking cures, rising and falling water treatments, hip baths in a very wide range of temperatures, herbs, essences, drops, natural methods, and hypnoses. The market had become as richly diverse as the patients' symptoms.

Of course all the patients, male and female, swore by their own personal doctor, and each of these doctors was held to be a great discovery, but they swore by Vogt as they would have sworn by a tailor offering the most refined needlework, the restaurant with the most unusual wine cellar, or the stable with the most reliable racetrack record. Their commitments were not exclusive: No oath of loyalty was taken. All too often a change in fashion, based perhaps on nothing more than a rumor, meant that the people who came seeking advice would suddenly consult another expert, one blessed with a greater degree of understanding, perhaps, one whose regimens were not quite as strict and who was a little more generous in defining what was acceptable, what was just barely tolerated, and what was absolutely prohibited—the edicts of abstinence, in short, which were constantly at issue.

Some of the more prominent doctors had found a way of coming to terms with these repeated shifts in loyalty; if they suspected their patients of wavering, they themselves referred them elsewhere, to colleagues who could be relied upon to refer new patients to them. This syndicalist system promised nothing but advantages to all parties. The patients were able to enjoy a wide variety of opinions, as well as a concomitant diversity of possible cures. But given that this diversity, in each individual case, was based on the judgment of an authority who expressly encouraged dissent, there was no chance that even self-contradictory diagnoses and therapeutic proposals would bring medical efforts as a whole into disrepute. Patients were accompanied along life's bitter journey by both the hare *and* the tortoise.

From time to time, unfortunately, there were also cases when a specialist who had recently been brought in at the request of the patient failed to abide by the tacit agreement. Once the merry-go-round of patients had come to a propitious standstill before the door of his practice, he failed to set it in motion again. There were various possible explanations for such a refusal, ranging from the insistence on a particular diagnosis to a base desire for material gain. Extreme situations occasionally arose: Some patients simply decided not to undergo any further medical care, offering the lapidary excuse, for example, that they felt much better from a subjective point of view. Such forms of refractoriness—on the part of doctors or patients—threw the complicated system of exchange into a dangerously critical state and generally led to violent academic and social tensions. They reinforced the fears of outsiders and newcomers.

Oskar Vogt felt that he himself had fallen victim to this intricate network of relationships when he was obliged to inform his colleagues Binswanger and Schweninger that the Krupp family had generously resolved henceforward to take him on as medical adviser. Krupp had, of course, left Vogt in no doubt as to who his wife's and his own quite personal confidants were in matters of physical and mental health. Not that Vogt needed this information—in Berlin, from a certain level of social visibility upward, one was as well informed about business connections of all kinds as one was about the intricacies of people's love lives, although the quality of that information often suffered from the breathless manner in which it was conveyed.

In any case, upon receipt of Krupp's letter, Vogt had immediately informed Binswanger and Schweninger that he had been granted "a certain competence in special emergencies," an intelligence which, to put it mildly, somewhat surprised the two gentlemen. All of a sudden their rather exclusive circle had been invaded by a younger colleague whom they had certainly not recommended—a doctor who, in addition, had not attracted attention by earning the customary academic honors. The man was neither a privy councillor nor a professor; indeed he did not even have a license to lecture. Both academically and socially the man was an upstart!

That much was, of course, quite clear to Vogt, and he was sensitive enough, as he wrote to Cécile, to "defuse any resistance from that quarter" by "making a gesture of humility." He did what all ambitious young people are expected to do, and asked his established elders for their advice. Thus little postcards, telegrams, and dispatches were soon flying like shuttles between Berlin, Jena, and Leipzig, weaving the fabric designed to protect the emotional life of the great German industrial family against the vicissitudes of everyday life, while none of the doctors concerned suffered the slightest financial setback.

By May 1899 Vogt was in a position to write to his mother in Husum:

1. Thanks to the Krupps, I am in a position to send you 100 marks until October 10 (enclosed).
2. As I need my brothers' policies as security, please forward a copy to me.
3. Frau Krupp has stated unequivocally that all furniture and linen were intended for me personally, or for the clinic. As Frau Krupp is coming around June 10, and as I should like to have the ground floor tidy by then so that she can see what it looks like, I request the prompt return of such objects as you took with you. As you have explained to me that you are out of linen, I am prepared to put a sum for the purchase of new linen at your disposal. But as the problems of the clinic seem to be taking a new turn, I must show Frau Krupp that I am capable of looking after any

furniture and linen left in my care, and can relinquish none
of it. I ask you to be so good as to send me Frau Krupp's
lists.

4. In view of the state in which you left the ground-floor
apartment, I am utterly unable to use it. For example, five
rooms are filled with your things. Some changes will have
to be made. The best thing would be for you to come here
in the next few days, so that we could discuss it in person.
The sooner the better.

He signed his letter "Sincerely," without a possessive pronoun,
"Oskar," making the final flourish of the *r* rise like a whip.

The decidedly curt tone that Vogt used in writing to his mother
was not prompted only by the sorry tale of the donations from the
Krupps that she had confiscated. In various letters, at first only in
a few casual references, and later in a more direct fashion, he
complained to Cécile about how little attention he had received
from this woman, throughout his life but particularly since the
death of his father—unlike his three brothers, who had not yet
"proved particularly impressive." He, Vogt, on the other hand,
had always tried to involve his mother at every stage of his career.
Thus he had sent her, "without fail," a copy of each of his publications; these had never been received with thanks or any form
of acknowledgment. She had taken them completely for granted.

Cécile had advised him quite simply to devote less emotional
energy to this particular matter. He would win enough respect and
straightforward affection from other people—from herself, for example, affection that she tried to express in all her actions and
thoughts, and of course in her letters. It would certainly be asking
a little too much of Mother Vogt to expect her to formulate her
gratitude in terms appropriate to the caliber of her son's work,
which would be difficult for her to grasp. But as he clearly did most
of the suffering in this relationship, and as Cécile's heart, "as God
knew all too well," beat for the son and not the mother, she also
recommended "for reasons of mental hygiene" the use of a little
acid—a bit of boldness could surely do no harm, even if it only
led to a temporary appeasement of Oskar's emotional state.

Taking courage from this advice, Vogt had written to his mother, and the actual occasion for doing so struck him as most appropriate. He was soon, however, racked by doubts as to whether the style and content of his letter might not have been too high-handed. But the letter had been sent; to send another, more conciliatory version in its wake would have served little purpose, and would also have appeared servile. In any case, this business about the furniture and the linen had really been a challenge and a half. Had Frau Krupp known of it, she might have mentioned it to her husband. He might, however, have frivolously informed Schweninger and Binswanger of the matter, and thus delivered the story to a very interested public.

The house in Magdeburger Strasse—and there could be no doubt about this—required strict and competent management. Vogt himself could not fulfill this task, since wealthy patients and prestigious conferences too often took him away from Berlin. And his fiancée, who was destined for this "inner sanctum," had not yet completed her dissertation. In addition, it was unclear whether her still less than adequate command of German would permit her, within the foreseeable future, to assume the position currently held, somewhat reluctantly, by Korbinian Brodmann, Vogt's assistant.

"Centralization and the division of labor": Vogt thought bitterly how easily he had used those words when describing the foundation of his project to Friedrich Krupp. He looked sullenly at the letters Brodmann had left him to answer before setting off for Brussels, for a basically quite unnecessary conference. Centralization and the division of labor—I'm everything all at once, but I don't cut a happy figure. Underneath a number of bills, which his assistant had neatly stacked together, according to the size of the sheet of paper rather than its importance, he found a short letter with AGENDA written at the top in capital letters.

. . . and please don't forget, on top of the tiresome tax concerns, to tell our colleagues in Vienna the theme of your lecture to the Society of Austrian Friends of Practical Philosophy. Professor von Mikula's private secretary has now asked

three times for a short outline of your proposed speech, and
has as many times mentioned your subject, strength and resolution of the will. He claims that he needs the manuscript
so that they—as you will see from your correspondence—can
complete the necessary organizational and intellectual preparations. I have so far replied politely, employing delaying
tactics, as I hope you would have wished me to do. But you
yourself should soon give them some sign . . .

This lecture in Vienna—and Vogt himself would not have been
able to say why—was burgeoning inexorably into a mighty mental
mushroom, a relentless gloom. And he had shone before other
audiences and with much less trifling subjects. Academies and
highly learned societies that had, despite his not even having
achieved the academic status of a German professor, given him
standing ovations. He had never encountered a situation like the
one in that story about Schweninger, who—it must have been in
Madrid—had been forced to watch when, at his opening words,
"Our duty must lie in discerning the mind through the body," the
whole front row of dignitaries had gotten up and left the hall,
cursing loudly.

Who, for heaven's sake, had told that story? And who had passed
it on with the additional remark, perhaps invented, that Schweninger had gone running after the gentlemen in question? To a
courtyard tastefully decorated with fountains, where the gentlemen
had sat down on a bench beneath luscious purple wisteria, and
Schweninger had stormed after them, clutching the manuscript of
his lecture, furious and anxious at the same time, and had blurted
out something terribly offensive and been unable to find the words
required to put things right. Had Schweninger been just as
blocked, perhaps, as he himself had been six or seven months
earlier in Capri when he had started collecting key points for his
lecture on strength and resolution of the will . . . ?

In 16 Magdeburger Strasse a bell rang, but Vogt paid no attention. He was not expecting any callers, and the maids dealt with
everything else. On this level, at least, the concepts of centralization and the division of labor must surely be sensible.

Back then, in Capri, he had taken leave of Krupp one morning to go in search of those key points—which were on paper in less than an hour—in peace, somewhere he could concentrate. Quite close to the harbor, to which he was brought by donkey cart, he had found a little inn—a dive, really. Wisteria had been blossoming there, too, fading at the edges from white to an ugly brown, and it had been unimaginably peaceful, peaceful in a way completely unlike the lobby of the Hotel Quisisana, at which he was staying as Krupp's doctor. Anyway, he was sitting with his papers on a bench in the shadows, the milky coffee was marvelous, and he had begun to write. The usual banner phrases. The honor of the invitation. The illustrious audience. The enormous importance of the subject for the times. Its lamentable neglect by others.

And then he had come to a halt. He had spotted a young girl's face behind his left shoulder. Someone might have been rattling the garden gate. This girl—Vogt tried to remember how she had worn her hair, whether his medical eye had registered freckles—anyway, the little girl had disappeared and he had only heard her whispering—presumably to her playmate—"He's writing!"

It was spoken in such distinct Italian that even Vogt could understand it. But he lacked the linguistic gifts to comprehend the subsequent children's whispers. All he could hear, quite clearly, was the excitement of the whispering, as if the girl who had discovered him were giving a proud account of a particularly unusual bird that she had been the first person in the world to see, although a fairy tale had long told of its existence.

While the bell in Magdeburger Strasse rang a third, and possibly a fourth, time, Vogt tried once more to reconstruct in his mind the precise sequence of events that had followed that first utterance of "He's writing!" Out of curiosity, and perhaps out of vanity, too, he had tried to decipher the children's discussion. But after only a few minutes, interest in the stranger seemed to have evaporated. Vogt had once more focused his attention on the paper before him, which was now only a quarter covered, and the top corners of which were already beginning to curl in the sun.

Suddenly he heard the girl's voice again.

"He's stopped writing," she said unmistakably. Vogt looked at the words "Resolution of the Will," and the owner brought him another milky coffee.

The doctor violently crossed out his heading. Now, at his desk in Berlin, the scene came back to him as clearly as a dream in full color: the sweetly scented wisteria swinging back and forth by the garden gate, children running suddenly away. He had waited for one of their little faces to reappear. He wanted to chase them away, to have the peace to formulate his fleeting thoughts appropriately. But the children seemed to want to go on tormenting him.

"He's stopped writing." Vogt heard the voice again.

"He's just sitting there," said someone else.

"Maybe he made a mistake," he heard a third say calmly.

Guiding his dried-up pen with the tip of his index finger, Vogt carefully underlined the sentence "The subject of my lecture today is, for various reasons, of indisputable importance," the only line that he had written and not yet deleted. He got up and walked to the tall window. In previous cases of sluggish mental flow or creative block it had always helped him to observe events in the street from a high floor. To imagine that the cabs, trolley cars, coach-and-fours, and of course the pedestrians, barging into one another and hurrying like specters in one direction or another, were all on their way to his lecture.

But that gloomy afternoon, his downward glance only confirmed his suspicion that the maid, Frieda, despite their agreement, had once more neglected to clean the windows.

Nothing was going well for him. No lecture, no article, no honorable appointment, not even the simple art of running a household so that it would live up to its reputation as one of the better addresses for the treatment of mental illnesses.

As far as he and his own abilities were concerned, he felt quite distinctly numb and inert, and believed that he could recognize irrefutably that the devil's horns of academic resistance had been clipped once and for all. Previously—only a few months ago—he had adroitly joined in every debate like an experienced gymnast going through his motions, certain of their precision, their daring logic. Now, on the other hand, he felt stiff and spiritless; he had lost his center of gravity.

Vogt sat down at his desk again. He carefully stuck the old sheet of scratch paper between the other sheets he had thrown into his wastepaper basket, pulled a new page from the drawer, and wrote again: "The subject of my lecture today is, for various reasons, of indisputable importance." He had put too much ink on the nib of the pen, and his words looked very broad on the page. And they didn't lead anywhere. They simply stood, much too extravagantly curved, on the paper, crying out for successors, for a reason for their own appearance.

Vogt dried the steel pen with a dark rag.

When the maid knocked at the door half an hour later to ask if she could go out now, he was still rubbing the shiny metal point. Then he dipped it in the ink again and drew a squiggle on the rough paper. His practice had also undergone a number of severe setbacks. The most embarrassing of these had been a case that Brodmann had written to tell him about before his departure. Like many of the disasters of the past few months, this one also involved Binswanger. Binswanger had notified him that he was referring a patient to him for treatment, a certain Janis Vigrabs, a forestry economist from Riga, a man, as Brodmann later discovered, "of crude mental constitution, with a tendency toward clumsiness, but also painfully shy, fifty-two years old, with a nose as red as the beak of an oystercatcher."

The recommended cure in Berlin was supposed to free Vigrabs from his disinclination to devote himself to the forestry business that he had so long neglected, and also to endow him with a more manly resistance to the temptations of strong liquor. Nothing out of the ordinary, then.

Of course Binswanger did not tell him why he had chosen Vogt for this routine matter. Afterwards, the most plausible explanation seemed to be that his colleague had simply found the case too boring and not lucrative enough. But it was also possible that Vigrabs himself had insisted on a referral to the capital in order to spend a few more nights, under the pretext of seeking medical advice, succumbing to those stimulants that were not to be found as a matter of course in Riga. At any rate . . .

"At any rate," said Vogt, addressing the still unbearably blank sheet of paper on his desk, "the whole affair, disagreeable as it was, is over and has nothing to do with the matter at hand." He read again: "The subject of my lecture today . . . ," picked up the sheet, and crumpled it. This time he did not bother to clear away the evidence of his failure, and simply threw the ball of paper on the carpet behind him.

Might he not, he wondered, having carefully folded the new sheet in half, have acted reprehensibly in failing to devote himself personally to Vigrabs? Nonsense, first of all, because his lecture in Lisbon had been much more important, or at any rate it had seemed so after he had read the names of the participants, and second, because Korbinian Brodmann was certainly competent to have a preliminary conversation with the patient, in order, if necessary, to begin a course of light hypnotherapy. It really was an elementary exercise.

But everything that could go wrong had gone wrong. Nothing had gone right over the past few months. Of course he had shone at that conference in Lisbon. His audience had given him ovation after ovation. But not for a second could that applause alleviate the feeling of disappointment that had descended upon him the first evening after his arrival, when he had discovered that no one even halfway important in his field had turned up. Some people had merely had their papers read out by their assistants, others had sent telegrams of apology, and some had not even bothered to reply.

He himself, Vogt wrote to Cécile a day after the conference began, had walked into a trap, and of late he had felt himself constantly surrounded by traps. Even in his dreams he was tormented by "nets like the ones used by inshore fishermen," as he wrote the same day to Amanda von Alvensleben. He certainly took this "newly fashionable, lively reliance on dreams" on the part of the "barons of the subsensory" with a hefty grain of salt, but there could be no doubt about the content of dreams and the feelings of oppression that they conveyed.

Cécile had not replied, and Amanda had sent him only a picture postcard from Bad Kissingen in which she said, in that friskily sententious way so typical of her writing, that announcements of misfortune were always more enjoyable, from the literary point of view, than announcements of joyful events, and that she would give this idea considerable thought on her immediately impending train journey to Berlin. Vogt had been disappointed with this answer, and annoyed that all manner of public servants could have cast their eye over this postcard, for which, to make matters worse, he had been obliged to pay additional postage.

Vogt began again, printing in capital letters:

THE SUBJECT OF MY LECTURE TODAY IS OF
INDISPUTABLE IMPORTANCE

As Binswanger had sent him only a very superficial account of Janis Vigrabs's case history, Brodmann had been somewhat surprised when the visitor from Riga had scheduled two appointments and missed both. He had then turned up at Magdeburger Strasse for his third appointment, but when he had rung the bell there had been no answer. It was a Sunday afternoon, at four o'clock, almost on the dot, and at that time of day Frieda had for a number of weeks taken to disconnecting all the bells in the house so that she could devote fuller attention to the sexual desires of Weppermann, the animal keeper, which were for the most part very unusual. Immediately after his birth Weppermann's mother, unable to see why she should give a child either to the world or to the child's father, whoever he might have been, had thrown him in a trash can, a blow which he had survived thanks to his powerful voice. This had left him with a fear of, but also a desire for, cans and barrels, which is why Frieda, time after time and despite violent protests—"But I'll suffocate!"—had had to clamber into a barrel while the animal keeper took her from behind. That, at least, is how the maid—in a tone of defiance rather than shame—later told the story when Brodmann confronted her about the disconnected bell.

Janis Vigrabs was baffled at first, and then was filled with a certain self-righteous fury, because he had not been permitted entrance despite a "number of attempts to establish contact." He snorted with vengeance. He had walked a few steps backwards on the pavement, to study the facade of the house, when his hat had fallen from his head.

By sheer chance, at this point, Brodmann had walked to the window to observe, in natural light, a slice he had that morning taken from the tissue of some spine marrow. In order to do this he used his pocket mirror, in which he caught the reflection of Vigrabs, or rather, of a stranger bending for his hat. Brodmann had immediately remembered the appointment, and reproached himself for failing to hear the bell, dashed down the stairs, and caught his patient just in time to keep him from disappearing into the nearest tavern.

The fact that the subsequent attempt at therapy in the treatment rooms on the second floor, hastily arranged and possibly not carried out with all the care that the law dictated, had led to disaster could surprise no one. Brodmann jotted down only the usual formula, "poor." But the first session, as any doctor could confirm, was always a step into the unknown, a two-sided examination without any guarantee of finding, in the doctor, the "rope ladder on which to climb out of one's own distress."

Why had Amanda written in such an indifferent fashion? Cécile—this much was clear to Vogt—only ever answered when she had given her letter the proper amount of thought. Presumably she was still brooding over it, concerned on the one hand about not hurting him and on the other about responding as his intellectual equal, and worried about whether she should write her letter in fluent French or in her German, which still relied heavily on phrases from her primer.

Vogt tossed another ball of paper behind him, which bore only the line "The subject of today's lecture is of indisputable importance." Presumably Amanda was annoyed because he had never so much as mentioned his relationship with Cécile. That had been stupid, feebleminded, foolish, simply idiotic, because after all he had informed Margarethe Krupp of his engagement, which gave the whole business the level of discretion of a "rumor from the very best circles" in the *Vossische Zeitung*.

After that unsuccessful therapeutic session Janis Vigrabs had gone back to his hotel and ordered a bottle of champagne to be brought to his room. He repeated the order an hour later. The alcohol made him thirsty for experience, so he set off and asked the porter where he could find "a good time." The rest of the evening's events were recorded in the police report, and the evening editions of the newspapers the following day published some of the more distasteful details. Apparently it had required the efforts of three policemen to subdue the rioting forestry economist.

Of course Binswanger had gotten hold of the relevant articles about his patient. In the letter that he immediately wrote to Vogt he quoted extensively from them. This letter was peppered with expressions such as "to my indescribable consternation," "severe infringement of the Hippocratic oath," "jeopardized further collaboration." Janis Vigrabs was not even mentioned by name; Binswanger referred to him only as "the patient specially entrusted to your care." That was the last Vogt had heard from Jena. Neither had he heard anything more from Schweninger, which forced him to conclude that both colleagues had decided to keep their distance from him for the time being.

When Frieda walked into the study the next morning to announce Amanda von Alvensleben's visit, she found the doctor lying outstretched on the sofa, his face buried in the cushions. The desk and the carpet were liberally strewn with sheets and scraps of paper, all of them bearing but a single sentence.

TEN

"At some point you are really going to have to tell me why the subject of your lecture is of indisputable importance," said Amanda. "If you want to introduce me to anything new ever again, that is. My first impression upon entering the room was: Here is someone trying to reconstruct the battles of the Armada with paper boats. Ever since the parliamentary debates about the German navy I've been thinking almost exclusively in nautical terms. If I've been thinking at all. The last two weeks in Bad Kissingen were hardly encouraging in that respect. It was bad form to use a word of more than two syllables at dinner. And on all the countless walks, the only topics on the agenda were coughs and wheezes."

Vogt stirred his hot chocolate. He had taken a bath and changed his suit, and a touch of pink was slowly creeping back into his pasty face.

"That was unforgivable," he began, "and I really can't imagine how it came about." He nervously put down his cup, and cocoa slopped onto the tablecloth.

"Are you talking about your little boats, your impending marriage, or the stain now decorating the lovely cloth? I don't understand the boats, the tablecloth can be washed, and the only thing that bothers me about your marriage plans is the fact that you didn't ask me my opinion of your future wife. I am not suing for my rights as a lover, but only for my claim to exercise a degree of authority in matters of taste. Certainly I have been shamefully passed over, but let's not talk about that, let's talk instead about marriage. Not yours, but the Krupps'. While a link is being forged between you and your fiancée, another such is threatening to come asunder in Essen. Which is where the doctor comes into it."

"Did the Krupps actually send you to Berlin?"

Amanda cheerfully stroked the doctor's sleeve. "I can quite understand your surprise, but you should learn to deal with it more discreetly. And before I continue, I should now like to take a glass of sherry, doctor's orders."

Vogt rang for the maid.

"I shall start again. First of all to satisfy your curiosity as to why Dr. Vogt should have been specifically chosen when—as Schweninger has told us—he was involved in a dreadful scandal in Berlin."

"But I wasn't in Berlin when it happened," Vogt said.

"A bad style of management, my dear doctor. Or that, at any rate, is how Schweninger put it. He raised his voice as he said it. And he was no less vociferous when it came to details. The two gentlemen were standing on their own by the fire. Frau Krupp had gone off, and some premonition must have warned them that strong words would soon take the story beyond the boundaries of good taste. In the next room I could hear everything with the utmost clarity without opening the door so much as a crack. And I must say that I was tremendously impressed by that patient of yours."

Frieda brought a decanter and two glasses. Vogt poured out the sherry, but then pushed his own glass away from him as if to distance himself from it.

"I am never more clearly aware of the restrictions imposed on my sex than when I hear such manly deeds discussed. It takes courage to chase five naked negroes out of a tableau vivant, armed only with the domina's whip. And, if I may say so, I would have been interested in the content of the tableau—and so would Herr Krupp, who did ask—but at that point Schweninger grew evasive, in his droning way. So, sadly, I never discovered whether they were all men or whether it was a classical scene, so my imagination was excited, but remained regrettably unsatisfied."

"But given that Schweninger spoke out against me, how is it that Krupp has sent you to me in Berlin?"

"I've gotten so hot again that I'm going to have to have your glass as well. Which supplies me with the key phrase: 'alcoholic excess.' In fact, after Schweninger, his pointy red beard dancing with excitement, had checked off your shortcomings on his table of Mosaic laws, he talked himself into such a state that he began, without transition, to speak of the sins of Herr Krupp. 'Abstinence,' he cried again and again, 'your abstinence, Herr Krupp.' It sounded as if he had found a new title for my mistress's husband: His Abstinence Herr Krupp has the honor . . ." Amanda paused, because she was now coughing with laughter.

"Herr Krupp became rather caustic and tried to interrupt Schweninger. But as always at such moments of excitement, he began to stutter, which must, of course, have made him even more furious. It was not difficult to hear that he was trying to say, 'Now will you make your point!' But he couldn't come out with the *p*, and Schweninger had no intention of interrupting his sermon, having moved on by now to the subject of diets—or, more precisely, giving them up—which then, after a few twists and bends dealing exclusively, and rather unimaginatively, with particular groups of fats, led him to his final chapter, bearing the sensational title 'Anal Bleeding.' "

"Pardon me?"

"Anal bleeding," repeated Amanda, raising Vogt's glass to her lips. "You, as a doctor, will have heard of it—causes, course, prognosis—I'm sure you know all about it. I, on the other hand, am a virgin where such matters are concerned. And if you have no wish to enlighten me, a virgin I shall remain, for as soon as the magic words were uttered, or rather, to be precise, a few seconds later, the door slammed and one of the gentlemen had left the room. I assume it was Herr Krupp. Then the door slammed again, and circumstances would lead one to conclude that this time the party responsible was Privy Councillor Schweninger. But as Herr Krupp could not hear it, I should echo my old governess and say: '*Quelle folie, mais quel grand geste.*' "

Vogt glanced with relief at the ugly steel pin, two thirds of which protruded above the brightly colored feathers in Amanda's hat. This—as Amanda had immediately remarked when she came in —"creation of veritably poetic tastelessness" had been left to Frau Krupp by Mother Vogt before she had moved out with her furniture and linen. Vogt had sworn to get rid of it straightaway, but had always forgotten or neglected to convert this resolution into action.

"So the Krupp family still wishes for my medical advice?" he asked, reminding Amanda of a little child being forgiven, to his surprise, for a great sin, without having to face a grueling inquisition.

"Since I have been paid not only to deliver a request for the earliest possible appointment for a consultation, but also to bring you certain intimate correspondence, I would—putting it cautiously—be convinced of it. But I am not a mind reader. And please do not stare at that terrible picture of Husum Harbor behind me. First of all, it undermines my confidence if you do not simply look at me, and second, it insults the memory of my devotion to you—fleeting though it may have been—that the scrawls of a second-rate Sunday painter should be more pleasing to your eye than my new hat."

Vogt leaned forward, and Amanda drew back.

"No need for airs and graces," she said. "I'm only the messenger." She drew from her handbag an oval powder compact crowned with a simple ornament, and two separately tied bundles of letters. She handed Vogt the little bundles, and the doctor immediately tugged impatiently at the bows. Amanda sprang open the lid of the compact and glanced into the mirror. "I would still like to know why the subject of your proposed lecture is of indisputable importance. So much meaning is contained in the very word 'dispute.' What is your putative subject? Do unimagined profundities linger in the prefix *dis-*? I'm afraid I'm expressing myself rather brusquely, which is why I must most politely refuse the invitation to dine which you have not yet extended to me. And it appears that reading your correspondence is so gripping that even the etching of Husum Harbor will have to feel neglected today. As I see, that is already the case."

She rose from her chair, walked around the table, and looked over Vogt's shoulder. His right forefinger had just reached the lines in which Margarethe Krupp summed up the current state of her emotions:

. . . thanks to the improvement in my physical condition, I am in a good position to keep up outward appearances, and according to the general opinion, I have probably not been so satisfied and contented for a long time as I am now, but for that very reason the goad within has rooted itself all the more firmly, and is burrowing ever deeper into the whole of my being, poisoning all those things that were good in me; if I did not have the children, and if I had no obligations toward them, I think I could take the extreme step, I think I could destroy myself . . .

Amanda turned toward the door. "A peculiar urge, to lay oneself so bare, and in such curious imagery: the goad burrowing within the being." She shrugged her shoulders. "I must dash. If you have any questions about the letters which you think I might be able to answer, do let me know. I shall be staying at the Bristol."

In the corridor Amanda bumped into Frieda, the maid, followed by a tall man with a huge beard. It was too dark to discern more than these outlines. In compensation, the smell of eau de cologne was all the more distinctive. "Herr Kautsky," Amanda heard the maid announce.

ELEVEN

The tavern where Amanda had arranged to meet the painter Max Landsberg was on the other side of the army canal, and it was an unusual place. That it was an artists' haunt was plain from all the frames which covered the walls from floor to ceiling. But the frames contained neither canvases nor boards. Instead they surrounded profiles of heads, drawn on the plaster in charcoal or red chalk. Most of them went no farther than the chin—or somewhat higher up—ending in shapes resembling feed bags, which were probably supposed to represent beards.

"I have never fully understood this enthusiasm for beards," said Amanda. "All too often they remind me of landscape gardening, sometimes the English kind, the wild variety, and sometimes of French pergolas. I, for example, can alter my face by making my cheeks a little more red or a little more peach-colored, as today's fashion would dictate. I can also paint my eyes to render them naïve or somewhat lascivious, not to mention all the other ways of applying mascara, if we assume that this way of playing with paints makes a woman fascinating. The crucial point is, however: I can change. And I can do it from day to day—what am I talking about, from hour to hour. Men with beards always strike me as much more immobile.''

Max did not seem in the mood to engage in a conversation about the fashions in men's hairstyles. A few days earlier he had received a written commission to design a title page for the magazine *The Samaritan*, the subject of which was simply to be mankind. The journal's editorial director had approached him so as to give ''an artist of the coming generation'' the opportunity ''to provide, as an antidote to the filth of the day, an allegorical representation of purity.'' Max told Amanda about the commission.

''A kind of Garden of Eden with flowing forms'' was how he tried to sum it up.

''No nudes, then?''

''Naked children in tall grass, naked man with a cloth around his waist, naked woman with long hair, in profile and leaning modestly against him.'' Max drew a quick sketch on the brown wrapping paper that covered the table.

Amanda considered the result and raised an eyebrow critically.

''I am not without vanity, but my nose is, regrettably, not quite so noble. And I cannot recall having gazed at you or any other man with quite such cow-eyed devotion.''

With a few swift lines, Max lengthened the woman's hair until it reached almost to her feet.

''Did you meet anyone else you knew at Vogt's?'' he asked as his pencil applied itself to the pelvis of Purity.

''As I was leaving, a certain Herr Kautsky was being announced. But I barely caught more than a whiff of him. A well-turned-out figure in the dark. On the stairs I wondered how I knew the name. Could it have been the famous Social Democrat? But then it occurred to me that Vogt tends to consort more with crown and altar—and of course with business magnates. Do you think he has secretly switched sides?'' She looked from her plate to the drawing, on which Max was still working intently. ''Max, please! It's getting vulgar!''

The painter drew a delicate veil over the detail on which he had been concentrating. Then he turned his attention to the woman's armpit.

"Vogt clearly has terrible problems," said Max. He took a little knife from his coat pocket and sharpened his pencil, making precise cuts. "At least that's what his colleagues say. And with a great deal of satisfaction."

"Money worries?"

"Sooner or later it all comes down to money worries. Why do you imagine I'm thinking about a dreadful subject like the allegorical representation of purity?"

"Because you want to lure me into your studio so that I'll model for you," answered Amanda without so much as a thought.

"You'd do that?"

"First tell me more about Vogt. And please tear that sketch out of the tablecloth before I do so myself."

Max drew a circle around his drawing with the knife, and then carefully separated the Garden of Eden from its surroundings. He cast his eye quickly over his work, folded it carefully in half, and handed it to Amanda.

"If I have understood correctly," he began hesitantly, "Vogt has made enemies chiefly because of his manner. You know him, reticence is not his strong point. Things went reasonably well as long as he remained unequivocally successful. But he must have botched a few cases in the meantime. Nobody will say so directly, of course, but everybody's happy to pass it on. Now Vogt, instead of waiting until the gossip has passed, has become vehemently defensive, and threatened supposed counter-revelations."

"Only threatened, though?"

"Threats were quite enough. Because immediately—I haven't the faintest idea who started it—a curious story went around, linking Vogt with stolen slide preparations of brains. No idea whether there's anything to it. From what I've been hearing, lately even famous researchers have been breaking the seventh commandment in their hunt for trophies."

"I simply can't imagine that of Vogt. The sixth commandment, certainly, and maybe a good selection of the rest. But why should he do that?"

Before Amanda could receive a reply, her conversation was shrilly interrupted. A guitarist had taken up position alongside their table, a lean man past the bloom of youth, with a reddish, pockmarked face. His head was covered with a rust-brown bandana, and from his right earlobe there hung a piece of cut glass that had probably once adorned a chandelier. A second figure moved like a shadow behind the guitarist, the hem of its pale blue fisherman's pants stopping a good eight inches above its bare feet. The shadow was holding a tambourine. "Liebhof and Gutzmann," cried Max in disgust, once the two musicians had passed on to the next table. "A year of landscape studies in Córdoba, completely useless of course, but in this place they serve up the romantic school for lunch. Let's go. More than half an hour of Bohemia gets on my nerves."

They set off toward Landsberg's studio. It must have rained while they were in the bar, but now puddles and shop windows reflected beams of sunlight. Amanda nearly bumped into a girl driving a hoop in front of her with a little wooden sword. She linked arms with Max and asked for a more precise account of Vogt's difficulties.

"Here you are with a beautiful woman on your arm," he said, drawing her even closer to his side, "but what does she want? She wants to talk about another man. That is the tragedy of my life."

All he could really do was pass on the gossip that was making the rounds at the moment, he said a few steps later. Perhaps there wasn't exactly a scandal as such, but only an attempt, born out of disfavor, to slander a medical colleague. Vogt, rumor had it, had announced in the very highest circles that he was planning an earthshaking discovery, a precise calculation of the exact position in the brain of the nerve cells that provide information about the genius of the bearer of those cells. Whether he had said this in so many words or had only suggested as much remained unclear. But there were plenty of indications that he had been working more in oils than pastels, and finally, at the moment in question, he had been awarded considerable sums from the public coffers, and it was generally known that Vogt's research post suffered from a chronic lack of funds. For example, he still owed him, Max, his fee for the etching "The Arching of the Body in a Major Hysterical Seizure."

"Who did you use for that?" Amanda interrupted him.

"I already had the position of the limbs. Cramps always look the same. The concierge's daughter sat for the head. She has a very striking chin," he added, as if by way of apology.

"Please continue!"

It could safely be assumed, Max went on, that Vogt, under the impression that he was now in financial straits, had actually set about drumming up support, and had made a considerable racket in doing so. Of late there had been a real explosion in more or less dubious academic projects, and in every case potential sponsors had been promised tremendous scientific results. As the whole world was now talking about degeneracy, about nervousness, decadence, and progressive enfeeblement—with all their implications for the health, resistance, and achievements of the nation—the only person capable of winning access to the coffers of industry and the court would be the one who promised to solve a universal riddle.

"So Vogt is setting his sights on discovering gold?" asked Amanda.

"That's putting it a little too strongly. To exaggerate somewhat, he is working on a new map of the brain. To develop your image of gold, an atlas of mineral resources. In certain places you find this, in others that."

"*Hic sunt leones*," Amanda said, laughing.

"Researchers have been doing that for decades, of course. They've been locating the centers of sensory perception, motor abilities, aesthetic receptivity, and all kinds of things. Vogt has now announced that he can represent everything much more precisely."

"So instead of a map of Germany we have a street map of Berlin? But there's nothing scandalous about that. In what way has he bitten off more than he can chew?"

Max freed himself from Amanda for a moment to look for his

cigarette case. "I'm a mere painter," he said, "and a craftsman, and not a scientist by a long chalk. I have to stick to what I can see for myself and what other people tell me. From what they say, the promise to produce this street map, as you call it, is bold indeed. But it's practically foolhardy to claim that you can locate not only every row of houses, but also the behavior of the inhabitants of individual floors."

"So these potential sponsors you mentioned, they've obviously understood Vogt's project to pin down a place in the brain—or a house, as you put it—in which new recipes can be concocted after the fashion of medieval alchemy? That sounds like a great deal of fun. It would have my instant support. I've always longed for more than one Mozart and, from the perspective of women's rights, more than one Don Juan. How perfectly ordered our world would be if we could stop overrating uniqueness as we do. There would simply be more justice in the world!"

She ran up to a woman wrapped in blankets, selling faded lilies of the valley from an archway. Amanda bought the whole basket, carefully selected two stems whose blossoms were still fresh, and guided the flowers into her friend's dark velvet-trimmed button-hole. Then she gave the basket back to the woman.

"Now, you're unique to me," she said. "The only flowers I like, in fact, are white ones; perhaps that makes me a desirable model for an allegory of purity. Please tell me more!"

Max pressed her hand. "If it were an allegory of silence I was after, clearly I'd have to look elsewhere."

Amanda cheerfully let her leather bag dangle from her wrist. "I have yearned and gazed into the distance too long," she declaimed, so loudly that passersby stared at the couple. "Too long have I belonged to solitude; thus I have forgotten how to be silent . . ." She lowered her voice. "And now back to our Dr. Vogt, if you please, back to the seventh commandment."

"I'm not quite sure whether I can share your enthusiasm about the improvement of mankind. As an artist, the geniuses who have lived and worked before me are quite enough. Whenever I confront an empty canvas or squat over a white sketchpad, these characters are peering scornfully over my shoulder. 'Scrawler,' they laugh, 'talentless little scrawler, thinks he's a painter.' "

"Max, your mind's wandering. But you're forgiven, because at last you're talking about yourself, for once. Even if it's nonsense, sadly—you know how talented you are."

"If Vogt claims," Max went on quickly, "to be able to track down the sites of genius in the brain, he must, of course, have made it seem plausible that he had appropriate material at his disposal. But this is where the chorus of evil voices come in. Over the past few months, at least in Berlin, practically no material that could be termed extraordinary has been left to scientific research. So if Vogt promises that he's hot on the heels of something, he must have gotten access to a brain that no one else knew about, or else he has gotten hold of preparations which were previously in other researchers' cupboards, or had someone else get hold of them for him.

"That's why a skillful crook will organize matters so that it looks as if nothing is missing. After he's helped himself, he'll simply put slices or blocks of some common or garden-variety brain back in the empty spaces."

"When you say 'slices or blocks' you sound almost like the nice old butcher in our village talking about his cuts of beef."

Max laughed. "In both cases it's a matter of preserving valuable material. Whether you separate out the fine pieces this way or that is—in this case—a question of scientific taste. Vogt claims that only a brain dissected into little slices can reveal its true greatness. Blocks, on the other hand, to stay with your image, are merely little canapés."

Amanda thought for a moment. "I could imagine something like that if I were, say, to switch one string of pearls for another. I wear the new one, and if someone expresses surprise, given that everyone knows about the miserable state of my finances, I just say that sadly, it's just a piece of costume jewelry. But in the case of a brain robber who wants to make his name, it's a much more sensitive matter. He will later have to say that he worked exclusively with material that was absolutely authentic, genius guaranteed.

And that forces him, as Frau Krupp says, so beautifully and so often, to *name names*."

Max shook his head. "Let us assume first of all that what our crook is looking for—the center of genius—really exists. Let us assume secondly that that center can be identified, as the doctor says. In that case the scientific proof will never depend on one single brain, but on a series of similar constellations. So our crook will say that he has"—Max raised his voice—"in a host of individuals"—and he lowered his voice again—"from the fields of government, the military, science, acrobatics, or whatever, observed a striking change at point *xy*. In the course of his investigations, however, he has had the most diverse slide preparations under the microscope or the microtome, his cutting apparatus, but he has concealed all of their names, of course, in order to guarantee the objectivity of his research."

Amanda clapped enthusiastically. "At last, a perfect crime. But what if the real owners of the elite brains, who don't know that what they've got is bad merchandise, sliced or diced, what if they examine our perpetrator's thesis and come to the conclusion that it couldn't be valid?"

"I've thought about that, too, but there isn't any great risk involved. Research like that would require a great deal of time, and it would take nearly as long for the opposite to be proven, *if* the opposite can be proven. But even then it would boil down to the refutation of a false or at least disputable claim. Nothing new would have been discovered. I myself would much rather do something new."

Amanda stopped and looked at him in astonishment. "That sounds like secessionist talk. Max, since our last meeting you've grown a rebel's horns." She took a handkerchief and wiped his forehead, which glistened with moisture. "And above slightly graying temples at that. My compliments!" They turned into a little side street that led off the Lützow Quai, and walked first through an alleyway and then through a courtyard. Max pulled out his key ring.

TWELVE

The good news from Essen unleashed a flood of energy in Vogt, the like of which he had not experienced for weeks. Having scrupulously worked his way through the Krupp correspondence, the crucial passages having already been marked in blue pencil, he pulled a fresh sheet of rough paper from the drawer of his desk and, almost in a single stretch, wrote a provisional version of his lecture on strength and resolution of the will. After writing only a few paragraphs he felt that this time he had captured the right tone. This feeling stayed with him right through to the conclusion, and swelled when he read out loud what he had written.

Frieda brought him milky coffee, but Vogt let it get cold without so much as taking a sip. The letter to Frau Krupp, the next thing on his agenda, took him only a few minutes, while the letter to her husband, to which he devoted a disproportionately greater amount of care, took him half an hour.

He rang for the messenger and had his mail sent off.

Then he flicked through his desk diary, picked up a form for a foreign telegram, and notified Cécile of the wedding date. He delivered this dispatch to the telegraph office in person.

THIRTEEN

She had, Amanda wrote in the morning hours of the following
day, visited many artist's studios (and there followed a list consisting partly of Christian names, partly of surnames) in the past,
but she had never come across such a neatly gruesome attic room.
Whereas other artists would have had more or less colorful mari-
onettes arranged around more or less threadbare armchairs and
cardboard pillars, with maybe a skeleton or just a death's-head to
provide a harmless thrill, and their distance from the bourgeoisie
was marked chiefly by dried-up paint pots and ashtrays that hadn't
been emptied for ages, Max's place exhibited "the depressing
sparseness of a shop specializing in first-aid products." Just as a
Tirolean wood-carver keeps his knives and chisels hanging on the
wall beside him ready for use, she wrote, the queerest selection
of pincers, enemas, saws, and bloatsticks was arranged along the
far wall of Max's high-ceilinged room; "It's impossible to speculate
about their purpose without worrying about what one's going to
dream in the night to come." Beside the window hung a broad,

"off-color" strap which she had initially taken for a chastity belt, but which, according to her host, was a new device in the treatment of umbilical hernias. Max had also shown her a wide variety of works that he had recently completed, all stored neatly in cupboards with a lot of drawers, and all, so far as she was able to judge, executed "extremely accurately and very realistically," but with a "rather sad, drained perfection."

Life modeling was not quite her thing, though it did satisfy a latent but urgent need. And she had clearly sensed how the painter's initial pleasure in her body had, during the "creative act" given way to a concentration on "unconnected details."

During this phase she stopped feeling like a person, and felt more like an assemblage of contours or "points of interest," and she was suddenly reminded of her favorite dog, a Labrador that had, tellingly, also been called Max, and which she and her father had had to accompany to the most important breeders' competitions. After modeling, she had found it very pleasant "simply from the point of view of relaxation and warmth" that Max's studio at least resembled the standard issue in being endowed with a wide couch. The view of two "flesh-colored artificial calves with knee joints" had been somewhat sobering, however. On the other hand, the bedclothes had smelled excitingly of lavender, a scent that she had not come across since her boarding-school years.

Max, "tireless if methodical," had lain dreamily beside her for a while, talking about a boxing match that he had seen the previous day, and then about the new career he wanted to embark on, a radical new beginning, as soon as his material situation allowed. He had had enough of executing official commissions imposed on him by other people, and wanted to follow his own vision to create something new, ideally in tempera, because tempera meant eternity as far as he was concerned.

Then he had draped a stainless white apron over his naked body and gone back to the easel to add a few details to the allegory of purity. He felt "an artistic aftershock," he said as he buttoned up his outfit.

Amanda looked around for something to read that would prolong just a little more her "cheerfully relaxed mood." But all she found on the two shelves next to the little kitchen, apart from a variety of books on anatomy and guides to the "suitable use of forms of vegetable nutrition," was a surprisingly wide-ranging collection of brochures about electoral legislation, economic policy, and "the social question."

That reminded her of Kautsky, and his relationship with Vogt, and the fact that Max still owed her some information on this subject. And she had also resolved to question Max about the key phrase "anal bleeding," but the painter claimed that his concentration must not be disturbed. Later on, when he was looking for a particular pen, he muttered only two or three very vague phrases, which seemed to indicate that it was always a good idea, "in times of crisis," not to put all of one's money on a single horse. Amanda laughed and answered that during the crises that had occurred in her life she wouldn't have been able to devote so much as a thought to horses. But Max would not be roped into a conversation, so she quickly got dressed and set off to visit her friend.

FOURTEEN

His bleeding must have started shortly before midnight. It could not have been much earlier than that, because he had distinctly heard and counted the chimes of the clock. At that point there had been no pain and no irregularities. Otherwise he would not have toyed with the idea of emptying the open bottle of red wine. Only toyed with the idea? At any rate, it must have happened after that.

But why had Francesco not noticed anything? Francesco, who always pressed so close to his back when he went to sleep that he could feel his curly head against his neck, and maintained this position until morning. Surely Francesco would have felt something and woken him up. Krupp anxiously examined the thick, dark stains on the pale blue silk sheets. The relevant passages in his *Compendium of Specialist Surgery* remained so clear in his mind that he could have recited them by heart. The words "slimy purulent discharge" on page 203 of that book had burned their way into his memory just as indelibly as the tightly printed characters of the word "impalement" on the previous page. But nowhere in the whole of the seventh chapter, entitled "The Rectum," could he discover the term "anal bleeding," which Schweninger had flung at him that evening in Essen.

Did Francesco really love him, or was he like the others, who only wanted to earn their bracelets and miniature gold cannon so that they could foppishly display them in the piazza later on? Or like Ottoline, that little rat from Spandau whom he had caught rummaging around in his private correspondence two days earlier. It had been a terrific relief to get rid of that ungrateful little tart.

Normally Francesco, awakened by some mysterious internal signal, left the bed without a sound shortly before dawn, slipped into his faded clothes, which always smelled rather excitingly of fish and tar, and then ran down the hill to the harbor to get the boat ready before Giancarlo and Franco turned up in Marina Piccola. Francesco was discreet, and he had never accepted a present. But why had he not shaken him out his sleep when the bleeding started? Perhaps he had been nauseated. Perhaps he had simply taken off abruptly, fearing that he might be accused of something. Or else he really hadn't noticed anything. But what else were lovers for? He would give Francesco a present. A tiny little one or a great big one, and today. He could buy him a new boat with tackle, nets, the works. If Francesco had a bad conscience he would betray himself and accept the gift. Then he would confront him.

But what if Francesco simply refused the present? If he looked at him with those hazel eyes of his, astonished, superior, thoughtful, possibly saying nothing that could lead to discussion or argument? If he then simply withdrew, leaving a proud or wounding word like a tip?

Krupp took off his spectacles, which he had picked up to examine the stains on the sheet more closely. Schweninger had written a few weeks earlier and, in a deliberately neutral tone, recommended a cure for mechanically injured hemorrhoids, one of the usual combinations of cold baths, enemas, and opium pills. All things he could have found out for himself from his book, and nothing that applied to him as a particular individual, apart, that

is, from Schweninger's tasteless formulation "friction between the
buttocks in particularly corpulent people subject to heavy perspiration." If one wished to place one scoundrel next to another,
one might juxtapose Vogt's letter from the previous day with this
one. It said the following:

> From the twenty-fourth until the twenty-ninth Frau Krupp
> had her period. I managed to bring it to an end within five
> days, to ensure that it was not very heavy. As was to be
> expected, an intensification of her emotional discontent nat-
> urally occurred during these days . . .

An indifferent spring sun shone through the open window. The
longer Krupp stared at the stains, the more striking and menacing
they looked. Immediately after breakfast he would write to
Schweninger and also to Vogt to tell them of his recent discom-
fiture. Here he was, calling upon some of the most expensive
doctors in the whole of the Reich, and they were unable to bring
any degree of stability to the state of his health.

A few days before, upon his arrival, he had still felt quite well,
apart from his asthma and the attacks of dizziness that continued
to afflict him. The business correspondence that the porter from
the Quisisana had given him had probably affected his nerves. He
was constantly expected to devote his strength to his work as a
company representative; in less than two weeks, on the seven-
teenth of April, he was due to return to Essen to open the military
display before His Majesty in Meppen. Then there were other
appointments, all of which his board had arranged without con-
tacting him directly. They were all tugging him in different directions and nobody showed the slightest concern for him.

At least these appointments kept him away from The Hill. He
had gotten off lightly on his last visit, at first. Margarethe had had
her hands full organizing the confirmation celebrations, but before
he had left, there had been another great explosion. It happened,
of course, because she wanted to go with him to Capri. He had
suggested other destinations in the south, but she vetoed them

out of concern for the children. That was a broad hint, as he very well knew, but he had simply kept quiet and set off.

Something had to be done about Margarethe. Vogt was competent, but so far he had only managed to offer palliatives, he hadn't actually brought about a cure. Or had Marga already won him over to her side? She was clearly very clever if she was able to play the humble victim. Not only had he experienced this first-hand, but many people had mentioned it to him.

Francesco would now be lying on the boat in the shadow of the sail. It was curious, was it not, that Francesco fished during the day. He had never thought about it before. Fishermen came home at dawn. People fished in the night and sold their haul at the market early in the morning. Did Francesco lead a double life he had never told him about?

The gentlemen from the local police force had been funny, practically ludicrous, when they had turned up the previous day, stammering and red in the face, to call his attention to certain rumours that they were obliged to investigate. Apparently articles had appeared in the press claiming that a German industrialist in the area was being somewhat careless in his choice of friends. The name Krupp had been mentioned later in the article, and a few fathers had gone to the police and complained that their boys had been lured into performing certain acts or participating in certain acts, exact descriptions of which they did not care to utter. Of course Capri was not Prussia, of course people were tolerant, and the complainants were probably only hoping for a degree of financial compensation. There was no proof of any kind, apart from a few photographs that had been taken from life. At any rate, the statements had very closely resembled one another, which could, of course, have been the result of a previous arrangement between the complainants. They had only wanted to keep Herr Krupp informed. The boys had, legally speaking, been very young. And rape was a crime that not even the Italian police could simply ignore.

Why had the uniformed police come to him of all people? When he had done so much for Capri—financing streets, concerts, the development of the grotto? The accusations had been pulled out of thin air. And they were arbitrary beyond belief. On such a pretext, you could have disturbed half the German inhabitants of the island. Why did they come here, of all places, to spend their money?

So he'd been taken in again. Taken in and informed upon. Either someone from the island was trying to play a nasty trick on him, or it had something to do with business maneuvers in the factory. In all likelihood it was the latter. The people in Essen had eliminated a competitor, and he was to pay for it here in Capri. Typical of his board that no one had thought to warn him.

He would send for his assistant, Korn, his go-between with the board. He would sort everything out. Korn was on his side, Krupp was sure of it. Korn would soon silence the troop of malicious letter writers and those little martinets on the police force. Korn knew who was who in this part of the world, and he had dealt with them successfully on every occasion so far.

Getting everything straight, that was what it all came down to. He would have to get everything straight. On the home front, where those verbal, intellectual, and physical gymnasts on his board played their tricks, and the same with Francesco, and finally with Marga.

Vogt would have to take care of Marga. Simply get rid of her. How could anyone be the head of a household with a nagging wife? There had to be some way of dealing with this problem in a clean and clinical fashion. Why didn't Vogt do anything? Yet again, everything depended on Krupp himself.

Krupp pulled his knees toward his chest, rolled on his side, and got out of bed. He stripped off his nightshirt and walked to the window. Even the sea was sparkling spitefully. Krupp drew the fresh air into his lungs and began his morning exercises.

FIFTEEN

Oskar Vogt folded up the report that he had written at Krupp's request, on the formal instructions of his assistant, Korn, concerning the case of Markus Jacobsen. Jacobsen, who had formerly been a servant at The Hill and was now the leaseholder of the Krupps' Kronenberg beer hall, "which fed him well enough," suffered, according to his former employer, from an "apparently hysterically ill wife," who had let him and the business down "with very great frequency," and who neglected the children to such an extent that Jacobsen was utterly desperate. Vogt was to decide what needed to be done "to save the man and his children (five)."

He had met the leaseholder in the Essener Hof on Limbecker Platz, and had then driven with the very soft, almost fishlike man to his tavern to get a clearer picture of the situation. A little later he had also met the man's wife, Maria, known as Itze, a strapping, Mediterranean-looking matron with a considerable growth of facial hair, who had been an actress in Düsseldorf before her marriage.

For a number of hours Vogt had patiently listened to accusations, justifications, and counteraccusations. He had drunk lemonade and eaten sweets, looked at children's drawings and family photographs. He could not rid himself of the feeling that he was witnessing an event that he would be able to understand only by deciphering a message in an impenetrable code.

Later, during the night, after he had climbed into bed with Cécile, he tried to explain his interpretation of that message. His wife listened to him in silence without voicing her support. Perhaps she was merely tired, but even so her behavior was unusual.

"My next step calls for courage," he repeated the following morning when they had already been on the train to Berlin for an hour. "Courage, application, and resolution!" Rich green shrubs, birch trees, and telegraph poles swept past the carriage window. "It's like a daring scientific experiment! We simply have to try it!"

Cécile said nothing. She had spread out a napkin on her lap, and was peeling an apple. Then she inserted the point of the knife into the fruit's greenish white flesh, cut it into little half-moons, and laid these out in a straight line on the cloth.

"If a conflict should arise," Vogt went on, the lilt of his voice echoing the rhythm of the rails, "a decision will have to be made in favor of one of the two parties. We have remained neutral for a long time, but it clearly cannot go on like this. There will be winners and losers, and we can't afford to be on the losing side. Even from the financial point of view it would be a complete disaster, it would be the end."

Cécile dabbed saliva from the corner of her lips with a pink handkerchief.

"Neither can we afford," she said in her hesitant German, "to back the wrong horse. If Frau Krupp wins a hearing with the Chancellor, a positive hearing, then she will be the stronger party. There might be a big scandal about the Capri affair, and there might be another about the profits from arms dealing. Ever since I've known her, Frau Krupp has been very much in favor of us. A patron of our research. One never knows which rumors to lend credence to and which not. But you alone must decide when the time is right for action, for commitment. Perhaps not right now, perhaps not until you return from your language course in England. And don't forget that Herr Krupp may be on our side, but he is not a robust fighter."

Vogt sprang open the cover of the gold pocket watch that Krupp had given him the previous Christmas.

"If the train is on time, we will be in Berlin in five and a half hours. I don't believe there will be a scandal. Even if there is, the court will stand by Krupp. No, we must act now. I shall take the first steps this very night."

These first steps were a report on the mental distress of Markus Jacobsen and an appointment the doctor arranged for the following evening.

A week later he received a written reply to the question he had put to the gentleman to whom he had talked that evening. To declare Margarethe Krupp incapable of managing her affairs, Privy Councillor von Simson, his legal adviser, wrote him, would not be a simple matter. Guardianship courts would be required to mull over "psychical abnormalities" and, in borderline cases, "temporary disturbances affecting only some of the brain's activities." The situation would be simpler, von Simson informed Dr. Vogt, "if the patient was deaf, blind, or dumb." But in the more delicate cases of mental disturbance, or feeblemindedness, the court would insist on a prior *causae cognitio*, which could hardly be carried out in complete secrecy.

This first page of Herr von Simson's letter sounded anything but encouraging. Caution was called for, the privy councillor stressed, since the courts generally only proceeded according to very clear ground rules. Thus "a mental disturbance rendering free determination of the will impossible" would, for legal reasons, be preferable to a case in which "the person to be declared temporarily incapable" had never been so declared, or had been placed under the temporary care of a guardian because such a declaration was imminent.

Vogt, who was well acquainted with legal writing, derived increasing pleasure from the style of the letter. This ponderous construction could only lead to a satisfactory conclusion. First the lengthy mock-attack on the project, then the pose of the learned dandy—surely the cat was about to be let out of the bag.

He was not mistaken. For shortly before concluding his analysis, the privy councillor finally recommended taking legal action. With reference not to paragraph 1676, according to which "the preconditions must be objectively discernible beyond a reasonable doubt," but rather to paragraph 1677, the formulation of which, bearing in mind the motives behind its incorporation within the civil code, took into account the particular conditions of this case, since it could also be employed in cases of "sporadic psychical abnormalities."

Herr von Simson had also added that the importance of Vogt's proposed letter to the guardianship court could be considerably enhanced if it was accompanied by the forthcoming report by Professor Binswanger. Privy councillor von Simson thought the idea of sending a report by Professor Binswanger at a later date somewhat risky. That would not make as good an impression in court as the simultaneous presentation of two reports.

But would Binswanger go along with this? Vogt folded the letter in half and placed it in his correspondence file under the letter *K*. It was possible that Binswanger would insist on being the front-runner. On the other hand, Binswanger was a ditherer. From the correspondence folder Vogt drew a letter from Krupp that had reached him three days before the privy councillor's legal notice.

Today I was in Düsseldorf, where I met the head of our council, who is a friend of mine. I cautiously informed him about my wife, and in response he admitted to me that on the same day that my wife had spoken out against the Chancellor, she had also talked about me in generally immoderate terms, saying among other things that I was a gross egotist, took absolutely no interest in my children, and had had no desire whatsoever to come home for my children's confirmation. He had not wished to say anything to me about it, but had intended at some point to tell my wife how unfair she was being in saying such things to other people, and how

grave the consequences of making such disclosures to third
parties could be . . .

Was that an adequate account of feeblemindedness? Would a
guardianship court deduce from a wife's claim that her husband
was a "gross egotist" that she was mentally ill, that she was suffering from a psychical abnormality?

That was for Binswanger to decide. He, Vogt, had dared to take
the first step, and now the others would have to nail their colors
to the mast. He alone had had the courage to take the initiative.
In any case he was going to be busy for a number of weeks now;
his language studies were taking him to England.

SIXTEEN

It was October, and the leaves of the maple tree were ablaze. What was a maple tree doing in Jena? It would never have survived in Essen, although other species—the cedar of Lebanon, the tulip tree, and the Japanese sickle fir—braved the climate there. Was there more than one maple out there? It was impossible to tell from the table, and even if one was to climb up on the table, it was not much of a help, since the little window was close to the room's ceiling. The little window was round and had bars on it.

Her brother, Felix, who had visited her the previous day, was still the sycophantic little creature she remembered from childhood. A compliant lackey to Fritz. And it had been she who had got him the contract for the frescoes in the dining room at The Hill—horrible frescoes, it must be said. It had also been she who had always spoken up on his behalf when the authenticity of the *objets d'art* that he transported to Essen was called into question. Not to mention the authenticity of the artists.

How curious to claim that she had thrown a fit and lashed out when the doctors and orderlies had taken her to the train. At the age of forty-eight, and after all the humiliations she had withstood, she would not go around behaving like a wild animal. But it was peculiar that she herself had no memory of the circumstances under which she had been brought here. They must have injected her with something that paralyzed her will and her memory.

But otherwise she felt fighting fit, just a bit tired. Numb, dull, tired. Nonetheless, she had written to Fritz, politely and firmly. He should know, she wrote, that she was not going to accept her fate without a struggle, and that she intended to refute, point for point, these monstrous accusations against her person.

Perhaps Fritz had even noticed the little barb, the little poisoned arrow, when she wished him a swift recovery from his cold. A man has his wife locked up in a sanatorium and she asks tenderly about his cough! Her husband probably hadn't noticed a thing, as usual. If she knew Fritz, he just had a case of the sniffles.

Not even the reading of newspapers was permitted here. She obviously wasn't supposed to learn whether the scandal surrounding Fritz had spread. She did not receive any personal communications until Binswanger or his cronies had read them first. She had a vivid picture of what happened to the letters that she herself wrote: They would be read and reread and analyzed, and passed on only if the addressee was conspiring with the people who had brought her to Jena.

They had all known about that dreadful business in Capri and no one had told her a thing. Neither Privy Councillor Binswanger nor Professor Schweninger, Admiral von Hollmann, or his wife, and least of all Professor Vogt. So this was her reward for her trust and her kindness, from the very people to whom she had turned for help.

But these gentlemen should not imagine that she would give up without a struggle. She had begun her last two letters: "Since my husband thinks that my nerves have been in a very poor condition following a taxing summer, I have decided, at his request, to undergo medical treatment in order to effect a recovery . . ."

That was a slap in the face, it fit the facts, it underlined her detachment from her husband's wishes and at the same time emphasized her readiness to obey those wishes if there were good reasons why she should do so.

She was not, of course, giving in to Binswanger's unseemly demand that she should view certain utterances, states of mind, and minor actions that were attributed to her as part of what he called her syndrome. Had she not been so tired all the time, she would have defended herself earlier. And then she would have foiled their fiendish plot, designed to make her see herself as an invalid.

So they required that she see herself, and herself alone—not Fritz—as the disruptive element in the marriage, with all the complications that this entailed for the household and the family, and particularly for the children. But she would take this ludicrously transparent sham as a challenge. She would call on witnesses. Vogt, for example, and Amanda von Alvensleben, to whom Fritz had obviously revealed years earlier why he shunned their marriage bed.

She would explain why she had simply had to tell the Kaiser that a man who neglects his family duties—in the narrower as well as the broader sense—who, in concrete terms, sneaks secretly away from home for a good six months of the year, is not fit to run the biggest company in the German Reich.

Had she really described Fritz as being of unsound mind? Was she really supposed to have claimed that a similar decline had afflicted his father twenty years earlier? It was quite unlike her to say such things; she would never discuss anyone close to her in such brash terms.

She must not forget that her dowry had not yet been transferred. The dowry was hers by rights, the sum had been agreed, and it was to be sent directly here, to Jena. She could no longer bear to be so dependent; not even her brother Felix would be able to persuade her that these claims were not legitimate.

She would have Dr. Vogt come to Jena. And Amanda von Alvensleben. Then she would go through the accusations with a fine-tooth comb. She would insist on having witnesses there at all times, and ensure that very precise minutes be kept. Minutes that would be valid only if she had signed them. Underhandedness was to be avoided at all costs; on no account could she allow herself to be isolated.

She had expected to have a lot of enemies. Fritz and his clique, that much was obvious. Her kind nature had simply blinded her to them. But the Vogts?

From a diagnostic point of view the results of the examinations were pathetic. On his way to the conference of neurologists from central Germany in Dresden, Binswanger made a provisional assessment of the current state of affairs. It was plain that a psychopathic change had occurred in the patient's emotions, as evidenced by a whole series of statements she had made in the presence of witnesses. Frau Krupp had lodged a complaint with the Kaiser, the Chancellor, and a not inconsiderable number of important people, which was designed to do serious damage to her husband's standing. She had used terms that implied an overactive imagination and a loss of memory, and perhaps also disturbances in her faculty of judgment. As this matter had been dragging on for more than five years, and as the attacks had become increasingly violent, the prognosis had to be unfavorable.

On the other hand, it could be argued that some of the accusations were not entirely without foundation, particularly those concerning the couple's private life. It was also easy to understand the emotional torment that a wife would undergo when—as had manifestly happened—anonymous letters were passed during a visit to the theater, containing billets-doux from her husband to other men. "Emotional provocation" was the term that best described Herr Krupp's behavior when, on visits the couple made together to Berlin or elsewhere, he had always insisted that his wife stay at a different hotel from his own.

Finally, not only did the case contain a large number of imponderables, which made it difficult to pursue a clear course of action, but he was also duty-bound to be discreet because of the social position of everyone involved. Binswanger resolved to tell Vogt of

his doubts and anxieties. When the train arrived in Dresden he
went into the waiting room and wrote to Berlin:

> . . . I now see my task as combating Frau K.'s emotional
> overstimulation, clarifying her judgments, and above all en-
> gaging her in some self-criticism. If I succeed in my task,
> everything will be fine. If not, the future looks bleak to me.
> Let us not forget that the symptoms elaborated overleaf are
> no excuse in law for resorting to compulsory restraint!

After he had posted the letter, Binswanger grew worried that he
had not expressed himself with sufficient urgency. He took a cab
to the telegraph office and sent a telegram to Vogt, asking him to
arrange a meeting in Jena as soon as possible.

SEVENTEEN

Simply ignoring the article in the *Augsburger Postzeitung* on November 8 had been quite the right thing to do. No question about it. Who could possibly take the slightest interest in what people in far-off Bavaria were printing concerning rumors allegedly circulating in Capri? And if "the name of a German industrialist of the very highest standing, whose close relations with the imperial court are well known, is, sad to say, very intimately involved in the affair," fine, duly noted, but this *Augsburger Postzeitung*—who read it, after all, apart from the supporters of the Bavarian Center Party? That band of bigots deserved a rap on the knuckles; the whole business would have sorted itself out in the fullness of time.

But when *Vorwärts* joined in a week later, and in its wake the *Volkszeitung* in Düsseldorf, the *Arbeiterzeitung* in Dortmund, the *Volkswacht* in Bielefeld, and the *Volkswille* in Hanover, a mere shrug wasn't enough. Without a doubt, it was a cunning plot by the Social Democrats to stir up the workers. There was an international strategy behind it. All these newspapers, apart from the miserable

Augsburger Postzeitung, were plainly organs of the left. And precisely the same was true abroad: *La Propaganda* in Naples, which had disseminated the so-called Krupp case, had long been known as a drum major of the belligerent Socialist press. *Avanti* in Rome— well, you had only to translate the word, and what did you get? Yes indeed, that vulgar and pervasive battle cry, "Forward, march!"—in German, *Vorwärts*! They were all members of the same rotten red clique.

Being cowardly, of course, they didn't dare confront their adversaries head-on. Instead they pretended their smears were aimed solely at the abolition of paragraph 175. How very decent of them! They were probably all perverts themselves, that band of muckrakers, faggots, fairies, sodomites, and shirt-lifters.

No, the only advice one could give Krupp was to let these guttersnipes feel the sword of Justice at their throats. No holding back, and no blindfold.

If Krupp was to bring an action against *Vorwärts* before the Berlin public prosecutor's office, and they decided to pursue the case "in the public interest," proof of the paper's statement—as in all legal cases—would be required. In other words: The defendant, *Vorwärts*, would insist on calling witnesses. If the court ordered the exclusion of the public from this portion of the proceedings, it could only do so on the grounds of a threat to public morals.

Then Krupp would be finished.

So if Krupp could be persuaded to bring a libel suit, and if the public prosecutor of the Royal State Court could be persuaded not to advise the applicant to bring a private action, and if the chamber was to present itself as the instigator of the proceedings, under no circumstances would the case ever be dropped.

And Krupp would be finished for good.

What would a trial mean for the company? For the company—and here it was almost impossible to raise a reasonable objection—the proprietor's extravagant behavior was clearly burdensome. The man had outdone himself. One had to answer for him everywhere one went. His stammering speeches. His unreliability in turning up for meetings. His cockeyed philanthropy, bestowed by turns on a former servant, a dancer, a gardener. Those expensive artistic and no less costly scientific hobbyhorses. And the marital discord that had dragged on for years. It was a running joke even in Berlin. And the company worked well enough without representatives. Enough, then! Better no representatives at all than representatives who constantly made a mockery of the board of directors.

Someone needed to persuade Krupp that he simply had to bring this action. There would be a scandal, but that could be kept within bounds. And Krupp would be finished. Not a bad outcome for the company.

He would save Fritz. He personally, Ottoline, the famous fairy from Spandau! That very day he would go into the editorial office of *Vorwärts* and explain to the gentlemen that, yes, Fritz came under the paragraph they were so keen to abolish, but he would also explain that his friend had only been an onlooker during those boys' games. That it was only Allers, the painter, Big-Brush Allers as they called him, who had arranged those tableaux vivants, all that cuddling and pumping in Tiberius' cave. Fritz had only liked to watch. And he had every right to do so, given the amount of money he put up.

Of course he, Ottoline, would never forget how humiliating it had been to be spurned so suddenly. It was only out of jealousy that he had rummaged through Krupp's letters. Lovers should have no secrets from one another. But Fritz could be so wonderfully hot-tempered. However, never again would he allow himself to be called a "pathetic little blackmailer." Fritz would eat those words.

No doctor anywhere in the German Reich would be able to help him out of this tight spot. What arguments could be employed to delay the doctors' notes, which everybody knew about? To the effect that Krupp, in all the time they had been treating him, had never shown any symptoms of contrary sexual feelings? That would speak volumes about the mutual trust between these authorities and their famous patient. It would amount to a simple declaration of the bankruptcy of their diagnostic abilities.

Should they perhaps say they had noticed the tendencies, but had managed to suppress this morbid deviancy by bolstering their patient's strength of will? Ludicrous! Too many potential witnesses were involved in this affair. Not only in Italy, but also in Berlin, Düsseldorf, and Munich. Even Krupp wouldn't be able to buy off all those witnesses.

The whole business would turn into a farce if the doctors tried to talk their way out of it by referring to momentary absences of mind. A man who was supposedly responsible for the weal and woe of Germany's biggest armaments company, the victim of momentary absences of mind! It was easy to imagine a lawyer greedily snatching at the idea: "And what cure did you recommend to the patient for these momentary absences of mind? Perhaps a lengthy visit to southern Italy? Even Capri, perhaps?" No, no one would expose himself to such ridicule in the courtroom. It was impossible to imagine any of his doctors getting Krupp off the hook on this one.

What, in fact, did one stand to lose if one broke with this member of the upper chamber? Irritation on the part of His Majesty, who was not keen on people kicking up stinks in his immediate vicinity, for fear of being tormented abroad. But that could be dealt with. It had always been dealt with before.

The whole business would have to be sorted out in such a way as to send out a few internal signals: to the regiments in and around Potsdam, for example, which were also entirely contaminated from the moral point of view. It would have to be made quite clear to those pansies just how little tolerance would be devoted henceforth to their Bulgarian pranks. The cleanup would have to start somewhere. There was not an army in the world that could survive if the man behind couldn't help staring, enchanted, at the bottom of the man in front.

If Krupp was sacrificed, vigorous action could be taken. The spread of decadence had become intolerable. What hope was there of winning the battles of the future with an army of perverts and degenerates? It was a form of degeneracy that had to be excised from the officer corps, and also from the ranks. Of course, one might feel sorry for Krupp. But then in such situations some poor bugger always gets it.

EIGHTEEN

The gray mists that had been hanging over the Ruhr Valley since early morning had grown increasingly dark. For an hour, the coachman and servant had been waiting by the Hill station for the two doctors who were expected to arrive from Jena. When the rain grew heavier and colder, the men pushed their way into the waiting room and stood by the little stove. "November weather," said the little groom with the flat nose, blowing on his cold fingertips. But no one responded.

They had to wait another half hour for the guests. A broken-down train had been blocking the tracks. At least that was what the station manager claimed. The rain did not let up.

Finally the signal light changed, the gates fell with an agitated jingle, and the train came in. It was empty apart from two gentlemen in fur-lined overcoats. Without uttering a word, these two gentlemen pointed to their luggage and climbed just as silently into the coach, which brought them to the Krupp estate.

The lord of the manor received his guests in the little library, also known as the Kaiser's nook. He had probably been sitting there for quite a long time, as the round table by the sofa was covered with letters and telegrams, pushed up against the silver ashtrays, the bottle of red wine, and the crystal goblet.

The visitors came directly to the matter that had brought them to Essen, and they did not bear good news. Frau Margarethe Krupp, Privy Councillor Binswanger revealed, had now pulled herself together mentally and seemed very calm and controlled. After a surprisingly swift recovery from the initial shock at being admitted into the clinic, she gave not the slightest impression of being frightened, insecure, or even regretful, but seemed instead to have a firm desire to break the Gordian knot around her soul, as she put it. He, Binswanger, had not stinted in his attempts to induce her to "examine her conscience" and thus self-critically analyze her previous statements and actions, but to judge from his efforts so far, he could only observe, with unconcealed distress, that the patient was reacting "in a calmly stubborn manner."

Frau Krupp's earlier "emotional disorder," Dr. Vogt agreed with his colleague, had become with amazing speed an "aggressive driving force." A few weeks earlier one might reasonably have assumed that "delusory behavior," and perhaps certain "galloping figments of the imagination," on the part of Frau Krupp provided the medical basis for legal action. Now, however, a dubious situation had arisen whereby although the facts, the scandalous list of Frau Krupp's misdemeanors, clearly spoke for themselves, the woman responsible for the facts in question was, to judge by her current state of mind, capable of acting like the epitome of the perfectly stable personality. The doctors treating her had thus reached the conclusion that at the present moment, from a legal perspective, the situation was most unlikely to produce a successful action in a court of law.

But they had also wondered, the doctors insisted, whether their own competence, which lay in the sphere of medicine rather than law, was adequate to the case in question. "My colleague Herr Binswanger," said Vogt at this point, with a polite bow toward the privy councillor, "has therefore considered it advisable—and I may add in all modesty that I consider this to be excellent advice—to try and involve another authority within our field. We are thinking of Professor August Forel of Zürich, who has been staying in Düsseldorf for the past two days. We have taken the liberty of asking Professor Forel to contact us here by telephone. You may remember Forel's excellent work a few years ago in the sad case of Crown Princess Luise of Saxony?"

"Get Forel over from Düsseldorf immediately," Krupp said. He rang for a servant and made the necessary arrangements.

"So you want to cover yourselves?" he then asked his guests.

The two doctors said nothing and exchanged furtive glances, each challenging the other to comment.

Finally Binswanger spoke. "We do not wish so much to cover ourselves in this matter," he began, "as to weigh the prevailing conditions in which certain courses of action are more appropriate than others. As things stand, and should certification proceedings be taken against your wife, we must prepare ourselves for two eventualities: Not only might the public, which is not especially well disposed toward us, take a keen interest in the case, but Frau Krupp might be forced to rely on that public. Of course we are all shocked and repelled by the malicious campaign by the Social Democratic press. We are also solidly convinced that you will succeed in putting a stop to these slanders. In any case . . ." Binswanger lowered his voice, as if he had with these words concluded a lengthy disputation.

Vogt put it more clearly, in a hesitant and laborious way: "We have arrived at the conclusion," he said, staring rigidly at the two rows of books in the glass case behind Krupp, "that in the event of a forthcoming trial, because of your supposed participation in that business involving a certain paragraph, it would appear less than opportune, such a short time after that trial, to allow Frau Krupp, in her present state of mind, outwardly—as we have stressed—so stable, to repeat certain accusations that might be unfavorably interpreted as being connected to earlier rumors."

Krupp filled the crystal goblet to its golden rim. "You can speak bluntly to me. Less of the fine talk. If I survive the first trial, the second one will break my neck—is that what you're trying to say?"

Binswanger and Vogt raised their hands in a defensive gesture. "First of all we want to consult our colleague Forel," said Binswanger. "Under no circumstances would we advise a hasty capitulation," added Vogt. "We simply feel obliged to take into account all eventualities. This does not indicate any change in our personal loyalty toward you. We are merely—how should I put it—diagnosticians of a particular situation that has come about without our assistance. A certain neutrality, quite out of touch with life, is often attributed to science. Nothing, as you will have been able to see for yourself, could be less appropriate to our own attitude. For this very reason, however, we also feel authorized to give advice which, if heeded, promises definite success."

Krupp raised the goblet to his lips and stared down at the liquid with stubborn defiance. "At some point you will also come across Dr. Pahl from Essen, who is at present treating one of my employees," he said, putting the glass down again and refilling it. "With your kind permission I shall now withdraw, the last few days have been rather trying."

Binswanger and Vogt rose. "We want to try to spare you as much trouble as possible during the time to come," Binswanger assured him.

"Then make a bit of an effort, gentlemen!" Krupp's tongue had grown heavy. He clutched the back of the sofa, made a hint of a bow, and departed.

The heavy curtains in his study were closed. The chandelier with its ten spheres and white porcelain bell, which had burned above the desk in the days when his father had done the accounts, had already been lit by a servant. The chandelier cast a bright light on letters, telegrams, and documents, family photographs and the bronze bust of his father, who cast a strict eye on his son.

Krupp sat down in the curved Moorish armchair and mechanically stacked the telegrams one on top of the other. Then he was seized by a coughing fit. He pulled himself up against the tabletop and walked unsteadily into the bathroom, where he kept his medication. It was only a few minutes before the morphine drops took effect.

The servant Erwin Bahlke, bringing him his tea early in the morning, was struck by a peculiar smell, sickly and acidic at the same time. Bahlke put his tray down on a little table by the door and switched on the light. His master lay motionless on the bed, his jaw hanging down as though it had nothing to do with his strikingly pink face. Beside the pillow, dark rings had formed around little cubes of vomit. The servant decided to call for Dr. Pahl at once.

Pahl found Krupp completely dazed, barely responsive. He reached for his pulse and placed his left hand on his forehead. Krupp's body temperature was unusually low, and his breath was frighteningly shallow. Pahl ordered the servant to call the other doctors immediately. Then he closed the door.

Vogt and Binswanger arrived at the same time. They repeated the actions that their colleague had performed, noted the slow heartbeat and the very small pupils. "Ipecac, we need ipecac straight away," Vogt said abruptly. He pointed to the two empty laudanum bottles on the bedside table. "Coffee first, then ipecac." Nine hours later the doctors abandoned their endeavors. Krupp was dead.

From the moment Frau Krupp arrived at The Hill from Jena, everyone had to act as though she were just returning from a rest cure. They were to inundate her with tasks and—no matter how dramatic the events—convey to her the actual normality of the situation. Maybe even a slight sense of guilt. A new regime had just been ushered in. It posed another challenge for the former patient. A kind of shock therapy. Above all, the doctors had to persuade her that it was in her own most general interest, in the interest of the family, the business, and even of the entire German Reich to forbear from requesting an autopsy. And not just an autopsy, but something much more important: criminal proceedings against the Social Democratic press. But that could wait for the time being. First, the needs of the moment had to be attended to; whatever the circumstances, Frau Krupp had to be treated as if—apart from the deeply regrettable demise of her husband—nothing, absolutely nothing, had happened. She must be reminded of her duty to the nation. Important ceremonies were coming up. But one point was urgent: no autopsy, under any circumstances! They would probably have to explain to her in the minutest detail why this was of urgent importance. They could only hope that she would understand.

If all four doctors signed the document, the board of directors would abandon further prying. To be sure, not only those gentlemen, but the Kaiser as well, would rather have read an autopsy report corresponding to the image of Krupp as an animal hounded to death by social democracy. Rumors were supposedly circulating in Berlin that the deceased had shot himself. But the diagnosis of a stroke was really the most that a responsible doctor could put his name to.

The four gentlemen agreed on a joint explanation formulated by Dr. Pahl:

To the Board of Directors of Friedrich Krupp:
For the following reasons the undersigned doctors have reached the decision that an autopsy on the corpse of F. A. Krupp should not take place:

1. The doctors were aware that Herr F. A. Krupp had for years been taking a large number of narcotic preparations to combat insomnia. These preparations needed to be taken in very large doses if the desired goal was to be achieved.
2. There can be no doubt that under the influence of the emotional disturbances of the recent past, Herr Krupp had relied on soporifics more often than before, and had probably increased the dose, particularly since his asthma attacks had been recurring during the last year and a half.
3. We found morphine in the possession of Herr Krupp; our

investigations, however, enabled us to ascertain that Herr Krupp was never in possession of morphine in sufficient quantities to have a fatal effect. We may assume that on the night of the twenty-first to the twenty-second of November Herr Krupp took morphine to combat his feelings of debility.

4. Under the prevailing circumstances it is more than likely that an autopsy would reveal the presence of narcotic preparations in the intestines. This finding would have precisely the opposite effect that the board would hope to derive from an autopsy. To put it plainly, it would only add fuel to the suspicion that a suicide by poisoning had occurred.

5. Given this state of affairs, we are convinced that the expressed wish of the head of the household and the direct request of the widow, to the effect that there should be no autopsy, should be fully respected.

[signed]
Professor Dr. Forel
Professor Dr. O. Binswanger, Jena
Dr. Vogt
Dr. Pahl

Why had nobody prevented His Majesty from making that speech at Essen Station? Vogt had not understood every word, because he was standing too far away from the speaker's improvised rostrum, and in addition he had that morning had the misfortune of standing right next to the Krupps' firemen's band when they had delivered a deafening rendition of *Jesu, meine Freude.*

As supreme head of the German Reich, His Majesty shouted, he had felt obliged to keep the coat of arms of the German Kaiser above the house and memory of the deceased. That would have been fine, in the old Nibelungen tradition, but his advisers should have warned the German Kaiser about the passage that followed:

A German to the core, who only ever considered the welfare of the fatherland, and particularly the welfare of his workers,

has had his honor impugned. This act, with all its consequences, is nothing less than murder, for there is no difference
between the man who mixes a poisonous brew and proffers it
to another, and the man who, from the safe hiding place of
an editorial office, sends out the poison arrows of his libels
and kills a fellow human being for the sake of his good
name . . .

Or perhaps one of these speech writers had simply heard something
about an overdose and had jumped from there to the idea of poison?
Was it possible that His Majesty was not in fact informed as to the
circumstances of the case? That would mean at least that the company's board of directors consciously wished to involve the Kaiser
on their own behalf. Frau Krupp, Vogt was convinced, had concentrated entirely on the part she was to play. But by the time
proceedings were taken against *Vorwärts*, some of the truth would
have come to light. On the other hand, Margarethe Krupp had so
far played along. It was painfully cold, here at the station in Essen.

As if he had read Vogt's mind, August Forel drew him aside.
"There will be no judicial sequel to this whole matter," he assured
Vogt. "I repeat, to this whole matter! I have received this message
from sources I can trust." He was obviously about to add another
sentence, but a brisk threefold "Hurrah!" interrupted their conversation. Then Forel disappeared into the crowd of dignitaries.

Jesu, meine Freude, sang the railway tracks as Vogt made his way
to the restaurant car. Since the train had left Essen he had been
unable to shake the tune from his head. Neither that tune nor
Cécile's accusatory expression, which she seemed to have brought
with her from Berlin for the funeral ceremony. Yes indeed, he
had, as she put it, backed the wrong horse, yes indeed, it had
been entirely his decision, but even afterwards he could not quite
put his finger on the point at which he had blundered or had cause
to reproach himself.

Of course Krupp had been susceptible to mood swings, but these
had always been a plus when it came to winning his support for a

particular project. Of course he had been dependent on morphine, alcohol, and perhaps on his sexual urges, but those had all been fundamentally calculable risks that anyone would run if they wanted to succeed and assert their superiority in this milieu.

Frau Margarethe had given his condolences a frosty reception. Amanda von Alvensleben, too, with her cool, businesslike manner, had at first struck him as extremely dismissive. It was a good thing, at least, that he had been able to reveal the truth of the matter to her before he left.

Krupp's brain might have been worth investigating. That combination of breeding and decadence . . . ? The cast-iron fishplates between the carriages beat out *Jesu, meine Freude*. That was the end, Vogt mused in the dining car, of the big money. Frau Margarethe would not be quick to forgive him his role in the Binswanger affair, and even if he could justify himself in appropriate terms, why should the widow support the deceased's academic hobby? And there were other candidates.

It was not too much of a shame about Krupp's brain. It might have supplied information on certain, somewhat exotic questions, but it would not have passed muster as an elite brain.

Cécile would need to straighten things out with Margarethe again. Cécile was not involved. On the contrary, she had, in fact, always stuck by Frau Krupp. Cécile would have to explain to Margarethe why he, Vogt, had not been able to act in any other way.

The waiter brought him the breast of veal he had ordered.

NINETEEN

Amanda von Alvensleben corresponded at irregular intervals with Vogt in Berlin. She usually sent little parcels containing bundles of jottings from the previous few days or weeks. She herself called them her scribblings, perhaps because she chose her subject matter as arbitrarily as she selected the paper on which she set it down. Thus, for example, Vogt had once found a description of her search for a fugitive tortoise on the back of the obituary of one of Amanda's aristocratic relations. Another time her fury over the vindictive behavior of a Geneva policeman, whose "custodial eye" had been blackened by a woman about whom nothing further was revealed, first wound its way along the edges of a restaurant menu before moving across the program of a lieder recital. Most recently, Amanda preferred to write upon the insides of the protective covers of bound books, which had just become fashionable.

Yearning was the title on the dust jacket on which she had chosen to complain—as she had done in previous missives—about her life as a governess in Geneva. Vogt briefly wondered whether on this occasion she had chosen the title on purpose.

"No one who has not felt it in their own body, their own emotions, or, more precisely, in the neglect of those emotions, will ever be able to understand the incredible boredom of life here in Geneva. Sometimes I am overcome by the feeling that all the people around me have passed through treatment with that colleague of yours—his name escapes me but not so his pungent breath—that man with the thin goatee and that incredibly showy practice on Alexanderplatz. They once told me that he rendered his patients docile by means of electric shocks, and I still remember how that amazed me, because electricity enlivens, after all, although after their cure these characters looked more like the cave dwellers in Greek philosophy.

"My thoughts are already back in Berlin. Last night I even dreamed longingly of puddles after a shower on Potsdamer Strasse, but I don't want to succumb to dreams now. I would rather provide you with an up-to-date picture of conditions here. The kindest thing that can be said about them is that they are in a state of absolute harmony. The peace seems imperturbable. 'In Zürich,' my acquaintances say—I have not yet made any friends—'in Zürich they lead a wild life.' Then, with the weariness of a well-fed tortoise, they will lower an eyelid and raise it again, and in the interval you could turn over an egg timer before they add: '*Mais c'est Zurich!*' which clearly explains everything.

"I have not yet been able to discover just what it is that is so scandalous about Zürich. Perhaps they lace their tea with rum in the wintertime, perhaps their women button their corsets at the side, perhaps the gentlemen there smoke cigars as they read the Bible. You will observe, my dear doctor, that try as I might to imagine something scurrilous, under the circumstances I can only come up with things with which I could not even have shocked Frau Krupp.

"And as for the wild Russians I had been promised in the city, there is not a single trace of them. How I long for a few anarchists—even bearded ones. And there is so much here that might be put right with a bit of dynamite. Russian Social Democrats are said to be staying in the city. The unfortunate Max Landsberg told me that. I didn't write in my last letter that he had turned up because—as he himself claims—he feels a new creative phase is on the way. Out go the anatomical portraits, then, and in comes unpopulated nature. I told him that with a name like his he would be well advised to give Alpine subjects a wide berth; of course he took this as the crudest mockery and reached for his brush none-theless, to capture the lake here at sunset. But paint as he might, even in oils, the lake persisted in looking rather like an inflamed liver. That, at least, is what I thought, but he said his oeuvre—when did he ever voice such an idea before?—was dictated by his inner eye. I got a bit annoyed at that point and said his inner eye must have developed a cataract, and he didn't call on me for two days after that.

"But what I really wanted to say—these Russian Social Dem-ocrats, or so Max explained to me, are bitter opponents of the anarchists and more inclined to support a program like the one represented by that Herr Kautsky whom I once met at your house in Magdeburger Strasse. That is, I didn't meet much more of him than a whiff of his cologne, but of course you will know who I'm talking about. So they are thinking about revolutionary upheavals, about what we used to call 'the great unwashed,' but I can't be more precise than that because the gentlemen in question never show their faces.

"My dear doctor, I'm beginning to chatter, and even the at-mosphere of this place is no excuse for that. I wish you and Cécile the very best, as I shall certainly do again in future letters, and every success, especially in your research."

This was the end of the first letter in the parcel, which Amanda, as always, had left unsigned, because, as she once wrote, it would never occur to her to conclude a conversation by repeating her own name.

The next layer of her letter consisted of remnants, or possibly samples, of wallpaper decorated with pale roses, which had clearly been cut out with nail scissors. It contained the news of a suitor, who was revealing his intentions only very hesitantly, married, of course, like everyone here over the age of twenty-one, but not quite a stick-in-the-mud like the rest. His name was Emile, which she found very passable, almost encouraging, in view of her sur- roundings. The only disturbing thing about him was his militant teetotalism, but what was charming, on the other hand, if some- what superfluous, was his intimate knowledge of German poetry. To give Emile a helping hand, a few days earlier she had asked him to recite two poems about the heart and two about the brain on his next visit. Perhaps he would come up with something that Vogt would find useful.

Max Landsberg, she continued, had gone to Munich for a week, hoping to win greater recognition for his work there, and even financial success. She was still skeptical about the whole business, but had found him in such an agitated state when she was giving him some provisions for the train journey—"two bottles of white for the first hundred and fifty miles, three bottles of red for the rest, a bottle of schnapps for the tunnel"—that she had even, "*à contrecoeur*," expressed the hope that she would see him at Princess Urussova's salon after his return. This princess's salon was the only "oasis of hope" in her existence there. In fact she had to underline the words "hope" and "only" a number of times, first because all the other social groups there had been dipped in "a flat gruel-gray paint," and second because there was no concealing the fact that Emile, her only channel of access to the princess, would receive an invitation, and finally because she, Amanda, could not predict how Emile would react if she proposed that he introduce Max to this celebrated society as well. Emile had a dark shock of hair, "a constitution so somber that he was practically a silhouette," which would almost certainly make him capable of showing certain "Othello-like characteristics," but perhaps he did not yet dare fully to reveal those traits so soon in their relationship.

A new sheet of wallpaper—"the roses," wrote Amanda, "remind me of some underclothes that my mother once showed me, and then locked away again with the remark that such things were 'for later' "—this new sheet dealt with painful setbacks: Her budding romance with Emile had reached an impasse the previous Friday afternoon, while the children in her charge sat at their German lessons, when he had surprised her reading *Les liaisons dangereuses*, in the rose garden of all places. He had presumably come—as requested—to deliver poetical information about the heart and the brain, but Amanda had not noticed him until he had "turned back again, crunching on the gravel." She had been too absorbed in the book, a work that she could, in passing, wholeheartedly recommend to Vogt: "Not only is it pretty strong stuff, as my father used to say when he locked literature in the glass case, it is extremely refined, exciting, and in a perverse way even moving." Presumably this excitement had been clearly legible in her face—red patches still tended to reveal her emotional stirrings.

"A day later," wrote Amanda, "a card arrived, and I can only hope that Emile copied it out of a moral philosophy letter-writing manual. The accusations read in every particular like one of those tracts that people here lend their friends on special occasions." Losing a suitor was not so painful to her as the fact that her chance to meet people other than the financiers surrounding her, with their savings-bank faces, had utterly vanished.

The third layer of Amanda's letter was immediately striking in its expanse: almost half a dozen sheets covered with her round cherry-pit handwriting, all bearing the name and address of a couple, unknown to Vogt, who lived in Lausanne. Also unusual was the fact that the day of the month was specified at the beginning. Amanda had even added a precise "05" to the printed century, "19."

"I can finally tell you about an exciting afternoon—as an eyewitness and with the events still fresh in my memory. You were so right when you recommended that I distract myself with the Russian soul. The scene of the action was the salon of Princess Urussova, who has moved into a country house nearby. As I wrote, I had been so hopeful that I would be introduced to it, but until a few weeks ago the princess was still in Russia, where she spends a few months every year, establishing contacts with absolutely everybody and presumably also instilling a bit of terror and humility in the administrators of her estate.

"Emile, whose name and basic characteristics I must have men-

tioned in my last letter, has been dealing with Princess Urussova's
finances here in her absence, which must mean that they are not
inconsiderable, although of course he would never talk about them.
Ah yes, I forgot to mention that Emile and I were reconciled after
our little disagreement. Flowers, chocolates, and volumes of poetry
changed hands, and cards that would merit the epithet 'devastat-
ing.' So utterly profound was his regret that he immediately gave
Max an invitation as well. Max could hardly contain his joy. Nobody had been able to do much with the products of his inner eye
in Munich, either, and he imagined that he had fallen into a patch
of bad luck, and that he was a victim of the bourgeois art market's
conspiracy against progress in art, and he was beginning to bore
me with his inane prattle.

"So Max was thrilled by the idea of being admitted into a house
reputed not only to value the unusual, but to measure it in gold.
His Jacobinism vanished like the wind, and all he could talk about
was the traditional role of the aristocracy as patrons of the fine arts.
Max even went so far as to ask Emile how much he could reasonably
ask for his inflamed livers and caseous glands and whatever else
he sees in nature. I just barely managed to persuade him not to
roll up a few samples of his art and bring them along. But then he
himself had the bright idea of making a few sketches during the
party, which he was later going to send the princess as a gesture
of thanks for the invitation—and perhaps so as to establish a more
stable relationship. I made him promise to show me the drawings
first; I was not going to have our hostess insulted by the impudence
of his inner eye. Although, in parentheses, I can hardly imagine
that the lady in question is very easily disconcerted.

"Max then disappeared into town to buy a new sketchpad and
one of those velvet items of headgear that identify the wearer as
an artist. These errands took him so long that we were almost late
in arriving, at least according to my sense of decorum. Emile,
however, consoled me with the information that different rules of
etiquette applied at Urussova's, and the somber tone in which he
said this gave me a pleasant feeling of anticipation.

"In general, my moods do not depend on the weather, but this time my state of mind received a tremendous boost from the fact that the sun was peeking through the ragged clouds. I would have said the foehn was blowing, but Emile won't have anything quite so simple as that, because the Genevois have more words to describe their winds than they have to flatter their women. But Emile too had noticed the bizarre cloud cover, and immediately came up with an appropriate quotation from Goethe: 'The truest herald of the clouds will scatter before he reaches that place we yearn for,' upon saying which, he gave me a puppyishly soulful look.

"Princess Urussova's estate lies in a little hollow, and in the past is supposed to have been used as a hunting lodge and perhaps for spicier purposes as well. What fascinated me was how so many rooms could be crammed into such a tight space, and how much could fit into those rooms. Everywhere the eye could see were samovars and busts and aviaries mostly filled with squawking birds; the walls were covered with the heads of dozens of members of the family, all of whom clearly considered it a blessing to have their portraits preserved in oils for posterity. It required a certain grace to maneuver around all these objects without doing any major damage. And the princess is anything but slender. Your friend Schweninger, according to Emile, was once entrusted with—as he put it—'resolving her dietary problems.' Without, it must be said, any lasting success. But neither is there any indication that the princess regrets the fact that when she gallops through the rooms, the leaves of the palm trees break off, Gallé vases topple from their shelves, and the crystal chains of the chandeliers go crashing into one another. This woman clearly converts her abundance of flesh into energy, and she also has a voice with which it is easy to imagine that she can penetrate the great expanses of her Russian homeland. She made a profound impression on me, particularly when, as she often did, she uttered the word *wunderbar*.

"I also found it agreeable that the *petit cercle* was not forced to follow a rigid schedule. Of course someone played the piano, in this case the princess's daughter, a startlingly soulful, almost consumptive creature, and she played unassumingly well. The instrument was not placed anywhere central, however, as there was no center, but in one of the rooms leading to the garden, and one listened only if one wanted to. Happily, people were smoking so much that no one hit upon the dread idea of striking up a song.

"In fact we were almost among the first to turn up. Only four gentlemen and a lady had arrived before us, Russians, we were to learn, and a very strict-looking man whose French immediately identified him as an Austrian. In a side room we also happened upon a Baltic gentleman of almost dwarflike proportions inspecting the porcelain in a state of happy abstraction.

"After making a meticulous bow, the Austrian introduced himself as a certain Herr Lanz von Liebenfels, and he immediately ushered me over to a sofa to enumerate all the von Alvenslebens whose paths had ever crossed his. This promised to be only moderately entertaining, which is why I quickly informed him that I had never taken an interest in any member of the family whose name I bear, apart, of course, from my father, who was, on the other hand, spurned by his branch of the family after marrying the daughter of a tobacco trader in Odessa who had fallen upon hard times.

"In response, this Herr Lanz muttered something in his Alpine dialect that sounded like 'Appalling mess—such relations!' but might actually have been 'Appalling miscegenation!' I'm not quite sure, because the princess had been passing by, making her own racket, to greet another Russian, a certain, if I heard the name correctly, Herr Plekhanov, who—I'm relying, as ever, on Emile's social information—lives in the immediate vicinity.

"To judge by the behavior of the other guests around the front door, it seemed that in the form of this Herr Plekhanov a very important person had graced us with his presence. Maids curtsied, lackeys bowed from the hip, and this immediately prompted Max to reach for his pencil and sketchpad. My Austrian neighbor on the sofa promptly lost all interest in Alvenslebens in general and me in particular. He stared at the new arrival like a nervous marmot perched on its back legs to sniff the air before beginning its warning whistle.

"Herr Plekhanov very pointedly paid no attention whatsoever to his audience. He was divested of his fur-lined coat and walked up to the only Russian to have come with a female companion. I can't of course swear that he had come with her, but at any rate, when I saw them for the first time, they were both standing together very intimately. Plekhanov kissed the woman's hand a shade too swiftly, and then he fell on the man's neck, as Russian custom seems to decree. This exchange of endearments reminded me of nothing so much as those rather formal ceremonies where the winners of bicycle races are honored by the mayor.

" 'You look magnificent, my dear Volodya,' cried Plekhanov, when he had finished his embraces. He spoke loudly and in French, as if one of the other guests had questioned the handsomeness or health of his friend Volodya.

"I had no means of comparing, but the word 'magnificent' would not have occurred to me. This Volodya—Emile claimed his surname was Talin, while Max knew him as Ulyanov; the Russian emigrants change their names every time they change their addresses—made me think rather of an actor who has to play a Chinaman in *Turandot*: His eyes were like nothing so much as slits, his head was peeled like an egg, and his complexion was an unhealthy quince-yellow. But what he really lacked, to be entirely Chinese, was a pigtail; very much so, in fact: Ulyanov—I shall stick to that name, it sounds more Russian to me—Ulyanov's head was covered only by a few reddish strands at the temples, which looked more like downy feathers. This made his head more imposing, but at the same time more vulnerable. As to the decorative use of hair, I should also mention that he wore his beard as if to give his chin some threatening extra weight. Later, on the way home, Max, Emile, and I argued about whether the glinting eyes beneath those Asiatic lids were black—as Emile believed—or cinnamon-brown—as Max said, relying on his artistic gifts. We agreed only that they had had a certain penetrating quality.

" 'The similarity between that man and myself,' Herr Lanz von Liebenfels confided to me after very maladroitly pouring me more tea from the samovar, 'is that in Russia his writings are as forbidden as my own.' No, he said in response to my question as to whether he too was dedicated to revolution, that would be to say both too much and not quite enough, he was indeed a revolutionary, but not in the same narrow sense as the Russians assembled around us were. He was concerned both about more universal themes and a different concept of time. 'Madame,' he then said in a very solemn tone, 'you are talking to the founder of theo-zoology.'

" '*Wunderbar*,' said the princess, who had just walked into our corner, 'I've never heard such a thing in my life. My compatriots will be fascinated! And by the way, do you have a request for some music that Larissa could play for you?'

"Herr Lanz was clearly quite willing to go into details about this doctrine whose name was unknown to us all. He was unprepared for a question about his musical tastes. So he quickly kissed the princess's hand and cried, 'Your Highness, you are, if you will permit me the observation, an impressive racial specimen!' Whereupon the princess, visibly baffled, thanked him and wandered away with two empty teacups.

"Since a woman can never count on a man to explain a situation to her more intelligently than he would to a four-year-old, I was glad when Emile turned up, his voice having been heard declaiming poetry in another room. I introduced the two gentlemen to one another and asked to be enlightened about the concept of theo-zoology, which was a mystery to me. But after this Herr Lanz von Liebenfels had been talking for five minutes I bitterly regretted having assumed the attitude of the *naïve*, because the theo-zoologist was talking to Emile as one profound thinker to another, and with an apostolic obsessiveness. As far as I could grasp, they were talking about a racial theory involving the decline of our culture, lamented by Herr Lanz as the product of the mixing of the most diverse races—this is clearly not the result of migrations and whatever else my history books might have said, but rather of a loss of energy. The gods and the angels—or at least this is how I understood it—were the embodiment of pure electricity, some of which they lost when they descended to earth. At this point I raised the perhaps rather superficial objection: 'Apart from the electric eel'—the conversation had already been going on for a considerable time, and I had been annoyed that the two men were quite plainly ignoring me, and given that we were talking about zoology . . . Anyway I got a not very grateful look from the speaker and a pained one from my suitor, and was saved only by the princess, who had joined us again and pounced on the word 'electricity' as if on a petit four on the servant's silver tray. That was simply *wunderbar*, she said, everyone in the whole salon was talking about electricity, her compatriots were forever discussing a magazine entitled *Iskra, The Spark*. The subject was clearly in the air. Like clouds before a storm, she added. Then she asked me to help her hand out the little buckwheat pancakes that went with the caviar.

"That took a few minutes, and when I returned to the corner occupied by the sofa, the two gentlemen were already huddled close together and absolutely failed to notice that I was able to follow, word for word, their excited conversation—hot blinis and caviar between their fingers—about dalliances and catamites. That is, Herr Lanz was chiefly up in arms about what he called Lupercalian fig-fauns, an expression that I liked very much, and then about Old Testament practices of sexual miscegenation between women and donkeys, and sometimes goats, the whole thing coming under the heading of racial degeneration. 'Rutting dwarves,' cried Lanz suddenly when the Baltic gentleman, fondling a little figure of Diana, had disappeared in the direction of the music room. Emile seemed to be gripped by the lecture, as I could see by the way the wings of his nose were twitching. But he was plainly not quite at ease, as his embarrassed, darting glances around the room revealed. After our little dispute over *Les liaisons dangereuses* I did not want to give him any new reason to see me as being too curious about situations he considered unsuitable for a female imagination, so I left unobtrusively, but caught myself thinking that while I had indeed loved my horse as a young girl, I had never exactly desired it. The same could be said about our dogs; of course it was fun, and a bit horrible at the same time, to watch them copulating, but I never really felt jealous, perhaps because I found it difficult to empathize with the role of the female. And swans—while we are on this particular set of subjects—rarely have such peaceable dealings with humans as the relevant depictions might suggest.

"These imaginative digressions brought me to Max, whom I had last seen in conversation with the princess. I wanted to remind him about the sketches he had said he was going to do for Princess Urussova as a souvenir; so far, Plekhanov's arrival aside, I had only seen him eating, drinking, and chatting. Now he was standing next to Ulyanov, who speaks thoroughly respectable German, complaining about the stubborn resistance to innovation in contemporary art, particularly in Munich. Ulyanov was listening attentively. He seemed to know the Bavarian capital very well, including the city's artistic scene, but then, quickly and surprisingly violently, he said something about the danger of indiscriminateness in the avant-garde, which prompted Max to deliver a long and heated reply, the conclusion of which I preferred not to hear. This Russian obviously has a remarkable gift for drawing the people who come into contact with him into sudden exaggerations of their own views, or perhaps merely into stating them more precisely.

"I made myself comfortable under a plaster statue, an allegory with the word 'Reflection' inscribed in gold on its plinth, and observed the two men from a distance. There are moods that do not become some people, and Max's is feverish excitement. It does not enhance his stature, but only makes him argumentative. Almost wistfully—perhaps the sad figure of the statue above me had upset me—I thought of the happy time—barely twelve months ago—when I was still modeling for him; the last time I was 'The Natural State of the Bowel,' and then 'Body Posture to Relax the Painful Parts in a Case of Violent Sciatica.' Of course he can't go on doodling illustrations until the end of his artistic life. There is certainly much to be said for his wanting to start all over again from the beginning, but so terribly earnest is he about his plan that he is threatening simply to change into a different person. His affectations depress me, he's too much the major general, as my father used to say. I do like eccentric people far more than uncompromising ones.

"I passed my time with these cheerful thoughts while watching Max and the Russian, and the way—their profiles against the window and the peach-colored evening haze, of which they were of course quite unaware—they faced each other like two fighting cocks. It would have been the right time to help myself to some vodka, but the Russian's wife was preparing to sit down next to me. She had kept out of the ladies' fashion contest by wearing a plainly embroidered blouse, almost a folk costume, over her dress. Before she sat down she gave me an inquiring smile, which made her face look curiously older rather than younger. All afternoon she had worn, or tried to wear, the same expression as her husband, but what came easily to Ulyanov with his Mongol slits was much more of an effort for her, her eyes being much too round. I indicated the cushion next to me, and was already looking forward to hearing about the life of the revolutionary in exile, but before she could take her seat she stood up again with a start as the noise of a loud quarrel reached us from the next room. Excited voices were roaring at each other in Russian, although unfortunately I didn't understand what the argument was about.

"But it did become quite clear that this was more than mere swaggering male bravado, because the voices sounded severely irritated, as ferocious dogs sound just before they bite. That is, of course, only my musical interpretation of events, but it can't be absolutely wrong because other guests also perceived the threatening atmosphere. Mr. Ulyanov brusquely interrupted his conversation with Max and stormed into the room where the argument had started. We heard him utter two rasping sentences—or at least they lasted no longer than two German sentences would have—and then everything fell silent until all of a sudden a piece of porcelain smashed very audibly on the stone floor. But the princess herself had obviously swept that from the shelf with the train of her dress; a few moments later she appeared with several gray and yellow fragments in her hands, which had formerly depicted a young boy pulling a thorn from his foot. This time Urussova's *wunderbar* did not sound quite so triumphant.

"In the corridor to the kitchen the little Baltic gentleman explained to me what the Russians had been arguing about. I'm afraid I can't capture his Lithuanian dialect in writing, so you will simply have to imagine the accent of that Vigrabs you once treated in vain. But I forgot, you never met that particular patient. Anyway, in the manner of all Baltic people he said: 'My dear young lady, you must simply imagine the Russian as a wolf or a wild duck. As a wolf he wants to keep his pack together, and as a wild duck he wants to be free to follow his instincts. Translate that into a revolutionary party. There too are wolves and wild ducks. Both feel, if you understand my meaning, the power of nature. The wolf wants to rule the pack, and the wild duck to triumph over nature.' He paused. 'You do understand metaphors, young woman?' he inquired anxiously. 'Good. This Ulyanov is a wolf. He has to make it clear to his party, these very wild revolutionaries, that they can only survive if they follow a leader, and that he is the leader of the pack. The pack does not consist only of wolves, however, but also of all manner of other animals: snipes and hares, buffalo, geese, and cranes. Our Mr. Ulyanov, where his party is concerned, sees himself as the leader, but not only of the creatures belonging to his particular species. And that is what makes him so dangerous. The capercaillie and the wild duck have just been having a set-to, which is why the wolf only had to bark once. But now I've bored you quite enough with my fables.'

"In the meantime visible tensions had also arisen between Emile and Lanz von Liebenfels. The two men had separated, and were looking at each other as if each was taking the measure of his companion. What had plainly divided them was Lanz's assertion that during some geological era our continent had been populated by animal-humans, whose appearance on earth was the result of 'human-female' lust, namely of women giving themselves to monkeys. In Siberia and the Himalayas, according to Lanz, these 'scaly witnesses' of past misdemeanors are still to be seen today in the form of Abominable Snowmen.

" 'In the Bible,' objected Emile, but in his rage he was speaking in far too controlled a manner.

" 'In the Bible, exactly,' Lanz immediately said triumphantly. 'Take Ezekiel: Thou hast committed fornication with the men of Misraim thy neighbors, whose members are great. And: For her lust was wild for their paramours, whose members are as the members of asses, and whose sperm is as the sperm of horses.' He grew quite red in the face. 'Is that not in the Bible? I repeat: Ezekiel!' Then Lanz named the relevant chapters and verses from the Old Testament, which I immediately noted down. Ezekiel has always been my favorite prophet.

" 'The important ones for me are still the descendants of Adam and Eve,' Emile tried again, speaking with great constraint, almost sotto voce, perhaps because he had discovered that Larissa, the princess's daughter, was leaning against the door frame, following the discussion with obvious attentiveness.

" 'And do you know what Adam did?' asked Lanz spitefully.

" 'He ate bread in the sweat of his face,' answered Emile after some thought.

"Lanz crowed with delight. 'He named the animals,' he cried, slicing the air with his forefinger as if to underline each of his words. To name, he explained, to name by name, is to do nothing other than to commit fornication. All serious commentators agreed on that point. In fact Adam sodomized the animals.

"With these words Lanz, who had risen from his seat on the sofa, dropped contentedly back into the cushions.

"I'm certainly no prude, but I thought that was the moment to invite Larissa to perform a piece for four hands. She thanked me rather distantly, cast a wistful glance at the gentlemen, and disappeared into her room in search of sheet music.

" 'Pig-swill!' Emile suddenly roared, then leapt up and walked from the room at a brisk pace. Lanz followed him and hissed something about the lush wood of the Lebanon cedar of Sodom, but before he could reach Emile he tripped over the knots at the

edge of the carpet, slipped sideways, and crashed amidships, so
to speak, into Mr. Ulyanov. This gentleman was at that moment
raising a cup of tea to his lips, as satisfied as a successful big-game
hunter. It all happened very quickly.

"When the chaos had subsided somewhat, the two gentlemen
were standing opposite one another, extremely taken aback, rubbing their thighs, on which large dark stains formed a curious
pattern. I still remember my astonishment at noting that a single
cup of tea could spread so much moisture.

"Lanz stammered confused apologies in German and French,
then Mr. Plekhanov suddenly turned up to announce that he would
immediately have new pants brought from his house, nothing special, but wearable, for they could not go back to Geneva in that
state.

"At this, the princess showed victim and perpetrator the way to
the bathroom, where they spent the next quarter of an hour until
a replacement outfit appeared.

"I quickly sat down at the piano with Larissa, to brighten up
the party again with a rendering of *Death and the Maiden*. Max later
reported that he had passed the bathroom a few times, and although
he had not dared to listen closely, the voices had sounded perfectly
harmonious. Emile, whose lack of scruples delighted me in this
context at least, was able to add that Lanz, without talking smut,
had been discussing the importance of elites for a nation, and about
the avant-garde role of enlightened people. Ulyanov had responded
very positively to the word 'elite.'

"When our four-in-hand drew up—I must now bring my story
to an end, or else I'll be accused once again of neglecting my
official duties—we were all in a thoroughly good mood. As we left,
I was struck by the unusually large number of coaches waiting in
the long shadows up to the turnoff for Urussova's house. Certainly,
we had been a very big gathering, but most guests had not come
alone, they had banded together into parties. I asked Emile for
an explanation. He was boisterously biting off the wrapper of a
chocolate bar. 'Secret agents,' he said, and spat the paper out the
window. He is slowly coming to understand the way my imagination works. We may well make a fig-faun of him yet."

*   *   *

Vogt put the parcel to one side and took another look at a newspaper report: "Revolutionary Uprisings in Russia," read the headline. The report dealt with a certain Ulyanov, alias Lenin, whom the Russian secret police were keeping under surveillance as a leading conspirator, and who was said to have been arrested in Switzerland.

T W E N T Y

It was a perfectly normal morning at 16 Magdeburger Strasse. Before going to school, the daughters of the house had practiced with Natalya Avdotyevna Suvorova their Russian irregular declensions, as well as pet names and pejorative expressions. "And don't forget," their teacher impressed upon them at the end of the lesson, "Russians do not like an affected and prissy demeanor, least of all at the dinner table."

Then the daughters had said goodbye to their mother, repeated the words "affected" and "prissy" in Natalya Avdotyevna's rolling accent as they went down the stairs, and burst into fits of giggles. Cécile Vogt was on her way to the laboratory to return to the cutting instrument with which she was dissecting a brain that had been sent to her from Portugal. This brain had belonged to a patient suffering from an extremely rare hearing disorder, and Cécile hoped to be able to produce preparations showing the cause of the disorder. She had begun this work two months earlier; if Oskar occasionally came to her assistance, she would be able to produce her first results two months hence.

But her husband was currently under a great deal of pressure. They desperately had to secure more money. Certainly, the practice had blossomed magnificently, so that they only needed to take on first-class or particularly unusual patients, but at the same time the cost of ambitious research projects had risen enormously. The price of a chimpanzee, for example, was now between one thousand and two thousand marks, not to mention five hundred marks a year for feed. But feed alone was not enough; chimpanzees, as they had learned from bitter experience, could only be kept in captivity over long periods if they were regularly distracted, which meant long-term human contact. This involved a considerable increase in financial expenditures, but no concomitant reduction in economic risk: Many of the animals delivered to the house had already developed repellent and genetically uncontrollable habits during their previous confinement, and the animals often required time to settle in before anything approaching normal reactions could be elicited from them. But some individuals—and other researchers complained about this as well—had to be eliminated as unsuitable only after a considerable amount of time had been wasted, while others—and Vogt could only confirm this too—died before completion of the research, sometimes as the result of operations. Of course it was cheaper to work with baboons, much cheaper to choose horses, donkeys, or dogs. But since they were engaged in brain research, in establishing ever more precisely the principles of a hygiene of our most noble organ, random animals were, of course, out of the question.

Vogt dismissed his patient, a wan young count from Westphalia with prematurely thinning reddish hair, whose indiscriminate sexual pursuits had developed into a nervous condition. The doctor had an hour free before he had to attend to his next case—an actress who had been much admired that season and who, for the past three weeks of treatment, had taken to signing her letters to Vogt "Your yearning Nibbly Mouse."

Vogt wanted to use his remaining hour to sketch out a proposal for his participation in the quarrel that had recently broken out over the allocation of research funds. Since it had been made known that a new central funding body was about to be set up under the very personal tutelage of His Majesty, with funds at its disposal that could only be described as lavish, arguments had been raging between experts and their opponents, hasty associations were forming, and scientific reports were circulating like stock exchange tips.

Among the physicists and chemists who were to be the first to enjoy the benefits of this golden cornucopia, an alarming amount of pushing and shoving and backstabbing had begun, just as if this were accepted practice. But in the biological sciences, where academic judgments could be made on a rather more speculative basis, individual researchers were setting upon one another like Burgundian jousters.

The Royal Ministry of Education and the Arts had asked precisely thirty authorities for their esteemed opinion as to which of the many biological disciplines most merited support from the Kaiser Wilhelm Society. The thirty answers provided precisely the same number of different suggestions. As the responsible gentlemen in the ministry had feared, each of the academics, most of them having come to a completely unbiased decision, had presented his own area of activity as especially in need of support. Otherwise they would not have dedicated a lifetime of research work and self-denial to their particular field of inquiry.

Were psychology and the various areas of psychiatry the legitimate offspring of biology, and as such entitled to maintenance? Of course the complete decentralization of the German mental health system so lamented by Professor Sommer (Giessen) presented a considerable problem, particularly when considered in light of hereditary theories and psychical hygiene—as Professor Sommer intended to do. But did it advance biology?

Should more backing be given to the future of experimental psychology? There was another interesting proposal in favor of this field, the authors of which promised to dedicate themselves to unlocking the questions of genius and the supernormal. In edu-

cational terms this sounded extremely promising. The English had
been carrying out this kind of research for a considerable period
of time, and the Reich had a certain amount of catching up to do.
The early and reliable identification of supernormality would also
be of indisputable importance from a political and practical perspective. Thus comparative anthropological studies were being
developed, dealing with the psychical constitution of the natives
in the new German colonies, their way of thinking, their sense of
touch, their understanding of music. Missionaries, big-game hunt-
ers, and businessmen would be valuable sources of information
here. Presented in such worldly terms, the problem might also
attract new sponsors to German scientific research. The initiators
of the new foundation, on the other hand, had established it first
and foremost in order to support basic research; could it really be
said that an effort to understand the unique qualities of the black
subjects of the Reich fulfilled this requirement?

The medical officer, Professor Waldeyer, supported research on
the ape-men of the Cameroons. Precisely because these creatures
were a hindrance to the advancing settlement of the region, and
were consequently an obstacle to civilization, "soon little trace will
remain of them." Research into this area was thus called for, Waldeyer wrote, but, he continued somewhat surprisingly, every bit
as urgent, if not more so, was the need to emphasize the human
nervous system. In particular, he considered the establishment of
a special brain research institute to be indispensable.

Vogt had read Waldeyer's deputation, and it had enraged him.
Waldeyer of all people, that psychopath, whom he had previously
caught hawking his, Vogt's, ideas on a number of occasions. Of
course Vogt would also be standing up for brain research, although
not in the general, hazy terms that his colleague had used to mask
his own easily discernible lack of concrete goals. And Vogt had no
need to use his academic contacts to contrive a connection between
his own projects and the progressive tendencies in biology. He
could simply refer to the name of his institute in the Magdeburger
Strasse, the Neurobiological University Laboratory, as the best
evidence of that connection.

With any luck Nibbly Mouse had not dabbed that Oriental perfume behind her earlobes today, since it should really have been prohibited under the current narcotics laws. She had shown him the bottle on her last visit: Nuits d'Extase, read the label on the emerald-green vial. Three sessions later, when Vogt was in the midst of treating a melancholic morphine addict, the young man had suddenly sat up on the couch, sniffed, and said, "You smell like my mother—I hate you!" The doctor had meanwhile kept the window open for a long time and only closed it again when the howling of the dogs from the cellar had become too audible on the second floor.

If only one knew precisely what the gentlemen on the commission would consider the most acceptable common denominator. These committees being the way they were, the final decision would be a compromise. This meant that applicants first of all had to express their own intentions in very general terms, and yet back them up with unimpeachable specifics that revealed the highest level of competence and stood the greatest possible likelihood of success.

Vogt had decided to stress the importance of a clinical examination of individual psychology. In his introduction he would look into the rise in nervous ailments, but at the same time explain that illnesses, from the theoretical point of view, were fundamentally nothing but "nature's experiments," enabling one to draw conclusions about normality. Not normality in the idealistic sense, of course, but as exhibited in rigorously materialistic terms, backed up with statistics. The proposal must not lead to just any anatomical brain research, but required an investigation into the *human* brain, or, where applicable, the brains of monkeys and carnivores if their structure provided information about the basic design of mammals in general.

For the sake of strategy, expenditure would need to be concentrated on anatomical research of the coarser, microscopic kind. This field had already yielded considerable results—in Vogt's own Neurobiological University Laboratory. Apart from that, studies would have to be carried out on the consequences of destroying the nervous process. Such an act of destruction could be undertaken experimentally—here Vogt jotted down the word "animal"—but it could also be found pathologically—Vogt wrote in brackets "human" and decided, in the final version of his proposal, to mention the lamentable shortage of first-class brains available for research purposes.

In any case, these very difficult and complex circumstances would not be corroborated by the study of guinea pigs. These areas of research were of the utmost importance as regards, for example—and here Vogt restricted himself to key points—achieving an understanding of inherited mental tendencies in individuals, the exploration of scientific bases for selective breeding, the influenceability of hereditary tendencies, and finally even the *creation of new hereditary tendencies.*

Shortly before—and he had omitted to enter it in his records— Nibbly Mouse had bitten him. It had been at the very end of the session, when he was running his hand over her face, without, of course, touching it. "You will now wake up," he had been about to say, but clearly she had been in a half-waking state, in any case she had snapped at his hand with her teeth, as fast as lightning, like a dog or a cat in search of attention, wanting to provoke a reaction.

When he washed his hands later on, the red marks left by her teeth were still quite clearly visible. Looking at these indentations, he had, with a pleasant feeling of warmth, remembered the shiver that her bite had caused.

Where was he . . . ? "CONCRETE VISIONS," Vogt wrote in capital letters, and beside it he put "concrete visions for a form of research that does not reduce the hereditary process to pure chance." It was along this line that he would group the phalanx of his arguments. The word "phalanx" reminded him of a conversation that he had had a few weeks earlier with a military officer who had asked him for psychological explanations of some of the animal experiments carried out by his regiment. A Captain or Lieutenant Most, who had told him in passing of a previous meeting and who had—very discreetly—asked after Amanda von Alvensleben.

Would it, in fact, be possible to involve the military as well, for financial and expert assistance? But if the military was on his side, what sympathies would that cost him in one of the other camps?

One could, of course, also deal with the crucially important social question. His research was fundamentally social in character. Normality, supernormality, and genius were, after all, questions of overall individuality. But it was important to remember that if one was to overstress social factors, a great deal of suspicion would inevitably be aroused among the conservative factions. At the very word "social" these gentlemen would show one to the door, as past experience had shown often enough.

Under no circumstances could one afford to be too modest in one's financial demands. Research—and experience had shown this too—only gained credibility with the sponsors when the sums requested reached a particular level. What had his former teacher Flechsig always drummed into him? "Set your sights on Cape Horn, my boy, not Bremerhaven!" Flechsig's career was eloquent testimony to his own advice.

The maid excitedly announced the arrival of the famous actress. Two white autograph cards protruded from the pocket of her white apron.

Vogt laid his pencil in the crystal bowl and stacked his notes into a pile. He walked to the washstand, washed his hands, and brushed his beard. The breath freshener that he sprayed into his mouth had a fresh scent of lemons, with an aftertaste of peppermint.

Nibbly Mouse's real name was Adele Schönfeld. In the signed photographs that she handed out, what met the beholder's eye was less the image of an enamored rodent than that of a determined governess. That might have been due to the pose—the coarse hand with the plain gem on the ring finger pressed against the right hip—or perhaps it was the wide mouth with its thin lips, or the hair pulled tightly back from the brow. In addition, the actress wore an outfit that fell like a simple pinafore and was only decorated at the neckline with a little white collar, which seemed to be in flight from her long neck.

At first Vogt had had some trouble putting this patient into a light hypnotic sleep. It was only a number of weeks later, after she had invited him, "to gain a more intimate assessment of her art," to a number of plays—in which she always gave very chaste, severe performances, the Maid of Orléans, for example, or Mary Stuart—that their relationship had become much less difficult. The patient suddenly seemed filled with such a vigorous creative will, her drives and mental energy were intensified to such a degree that Vogt often feared he could no longer distinguish properly between hypnotic self-portrayal and artistic performance.

Certainly, this abundant willingness to participate could be called a medical success on every level, even reaching beyond the goals of therapy as they had been established at the outset. But Vogt preferred to be in control of the process. With Nibbly Mouse there were always moments when he could see his control coming under serious threat.

On the other hand, the patient, who was now flicking through a magazine in the waiting room, bolstered and defended his reputation in society, and she did so with the same vehemence that he had observed in her behavior during more intimate moments. Just two weeks ago, for example, at a reception given by the French ambassador in honor of a pianist visiting the capital, Vogt had witnessed Nibbly Mouse's rebuttal of a skeptic. She was sitting in the supposed seclusion of a group of armchairs separated off by potted palms, on her left-hand side a celebrated operetta conductor, on her right the Italian cultural attaché, and, sitting opposite, a baron from the Royal Education Ministry, already slightly inebriated. As she often did on such solemn occasions, Nibbly Mouse was wearing an outfit that quite relentlessly followed the contours of her body.

The tipsy baron from the Education Ministry had resolutely spoken out against the hypnotic method.

"Rat experiments, my dearest young lady," he said excitedly.

"On such occasions you are being made the victim of rat experiments!"

"Are you suggesting I'm a rat?" Nibbly Mouse had replied.

"That's how you're being treated, my dearest young lady. You don't count as a human being, you count only as a form of behavior."

Nibbly Mouse had given the gentleman a withering glance. "Three sessions and I was able to stand center stage again," she said in a firm voice that rose as steadily as the red patches spreading on her cheeks. "I repeat, only three sessions. Before, the stage manager had to shove me out from the wings. If I dared to take as many as two or three steps farther, I fell into a panic, you can't imagine. Not even during the applause at the end did I have the courage to let go of the edge of the curtain."

"Amazing," observed the celebrated operetta conductor. "That has never happened to me. That is to say, for a conductor, for a conductor, that is, the danger would be that much greater, because he always has to be in the center. In other words, for me—"

"Rat experiments," cried the baron from the Education Ministry again, without waiting for the conductor to reach his conclusion. "My dear, my sweet Fräulein Schönfeld, you have not understood your mental suffering with your heart, you have merely obeyed with your body!"

"I don't know any obedient rats," interjected the Italian cultural attaché, and bowed politely toward the lady on his left. The conversation reached a lull for a moment, and all that could be heard was the dance band playing in the distance.

"Sexual arousal," said Nibbly Mouse suddenly. "After five more sessions I experienced the sudden thawing of a four-year freeze." She crossed her arms over her chest and stood as rigid as a pattern in frost. "Before, I was a creature carved from wood, from wood, glass, or stone, but not from flesh, blood, skin, or nerves. After those five further sessions with Dr. Vogt, I simply have to tell you—"

"So his name is Vogt?" asked the Italian cultural attaché abruptly, before Nibbly Mouse could tell them what she simply had to tell them.

"You must tell me more about it," said the baron from the Education Ministry.

At this point Vogt quietly walked away.

"The article about the balloonist was fascinating," said the actress, after Vogt had kissed her hand. She held the magazine open like a little tent with the very tip of her left forefinger. "All these articles about technical advances and brave pioneering deeds enthrall me, especially when they have so much in common with dreams, like the art of ballooning—lifting off, soaring, wonderful!"

Vogt pointed to the couch. "Let's consider horizontal matters for the time being," he said, and sat down at his desk. He glanced at the files containing his patient's records.

"What am I being trained for today, then?" asked the actress, after she had smoothed her skirt.

"Trained?" Vogt looked at her in astonishment.

"Recently, at a reception given by the French ambassador, I met a senior member of the Education Ministry who tried to have me believe that my little doctor was carrying out rat experiments on me. We subsequently met a few more times, and I am utterly convinced that I managed to persuade this gentleman of the wonders of your method of treatment."

"So he's now a great fan of rat experiments?"

"I'm not sure. The day before yesterday he called me his little mouse, and he also proposed a few experiments." She paused briefly. "But he had a great deal less experience than my doctor," she added thoughtfully.

"I hope you didn't tell him that."

"Your name cropped up two or three times, but in a quite different context. You are clearly up for a scientific prize, a medal, a garland, or something or other. No"—the actress slapped her forehead with the palm of her hand—"now I remember. He said that you should concentrate your powers. 'It would be better,' said my acquaintance, 'if Vogt could dedicate himself to one thing and one thing only.' "

"You're making me curious about the name of your acquaintance."

The actress mentioned the name. Vogt raised his eyes gratefully to the crystal chandelier in the stucco ceiling. Then he addressed himself to his patient with all the single-mindedness that the circumstances required. An hour later he felt quite exhausted.

He was rubbing his hands dry when Cécile came into the surgery very agitated. To his relief her agitation was due to something she thought she had discovered under her microscope. "It's significant, the change," she said on the stairs, "you'll see, very small but quite discrete. And I didn't find it on one slice alone, but three."

After Vogt had had a look at her discovery—there really was something to see, and he suppressed a slight feeling of resentment at not having seen it first—he went back to his desk.

Nibbly Mouse as an ally with connections to the ministry—that wasn't bad at all. But of course you could never know whether such connections would last. How perfectly she had performed that little scene when, at the request of the ministry man, she had imitated a timid doe being pestered by a buck. However, Cécile bent over the microscope, pure research, that was where his real destiny lay.

From the drawer he drew his plan for a Kaiser Wilhelm Institute for Brain Research. "More research material," he wrote rapidly. "If we are to have a precise series of neuroanatomical experiments, we urgently require an improvement in the supply of brains of the most diverse grades. At present, elite brains are as good as impossible to obtain. These specimens must be shown to be particularly valuable, first because of their indisputable uniqueness, second because their history, their family trees, etc., are in most cases the most thoroughly documented."

Vogt wondered briefly whether it would not be better, more objective, perhaps, to recommend another field of research as well as his own. That might make him appear more impartial to the experts.

He poked at his beard with his pencil a few times, and then

noted: "Finally, the elaboration of a special hygienics of the workers strikes us as a project well worthy of support . . ." The minute he had the time he would explain that this was a matter of weighing the social against the scientific points of view. One never knew, after all, what decision a committee would reach. But they would have to understand: Brains were of great scientific importance. To be studied in a way that was only possible in his laboratory.

T W E N T Y - O N E

The stranger was not to be kept too long in the waiting room, the professor had said. Vogt, who was still held up in his neurobio-logical institute, would collect the guest in an hour at the most, perhaps in as little as half an hour. And should Vogt, for what-ever reason, be delayed, she, Frau Lotze, was to accompany the gentleman in person to a particular tavern near Friedrichstrasse Station.

The professor had written the exact address on the cover of the experimental records that he wanted written up by lunchtime. But the professor had not mentioned the stranger's name, nor his na-tionality, neither had he said in which language she would be able to communicate with him.

Now the man was sitting in the worn-out leather chair from which the professor usually delivered his dictations. The stranger had taken his seat in silence, crossed his legs, and drawn from his pocket a pamphlet that he was now reading with the utmost con-centration. When he placed the pamphlet against his thigh, with the fold exactly aligned against the crease of his trousers, Frau Lotze had noticed the Cyrillic script.

She had offered the guest a coffee, first in German, then in French, then in unmistakable gestures. But he merely shook his high-domed, egg-shaped head and raised the palm of his left hand in a gesture of refusal.

Frau Lotze bent over the manuscript and the paper for the fair copy. On the left-hand side she drew a column with a ruler, above which she wrote "DATE" in capital letters. Then she turned to the heading. "Guinea Pigs: G.P.5," she wrote, and picked up the ruler again, drawing two India ink bars underneath it. It was beneath these bars that she was to place the description of the object under examination: "Sturdy animal, shaggy hair. Color brownish black. Sex: male. Weight: 575 g."

Frau Lotze looked up quickly and noticed that the stranger had clamped a gold-rimmed monocle in his left eye socket.

"December 14, 1912," the secretary entered in the left-hand column. "The animal is given three not excessively strong blows to the forehead with the percussion hammer every day."

The next result dated from the first day of the Christmas holidays. Frau Lotze copied: "While for the first few days the animal skipped about merrily almost immediately after the blows and ate heartily, it has now grown quieter, and sits for hours in one place staring straight ahead. Its appetite has diminished."

On the second day of the holidays the professor had noted in the records: "The animal keeps still while the blows are being administered, so there is no need to hold it. From today, three light blows three times a day."

The professor and his wife had spent New Year's in Budapest, and the animal handler, Wussow, had carried on the experiments according to their instructions. On January 4, the professor resumed his experiments. The same evening he scribbled in his notebook: "In the morning, the animal is found lying on its left side with its front feet extended, and makes no attempt to defend itself when touched. In the course of the day it recovers, but only eats a small amount and stops in the middle of eating without changing its position. Its psychical behavior is strikingly different, its facial expression distinctly idiotic."

Had the stranger cleared his throat? If he had, he was one of those curious people who clear their throats inwardly, so to speak, without giving any outward sign. His face hadn't reddened in the slightest. Who apart from the Russians still used Cyrillic script? That's right, the Bulgarians. But the two or three Bulgarian colleagues whom the professor had invited to lectures or colloquia over the past few years had not been so unobtrusively elegant as this bald-headed stranger.

Frau Lotze returned to her writing.

On February 20, after a good ten weeks of constant hammer blows to the forehead, guinea pig G.P.5 had given indications of progressive psychic decay. Somatic changes were barely apparent. The professor had, however, been struck by the fact that the animal was being attacked by its cage-mates, "which encountered no resistance."

During the months of March and April the animal was hammered and pinched. Sometimes it had attempted chewing movements, and sometimes it merely blinked for a moment. Cramps followed by scratching motions with the left rear paw were increasingly frequent.

Frau Lotze's pen glided faster across the paper. In May the guinea pig twitched as soon as it was put on the examination table. At the beginning of June the same reaction was apparent when it came into contact with the straw that covered the bottom of its cage. The professor had managed to provoke an "epileptic seizure" simply by stamping his foot hard on the floor. The records for July 4 said: "Handclap also provokes a seizure (effect of fear?)."

This stranger clearly didn't notice when people were staring at him. Or else his self-control was such that he registered that he had become an object of curiosity, but could still remain entirely calm. Most striking were his eyes. Almost transparent, and quite low on the head. Next to his earlobes, his two slightly curly sideburns looked like a trimmed bush of pubic hair.

"Urine passed during seizure," noted Frau Lotze for July 17. The professor had not written "passed," but after two hundred

entries Frau Lotze knew her guinea pigs. She only found the date
noteworthy—it was her sister's birthday.

If the man was not Bulgarian, he must be Russian. Professor
Vogt was well known for his contacts with Russians. But if he
actually was a Russian, why was he sitting so still in his chair? The
Russians with whom Frau Lotze had come into contact tended to
behave like restrained Frenchmen. Too obvious, somehow. And
only very rarely did they wear such finely cut suits.

In the meantime, things did not look good for guinea pig G.P.5.
Frau Lotze, who had translated all the relevant experimental records into a legible form, knew that the animal's days were num-
bered. It was astounding, in fact, that it had survived for so long.
She checked that no errors had occurred in the dating.

The Russian took a gold pen from his waistcoat pocket and wrote
quietly in the white margin of his pamphlet.

On July 27, the guinea pig began to have severe seizures at the
slightest, even involuntary, stimulus. "Tickling behind the ears,"
the professor had added, "provokes severe seizures of relatively
long duration (one to one and a half minutes), hoarse cry at the
start of the seizure."

The Russian had put the gold pen back in his pocket and closed
the pamphlet. He held his head tilted slightly to the right, as if
he were listening for a faint signal meant only for him.

There was a short hammering at the door, it was then pushed
open, and Vogt was standing in the room. He carried a white lab
coat over his left arm and waved heartily to the stranger with his
right hand. "My dear Semashko," he said, "I feel terrible about
leaving you waiting here. But sadly the matter at hand could not
be postponed. And as always when one is in a hurry, the whole
business takes a particularly long time. I now insist that you come
out to dinner with me. There's a car waiting downstairs."

"My wish is to spare you as much trouble as possible," said
Semashko in very careful yet very firm German.

"It's my pleasure, my dear Semashko," said Vogt, laughing.

He walked to the desk, playfully pulled Frau Lotze's ear, and
glanced at her records.

"Epilepsy in guinea pigs," he said appreciatively. "You'll have to send me that the minute the professor gives his blessing. It looks like a terrific piece of work." He turned back toward his guest. "You see, that's how quickly you get caught up in new things! But your stomach must be starting to growl by now. My respects, Frau Lotze, and my best regards to your boss."

Vogt took Mr. Semashko's elbow and guided the Russian out of the room.

After the door had closed, Frau Lotze sat back down to her work:

> August 1, 1913: Numerous daily seizures in the cage, apparently without particular cause.
>
> August 7, 1913: In a severe seizure preceded by six medium-severe seizures, death occurs.

Frau Lotze wiped her pen and placed it in the bowl set aside for that purpose. She took from her handbag the metal container in which she kept her lunchtime sandwiches.

TWENTY-TWO

Before Max Landsberg boarded the military train that was to take him to the Western front, he had had a dinner appointment with Amanda von Alvensleben on the Kurfürstendamm. It had not been a particularly agreeable meeting. Max had wanted to tell Amanda a little about his enthusiasm, his unease, and also his fear, but she seemed, unusually for her, somewhat aloof. He tried to overcome her reserve by being effusively sincere.

At forty-four he was, he confided, no longer the youngest of men, and he lived in constant fear of leaving nothing behind that would give the merest hint of his talents and his artistic project. This was why he had so tirelessly gone out in search of new challenges. A light that would illuminate what had so long been hidden. Whether he was up to the physical privations and nervous tension of a life at the front was something, of course, that only time would tell. The challenge of art was, he felt, a more serious matter. Blood, exposed bones, corpses—he had had to grow accustomed to all that twenty years earlier. He was as familiar with that as other artists were with the apple, the piece of cheese, and the wineglass which they used in their still lifes. But out there in the hail of fire, details mattered less than a vision of the destinies of men, captured in an instant, of man's struggle to survive, one might say, as a theme of world history. In purely technical terms, a painter of battle scenes was doing the same work as a painter of operations. But his responsibility as an artist did not lie so much in capturing details—although he had over the past few weeks been studying closely the various kinds of weapons and ammunition—as in attempting to portray the historical context, the forces of the will—and, of course, the phenomena of impotence, of failure. From both perspectives, that of triumph and that of defeat, he would presumably always be able to rediscover a small part of his own soul, but this could only be achieved at considerable risk to his own life and his own work, which perhaps boiled down to the same thing.

Amanda had replied only: "I'm afraid the wine is corked."

An old waiter brought another bottle and apologized, remarking that nothing was what it used to be. All the waiters in the restaurant were old men. Any information about the young came through the forces' postal service and the newspaper obituary columns. In restaurants one only came across fathers or grandfathers—one did meet other characters as well but they were not particularly well thought of.

"War is rather a high price to pay for art," said Amanda. "I'm not going to get nearly as nasty as I feel, maybe I'm just afraid something's going to happen to you." She drew four sharp lines on the white tablecloth with her silver-plated fork. "If I had kept my child that time, if he had been a boy, he would have been at one of these fronts by next spring. Before then he would have been with me in Paris, in Scotland, in Geneva, and probably in St. Petersburg as well. We would have made friendships, perhaps even developed deep antipathies." Amanda drew back the fork. "If my son had been eager to shoot those people or their friends and relations . . ." She shook her head. "Well, if I'd discovered so much as a hint of my son getting excited about uniforms, brass bands, or marching columns, I'd have put him straight into the Salvation Army."

The wounded soldiers attempted to adopt a military attitude when the doctors came to do their rounds. They tried to sit up in bed, to find the center of the wall behind them, and to keep their arms stretched rigidly out in front of them, their palms facing downward on the white blankets. In Ward 16A of the Berlin-Buch clinic, brain surgery department, discipline ruled. This was seen to by Sergeant Otto Jänicke, himself a patient, who, in a crude piece of raillery, liked to call the ward the bedouin camp, because of all the turban-like bandages.

Jänicke, who had been hit in the right temple by a Russian bullet, which had wormed its way like a jumping jack to the back of his skull, delivered a military report every time the doctors did their rounds: "Ward 16A, fourteen men, five newly operated on, two undergoing surgery, ready for doctors' rounds. Ward aired and cleaned. Sergeant Jänicke reporting."

The sergeant had thought up the report all by himself. It reminded him of a familiar world still governed by the dictates of military clarity and the availability of soldiers. It was the world he had lived in before his head wound, and it was to remain his world.

The other patients had complied with the sergeant's behavior. Some uncomplainingly, some morosely, yet others with humble overeagerness. After three years of war the idea of a private order of things had been extinguished in most of these men.

Apart from that—and everyone had to admit it—things in the clinic were simply splendid. One had only to remember conditions in the military sick bay. If one could remember anything at all. And at the civilian hospitals in which most of them had spent time, nobody had taken much notice of their special situation. Certainly, they were washed and cared for there, their bandages were changed regularly, and a vicar had visited to deliver uplifting words of spiritual preparation.

But here in Berlin, here in Ward 16A, the wounded were not just patients like so many others, they were the object of scientific study. Professor Vogt, who led almost all the doctors' rounds, had explicitly assured them of this. Some of them had not understood his choice of words, but the man radiated something so impressive, something so infectious that even the weakest of the patients felt like participants in a new and extremely important operation.

Upon arrival, the wounded soldiers had to sign a document, a kind of will according to which "in the event of their death," they ceded to the responsible hospital doctor "sole power of disposal over their brain."

Professor Vogt had explained to them, however, that this was done only in order to clarify the legal situation. They were about to make a patriotic contribution to research, he told the patients; they had heroically sacrificed their health for the Kaiser and the fatherland; for the German nation they had thrown their lives into the breach; but now they had the unique opportunity to use the suffering they had endured to make a contribution that extended beyond their own lives. For if a wound could be properly under-stood according to the rigid rules of science, it would not only save the lives of many of their comrades but would be an indispensable contribution to the progress of medical research in Germany. "Bas-ically," Vogt had said toward the end of his disquisition, "you have, gentlemen, by means of the exploration of your physical composition, become fighters in a much greater battle, beneath the banner of German science."

Sergeant Jänicke had answered briskly: "If it's against the French, we're all ready for anything. And I can assure you of that in the name of my comrades." Then he had the whole ward lie to attention again.

Every Wednesday morning, Vogt would introduce his rounds by demonstrating to the men of Ward 16A, with brains prepared es-pecially for the purpose, the damage done by the precise trajectory of an enemy bullet or an enemy bayonet. At first the patients had responded with horror and disgust; clearly it was hard for them to recognize their own brains in those oversized walnuts that were presented on gleaming metal trays by a stiffly smiling nurse, and which, as they knew, had been taken from their erstwhile neigh-bors in the ward.

But after a few weeks those who were still capable of speech discussed details of the anatomy of the brain just as they had discussed their fortifications, trenches, and bunkers at the front.

"We are now," Vogt wrote in December 1917 to Korbinian Brodmann, who had left Berlin and become head of the pathology department of the regional hospital at Nietleben in Halle on the Saale, "splendidly equipped to make the observations necessary to establish a theory of average performance. Given the nature of things, most of the brains come, of course, from the class of private soldiers, which can be differentiated regionally, but not, in any reliable sense, socially. It will be years before we can make professional assessments of all these findings. But I have already made some initial and far-reaching conjectures. Various foreign universities have already asked me to deliver seminar papers, but the war makes it almost impossible to follow up these invitations. Thus I have received from our old friend Bechterev, for example, a request for advice on the rebuilding of his institute in Moscow. They seem to have very exciting projects there, after the revolution. Perhaps a favorable opportunity will arise soon, now that we are at peace on that front at least."

TWENTY-THREE

A few weeks after his letter to Korbinian Brodmann, Vogt and Bechterev met in St. Petersburg, which was now called Petrograd. Chance had ordained that an East Prussian nobleman with the very best connections in the Berlin court had asked the Kaiser Wilhelm Society for a neurologist to treat his son. Vogt had been urgently requested to take charge of the case. Before he gave his consent he visited the Society's general secretary to inform him about a convention of Pan-Russian neurophysiologists to which he had been invited; he lacked the necessary foreign currency, however. The East Prussian patient, who was suffering from one of the countless kinds of combat neurosis, struck the secretariat as so important that Vogt was given the necessary funds without further ado.

He had not had to stop for long in Königsberg. The young nobleman—and Vogt had treated far more serious cases—was chiefly suffering from a lack of sleep. The doctor was an expert on that.

* * *

It was snowing in Petrograd, and the Neva was frozen over, so that it was possible to reach the opposite bank by crossing the ice on foot; on that side lay the university where the convention of physiologists was being held. Becheterev had made the reverse journey to collect Vogt at the station. As if he had felt compelled to demonstrate the high esteem in which he held his younger colleague in an utterly incongruous manner, he had turned up at the hour shown on the railway timetable. He spent the hours that followed in the unheated waiting room, first correcting his assistants' reports, then designing his own, quite new project, which he wanted to discuss with Vogt. Concentrated work, he had always drummed into the heads of his students, induces a marvelous form of hallucination which excludes physical discomforts such as cold, hunger, and thirst from the field of perception.

The train arrived five hours late, but its arrival was celebrated as if it meant the return of a victorious army. On the platform, Bechterev caught himself applauding along with the crowd and then waving his fur cap.

A cab took them to Vogt's hotel on Nevsky Prospect. During the short journey Bechterev repeatedly clutched the hand of his German guest, and shook it heartily. "It has been five years," he cried solemnly, "and so many great things have happened in science, so many terrible things between our countries, and so many wonderful things in politics."

Had the revolution transformed the hotel business as well? No outward changes were apparent, at any rate. Vogt had a servant bring his luggage to his room. In his hand he held only the little leather suitcase in which he had packed the offprints, work notes, and reports with which he intended to surprise Bechterev. No, he reassured Bechterev in response to an anxious question, he had had ample opportunity to rest on the train, he had also been able to wash his hands in the restaurant, and now he was simply looking forward to having a conversation with his colleagues. But Bechterev must permit him, as a small kind of compensation for his long wait, to offer an invitation to dinner. That too was a very selfish desire, however, because it was certainly he, Vogt, who was the hungrier.

Perhaps something had changed in people's postures, a steadier eye, a more erect gait, something that one might spot even here in the restaurant? Anyone with such a finely tuned sensibility as Vogt's would surely be able to sense the breath of history here. Ten years ago, the last time he had come to this hotel—Cécile had been with him that time—they had later talked for ages, in Berlin, about that Russian and Tartar mixture of pride, rebellion, and humility that had struck them so. But then St. Petersburg really had been on the western edge of the Russian Empire. They wore the same fashions, bought the same knickknacks, and danced the same silly dances as they did in Berlin.

On that visit, however, the Vogts had of course paid special attention to the appearance of all the things that were strange to them: unapproachable priests, half-naked beggars fighting over a rag for their feet, coaches displaying an elegance that one hardly ever encountered even in Berlin. Bechterev, who had guided them through the streets on that occasion, had shown them faith healers, flagellants, and witches who brewed philters; he wanted, he had explained, to make his guests aware of the hidden side of almighty God.

After the fish Vogt reminded his colleague of that remark.

"You know, back then under the Tsar," Bechterev said, laughing, "and right through the war years, I was a little inclined, on very particular occasions, to stress the social, and sometimes the metaphysical, factor. Why? Because it was a form of opposition! Admittedly it was not a particularly courageous form of opposition against the prevailing conditions, a flyspeck in comparison with the heroic deeds of our social revolutionaries. I myself was not persecuted, beaten, or imprisoned. But it was my modest contribution to subversion."

Bechterev briefly lowered his heavy head, and Vogt looked with envy at his old friend's thick, wavy hair.

"Let me give an example," Bechterev continued, and filled all three of the glasses that stood next to Vogt's plate. "Let's take criminals, our criminals, all criminals. At a certain point in history criminality becomes a question of definition. Someone steals a bag of rubles, someone else beats his wife to death—or the wife her husband—a third plants a bomb to blow the chief of police to bits. I ask again: Why? And I can give a number of quite different answers. I can say: There is the criminal type." Bechterev waved his hand as if an unpleasant insect had settled on it. "That would be the theory of our Italian colleague Lombroso, may he rest in peace and his theory with him. Let's take an assumption that would not be too remote from your ideas—and sometimes from my own—and accept that there are certain emotional sensitivities that are highly developed in some people, less so in others. We can assume this, but we are unable to prove it. The judges look at us, and we can only shamefacedly show them our empty pockets and wait for better times."

"Our loyalty is to science, not to justice," said Vogt, who was struggling against the disagreeable sensation that where Bechterev still had thick black curls, red dots were slowly spreading over his own head. "We can only struggle to ensure that justice, and society with it, will one day be subordinate to science," he added bravely.

Bechterev wrapped his broad right hand around the German's upper arm. "I have tried to do just that, with the force of a little chicken," he cried happily. "I wrote a small, insignificant essay entitled 'Criminality in the Light of Objective Psychology,' a pamphlet, in fact, and in that I proved"—Bechterev opened his arms apologetically—"I should have more respect for the word 'proof,' but I've always claimed that the source of evil is not to be found solely in the brain." Here the Russian tapped the handle of his silver fork against the point on his high forehead from which there sprouted a magnificent bush of hair. "We must rather, I wrote, seek its causes in the capitalist social order."

Bechterev cheerfully broke a dry slice of white bread in two, dipped a corner in his vodka glass, and contentedly chewed the damp lump with his white teeth. He flashed a complicit smile at his companion. "Of course I was only able to write the words 'capitalist social order' because at that time we were living under the rule of our Tsar. If I produced a critique of capitalism I could certainly rely on automatic support from the aristocracy, the church, and the military. For they saw capitalism as something threatening from the West, something bourgeois, godless, something that was at any rate profoundly contemptible."

In fact his hair was far too black, it occurred to Vogt. His beard, with its extravagant curls, tended toward a mixture of salt and pepper. Was it possible that Bechterev was wearing a sophisticated and realistic wig? Vogt did not have the exact dates in his head, but nonetheless the Russian must be at least a decade and a half older than himself. And he did not seem to live especially abstemiously, at least if this evening was anything to go by.

"Don't be too deeply disappointed in me," his colleague said, laughing, "or are you merely tired? But I forgot, you had a rest in the train. In a good hard bed, I should imagine. But to return to our subject: Of course our social revolutionaries understood what my real message was. Their sensoria reacted to the word 'capitalism.' So they felt they had some support. You see, my dear friend, I have not acted courageously, I have merely acted in a worldly way. Like the serpents in the Bible."

He removed the napkin from beneath his beard to reveal a slightly yellowed wing collar. "All that worries me is the notion that I might be about to bite off more than I can chew as a scientist. That we as researchers can say nothing about certain forms of supernormality. At that point I thought of you, and I should very much like to hear your opinion on this matter, but perhaps we might drink another little glass first so that we can talk to each other more openly. You must understand, I am an old man, full of hopes, and maybe for that reason I'm an old fool. But I still have these hopes, which I shall talk to you about in a moment."

He called the waiter.

"If I can collect my thoughts on the subject," Vogt began, but then he felt Bechterev's firm grip on his upper arm again.

"Let us talk first of all about our disappointments as researchers over the past few years," his colleague interrupted. "A thousand apologies for interrupting you again before you even begin, but let us first of all get the unpleasant things out of our souls. If you wish, I shall start, and that will make it easier for you. Sweeping etiquette aside, I shall claim the privilege of age. And my first assertion is as follows: The recent war was a disgrace as far as brains are concerned."

Vogt tried not to look even more baffled than he felt.

"I'm not talking about the social costs, I'm not talking about the unspeakable horrors, I am only talking as a scientist now, and as a scientist I just have to say that I found it almost unbearable to be forced to discover how unimaginatively man's brain, that noblest of all organs, reacted if hit by a bullet. I repeat, unimaginatively. I have had to examine hundreds, maybe thousands, of cases, and wherever the bullet struck, the wounded men always reacted in the same way: When they became excited they tore the bandages from their heads and charged through the wards or, if nobody stopped them, down the corridors. When the patients were quiet, they were barely responsive. In fact they behaved like our alcoholics—heavy perspiration and high blood pressure. But as a psychological phenotype they were apathetic and pitifully inarticulate."

Bechterev drew up his shoulders as if trying to shield his ears from bad news. "For decades I have researched, taught, and published the way in which real damage to equally real nerves affects a creature's behavior. I had never worked on a human being, of course, but the war supplied that opportunity. An abundance of material. God rest their souls, but that's how it was. And I had always hoped that nature would have come up with something particularly cunning or"—Bechterev searched for a new word—"something particularly quick-witted for such a complex organ to be able to do. In all my research I've never come across it. Or was that only true in Russia?"

Vogt's gaze had rested for a moment on a very gaunt woman at the next table—she could not have been older than thirty—who was emptying one glass after another as mechanically as a marionette, with no visible reaction whatsoever.

"No," he said quickly, as Bechterev's eyebrows were still raised inquisitively. "As far as I know—and I think I have a reasonable perspective on the matter—your description quite precisely matches our own experiences. So I have brought you a few initial publications of our provisional results." Vogt slapped the little leather case beside his chair, as if giving a dog a few friendly smacks on the flank. "You must consider these essays a kind of contraband," he said with a conspiratorial smile. "I have been much less courageous than you: defying only our customs officers, who still hold the exchange of scientific information, of which of course they know nothing, to be a punishable offense."

Suddenly the gaunt woman at the next table slumped silently in her chair. Two waiters immediately rushed over and grabbed her by the ankles and shoulders. They carried her out of the restaurant like a freshly bagged deer. Vogt caught himself staring at her thighs, exposed by the hitched-up hem of her skirt. No one apart from Vogt seemed to attach any particular importance to the event. At any rate, the cheerful banter at the other tables hadn't stopped for so much as a moment.

"We have been trying," Vogt resolutely continued, "or rather, I have been trying, to focus my experiments more precisely on the importance of the elite brain. For quite a long time now I have been convinced that studies of the mediocre can provide necessary, but never sufficient, data for the definition of man's highest capacities. When Marx says"—and Vogt bowed in an unspecified direction—"that we must understand the apes through man rather than man through the apes—I'm quoting from memory—but if we are to remain faithful to this idea, our task must lie in seeing elites as the sole valid form of humanity. Within strictly scientific categories, of course. But the elite, whatever form it may assume, is characterized by a quite definite combination of cells. Strength in one particular area, of course, is won at the cost of strength in another; major revolutionaries are rarely pianists of genius, excellent cooks, or imaginative courtesans. You will forgive the extremely clumsy comparisons, selected very much at random. I'm using them only to clarify an assertion that I find very important,

and which is as follows: There is a form of concentrated consciousness, there are control centers that can be represented anatomically
in the form of bulges, and in our work we should direct our attention
toward those particular centers."

Bechterev regarded his German colleague with unconcealed delight. "You are speaking with a profundity, knowledge, and determination," he said solemnly, "of which I know but a single
historical example. I raise my glass in deep respect."

Bechterev raised his glass, and Vogt raised his in turn.

"In our technical language," Bechterev continued, after he had
refilled the glasses, "you are saying the same of the brain as our
Comrade Lenin said of the role of the Communist Party—the
importance of the avant-garde, the concentration of a particular
consciousness, as you have just depicted it. It is concentrated in
a presidium or a central committee, the individual forms are
unimportant—all that matters is the fact that it is concentrated."

"That is what I mean by the elite," said Vogt triumphantly. "It
is not formed by chance or society, it can only be seen as a material
that exerts a powerful influence on consciousness. I repeat: Elite
lies in the brain. Brain creates elite." He fell back in his chair,
from which he had risen a few inches. "But enough of that. Tell
me about Lenin. Have you met him personally?"

Bechterev did not answer immediately. He drew such a deep
breath that his shirt stretched across his chest. "Vladimir Ilyich,"
he began in his rhapsodic style, "our honored Comrade Lenin, is,
as far as I am concerned, the incarnation of genius. Not one iota
less. Such resolution! Such vision! Such speed of association! My
dear Vogt, you were saying a few seconds ago: Brain creates elite.
That is a sentence that could have come from Lenin himself. You
are not a philosopher, if you will forgive me." Bechterev ran his
napkin over Vogt's hand as if to pacify him. "You are a philosophical
thinker, but your thinking is sharper than that of any German
philosopher I know, and that is why you will appreciate the following little example. Where a German philosopher, a complete
academic, would think up the phrase: 'Introductory considerations
toward a possible critique of practical judgment' "—the Russian's

voice had grown scornful, and he waved his hands up and down like a pair of imbalanced scales—"on a subject such as this, our Lenin writes quite simply: 'What is to be done?' " Bechterev struck the table with such force that the drinks did an excited little dance in their glasses. "True genius, as I see it, can also be defined as the shortening of time. Lenin can shorten time."

The inevitable dance band had begun to play the inevitable tunes. Vogt edged his chair closer to Bechterev and asked: "How would you describe him if you saw him as a patient?" Before he had finished speaking, he was overcome by a slight fear that he might have said something utterly tasteless. So he added: "I mean, what is your strictly objective opinion?"

"If I had to describe him at this historical moment," Bechterev answered, leaning toward Vogt, "quite objectively and in terms of his appearance, I would say, I swear to you, that he looks like the man sitting opposite me." The Russian briefly laid his hands on Vogt's shoulders, shook him, and sat back in his chair. "You have the same head, the high forehead, the resolute profile, you are also similar in build, you could even have copied his beard. But much more important than that, even in my objective opinion, as you say, you also emanate much of his power, his intensity, his attitude. As I have with his career, I have followed your work very closely; like Lenin, you have, even at an early age, stood up to the power of your superiors."

"Well, I wasn't banished," Vogt objected with a laugh. "I only fell out with my teacher because he stole my intellectual property. I wasn't sent to Siberia as a punishment, I just wasn't allowed to lecture; not on that occasion, anyway. But scientific heroism—this much was plain to me even then—lay in bold resistance."

Bechterev emphatically drummed two fingertips on the table-cloth. "You had the massed armies of the academy against you, and you won."

Bechterev refilled the glasses, and then said slowly: "I drink to the victor. And I drink to the man who shares with Lenin not only the year but the very month of his birth. Of course I hold astrology in contempt. But only privately; as a scientist I still await con-

vincing results. Yet when I noticed that your birthdays were only
two weeks apart, it made me think."

"Lenin was born in the same year as me?" Vogt asked delight-
edly.

"The same year and the same month of April. But that is not
why Semashko—who will be, or is already, our new Commissar
of Health—and I decided to involve you in our little plan, which
I shall now explain to you. You once met Semashko in Berlin,
before the war, and you must have made a strong impression on
him. Such an impression, in fact, that he now claims to have
discovered you. Be that as it may—come a little closer, the music
is getting more and more intolerable. I didn't really want to tell
you until tomorrow, but anyway, what Comrade Semashko and I
have planned is in the service of national enlightenment. We are
concerned with the propagation of the very ideas we were discussing a few minutes ago. Why would we want to do this? Because
as far as our working masses are concerned, thought in its concrete
form, the brain as an object of research, is sadly still alien to them.
The masses are trapped in ideas of the soul and of mystery. We
want to change this situation as radically as possible through a
project that is concretely symbolic, we might even say artistic."

Bechterev drew a brownish envelope from his jacket pocket,
and from his waistcoat a silver pen, which disappeared like a tooth-
pick in his massive hand. He ran his fist over the back of the
envelope a few times and then showed Vogt the result.

Vogt looked at the sketch, which vaguely reminded him of some
abortive creation by a pastry cook. It might have been a collapsed
sponge cake, or perhaps a little cinnamon bun.

"A design of genius," Bechterev said respectfully. "The famous
Tatlin drew it for me, but sadly my reproductions suffer terribly
from a lack of artistic talent. But of course you will know what it
is."

"Interesting," observed Vogt. He took off his glasses and wiped
the lenses. Then he dried the sweat from his forehead.

"All around the republics, we are seeing exciting works in a new
architectural style, which we call fantastic revolutionary architec-

ture," said the Russian savant. "Architecture in the form of a pyramid, of a tilted cylinder, hemispheres rotating on their own axes. New forms for the New Man. Towers and shapes like pointed sails, but much more monumental. The workers will be roused from their slumbers by new forms such as they have never seen in their lives." He added a little stick man to his sketch, to express the proportions of the work. Beside the bun, the man looked minute.

"An architecture like that of the brain," said Vogt, who felt that a comment was now required of him.

"You have the gift of seeing before other people," said Bechterev with admiration. "It is, in fact, an architecture *for* the brain. Semashko and I plan—with the vigorous support of the architect Tatlin—to erect a Pantheon to the Brain." He paused briefly, to relish the effect of his words. "A gigantic museum that will be devoted to science with respect to its working function, and to demonstration with respect to visitors. According to our current plans, it will display at least five hundred brains in the greatest variety of forms, like precious paintings or sculptures. Can you imagine the tremendous educational effect that such a massive exhibition will produce?"

Vogt nodded. "The crucial question, of course, is what selection you will use."

"Here, too, we have had some preliminary ideas. The scientific and political points of view must be brought into harmony. We are thinking of dividing them up first of all according to racial categories, as in a well-run natural history museum, and then differentiating them according to the contribution that the owner of a particular brain has made to the revolution. And the crowning glory of our collection"—Bechterev tapped with his pen on the top of his drawing—"the noblest jewel in our treasure trove, will, of course, be the brain of the man without whose life and work none of this would have been possible."

"But Lenin is still alive," Vogt objected.

"Lenin is still alive, and happily so, I may say. But even the pharaohs made provisions for the world after their demise, long before they died. What is revolutionary about our idea is that we are employing a strategy of transparency. We are not sealing up pyramids or Chinese imperial tombs, we are doing everything scientifically, concealing nothing. No mystery, nothing that might be transformed into a miracle if hidden from view. Our secret, if you wish, lies in our transparency. My dear friend, you know that from your own research, we generally fail to find the solution because it is too obvious. This time we are turning everything around and revealing the solution in all its directness. This solution to the riddle of our history is called: Lenin's brain."

"But how can I help you with this project?" asked Vogt. "I'm impressed, you might say enthralled, by your plan; it shows greatness, courage, and a brilliance that is the mark of the visionary. I am also attracted by the idea of transparency. I call it enlightenment through demonstration, and have, using this process in my own work during the war years just passed, achieved considerable successes. But what you plan is on a quite different level. Except, if I may say this, it is borne on the most competent of shoulders. So, once again: What can I, with my modest powers, contribute to its success?"

The band was playing a gypsy waltz, and a few couples were twirling on the dance floor. Bechterev brushed a strand of hair from his forehead. Then he rested his chin in his hand. "I'm an old man," he said dramatically, "and whether I will live to see this task completed, or whether I will have my wits about me when it is finished, seems to me more than doubtful. As scientists we are obliged to take a realistic point of view, precisely when we are dealing with ourselves, which is always particularly difficult."

"You can't deceive me," Vogt interrupted him. "Even here on the dance floor you'd wear these young people out as you galloped around. All the work we have done in this area shows that intense activity noticeably slows down the aging process. Physical, intellectual, and emotional activity. You have always been a model to us, in every area of life."

Bechterev's only sign that he had been listening to Vogt was a brief smile. "So I have been wondering," he continued, "who could take on this task with me and later complete it. In our circles all that counts is strict qualification, specialist competence, and the strength to see things through. Like the Marxists, we scientists are also internationalists. The former hostility between our countries"—the Russian picked a crumb from his lapel—"was tragic, but has already been overtaken by events. I have looked around and listened around, and you, my dear Vogt, are a unique authority. A unique authority and a unique force. And the way you have immediately grasped the intricacies of our little plan— if I ever had any doubts, they would have been swept aside by that alone. Of course we have a few good people here too, but I repeat: no one of your brilliance, with your energy, and with your contacts. Hence my quite solemn request: Join our commission, support us, and remain true to this fantastic project when I no longer can."

"It would be an honor," Vogt answered curtly.

Bechterev rose to embrace the German.

In the bathroom at his hotel, Vogt sat down on a thickly upholstered stool. The dressing-table mirror had two extendable wings and was lit like the mirror in an actress's dressing room. Vogt looked to the right and to the left and repeated, in Bechterev's deep voice with its rolled *r*'s: "The same head, the high forehead, the resolute profile." Then he shook a headache powder into his toothbrush glass.

TWENTY-FOUR

Your Christmas and New Year's letter took more than three months to reach me here," Amanda von Alvensleben wrote to the Vogts from Budapest. "As I counted up the weeks and wondered what the envelope and three pages had been through, I felt a deep respect for the plucky little frontier-crosser. I myself have just had a few weeks during which I hardly dared undertake the journey over the bridges from Buda to Pest or the other way around, a difficulty at first compounded by the fact that I could never tell on which side of the Danube lay Buda, and on which Pest. At some point, however, I got my hands on a *Guide Bleu* in the billiard room at our hotel, which explained to me that Buda had been the seat of a pasha in the sixteenth century. The word 'pasha' made me think of Sir David, the father of the children I have been looking after for a year, and since then Buda, pasha, and the Hotel Gellért have fused into a single unit for me. These children, I should add in a quick lament, are the real reason for the gray streaks that are becoming more and more conspicuous each time

I look at myself in the mirror in the morning, and which give my face the expression of a rather ill-tempered Pietà. Never have I so easily understood why the Scholastics had such trouble distinguishing angels from devils; never have I wondered more why a person such as myself, by nature so devoted to enjoying the fruits of civilization, should find herself repeatedly compelled to take up arms against the savage nature of children.

"These children could have come straight out of an illustration that Max once did for *The Jungle Book*. I shall tell you but one of a series of examples that could be continued ad infinitum. Shortly before Christmas, when Sir David was with us in Calcutta doing his arms deals with that air of calm so typical of him, they excused themselves from riding lessons in order, they said, to help the mission sisters pack presents for the leper colony. They had clearly noticed that I used to meet a British officer during these riding lessons, a pink and blank-faced man with a very finely trained tenor voice, who was also able to conjure away the hopelessness of his own existence with his very inspired piano playing. So while I was slowly beginning to forget the heat and dampness of the climate in the company of Captain Simms, the children set off, not, of course, in order to pursue good works, but in search of a beggar, some kind of Hindu, who had been hanging around in front of our estate for weeks—accompanied by a five-legged cow. Any beggar who could manage to reach our district had to have something striking to show for himself, or the guards would have shown no mercy in chasing him away. That repulsively striking cow gave its owner free passage. The fifth leg—and I shall write this promptly because I can already feel your skeptical scientific eye bearing down on my lines—looked, incidentally, rather like a long tail with a hoof. But the cow also had a tail without a hoof, and that is why this whiplike thing, utterly ill adapted to walking, was presented as a leg. And every morning the porter would ask me for a graceful donation for the five-legged cow, which must have fired the curiosity of the children, like everything else involving easy money. Max Landsberg—to return to him—could just as easily have represented them as an allegory of the classical doctrine of heredity. By the way, Sir David, or so he once told me, wanted to wait at least five years before he initiated Peter, who was then ten years old, into the secrets of his business. Perhaps he had already recognized that Patricia, the sister, only eighteen months younger, would not be needing any such initiation. In a state of mounting concern that afternoon, which was rapidly slipping into a pitch-dark evening, I roamed through districts of Calcutta of which my guidebook very accurately observed: The white woman is well advised not to set foot in these places. Thank God Captain Simms was by my side, clumsily holding my upper arm and whistling Flemish madrigals to give me courage. At last we found the children. They were squatting with the cow's owner, the father of a very large family and clearly also the owner of three more cows that could have been passed off as five-legged, in a lean-to made of boards and tarpaulin. As it turned out, Peter had given the Hindu a very valuable pair of mother-of-pearl-inlaid dueling pistols belonging to his father in exchange for one of these cows. It was only the very timely arrival of my captain that brought this deal to an abrupt halt.

"In Budapest the children merely went running after a stray donkey they had found on the hill near the hotel. That would not in itself have been a major problem, since that part of town has nothing but the fanciest villas; it's very easy to keep an eye on, and people there shoot only for sport. But as ill luck would have it, the sweet little things had just been playing India, so they had dressed up—or stripped down, perhaps—with a scarf for a loincloth and a number of their progenitor's ties around their heads. They must have looked like wandering gypsy children. This was cause for alarm—not, as a doddering old nurse tried to explain to me a number of years ago, because real gypsies will put you in a bag, but because of the revolutionary social programs of the Soviet government here. It is passionately concerned about the neglected and the snot-nosed, it puts them up in homes and sends them, bathed and brushed, to the former spa towns on Lake Balaton, in order to turn them into useful members of society. That is, of course, very praiseworthy and, to use the currently fashionable expression, progressive, but as I myself am being paid to raise children according to their parents' ideas, I am obliged to spurn such competition.

"After two frantic hours of searching I finally found the children in a freshly tilled front garden. They were helping a very respectably dressed man build a duck pond. All the respectably dressed people hereabouts seem to be busily eliminating their ornamental gardens in order to make room for poultry breeding. Sir David has told me that he has never experienced such an exciting form of economic warfare between such diverse strata within a single nation as the one being waged today in Hungary. They do not fight one another with arguments, they devour one another's goods. I have not experienced much of this in the hotel, but there is a rumor going around that vegetables such as peppers, white cabbage, and beets are being rationed in the city. The Soviet government has responded, of course, and is permitting the sale of vanilla ice cream at a ridiculously low price on every street corner and in every square. A revolution fought with *bombes glacées* naturally loses a little of the terror that the idea of revolution otherwise tends to convey.

"That aside, this revolution seems to be unleashing powerful forces among the poets. In every coffeehouse, nervous poets are brooding over their odes—a friend of mine claims that in certain establishments your mocha comes served not only with water but with an inkpot as well. As soon as their works are completed, a deft handpress ensures their reproduction. If you study the other side of my letter, you will find a model example of such an ode —at least this is what my friend claims, and she, unlike myself, understands the language."

With a little pin, Amanda had fastened to the work of the unknown revolutionary poet a folded sheet which said simply, on the outside, "For Cécile."

"My dear Cécile," this letter began, "I hope you are no longer cross with me because of my quick marriage and equally quick separation. I know you think me a little frivolous for the way I lead my life, but I can assure you that I really did love your nephew very much. If I did at some point say I wished he was a Swissified Frenchman rather than a French Swiss, it was just the kind of foolish nonsense that one sometimes comes out with in the powder room. I'm very sorry if it got back to you. I may have been referring to the fact that Antoine was trying so terribly hard to establish an appropriate life-style for us. He certainly wanted that for my sake at first, but I noticed with trepidation after only a few weeks that he himself was slipping into this new role as into a custom-made glove. You know me, dear Cécile, there are certain kinds of excessively conventional behavior that I find neither easy nor natural. Of course I was ashamed every time I skipped those afternoons when—for the sake of our future happiness—I should really have been with his women colleagues wrapping bandages for the Red Cross. I only mention this business because it seems to have become so important to Antoine later on. Those evenings he always looked as depressed as if he had been betrayed by a fellow Swiss confederate. And we stopped reaching out to one another. Which was all the more serious in that he was actually very successful, but he wasn't succeeding sufficiently quickly to have a wife like me so early in his career—economic matters were no longer an issue, but I was a foreigner, and a good five years older than he. Please trust me, my dear Cécile, when I say that I have no wish to load the guilt onto someone else's shoulders too hastily. But please trust me, too, when I say that I quickly came to feel that I had woken up a prince with my kiss, sadly not the romantic prince I had dreamed of, but a prince of real estate. In a strange way Antoine sucked in my passion and poured it into the pursuit of new conquests in the housing market. I assume that he himself was initially unaware of what was happening to him, but he would suddenly grow radiant, in a way that I found quite inexplicable, when as disagreeable a word as 'foreclosure' passed his lips, while I was increasingly overcome by a yearning for that young man who had once demonstrated to me how to play the oboe while standing on your head.

"Of course we separated at my request, but all I did was express something that would inevitably have led to unpleasant arguments a few weeks later. For my part this was neither generous nor mean, it was simply sensible, and as a memento I still have a few wonderful months in Geneva, I still have his name and his country's passport, which has been extraordinarily useful to me over the past few years."

Toward the end of this letter, Amanda's handwriting assumed a pointed, almost Gothic shape unusual for her. "You, my dear Cécile, once asked me, in the kindest of terms, to consider whether the self-love that I demand did not stand in the way of mutual love. I cannot answer this question in a very abstract way, but my experience so far teaches me that, in old-fashioned terms, I can only give happiness when I have felt it myself. I turn into a tense, dull, and wooden creature if I feel I have to live up to someone else's expectations. And for that reason I ask you once again not to give up your friendship for me, I assure you that our separation was as important for your nephew as it was for me."

In the last part of her letter to both the Vogts, written on the back of a piece of paper in which Max Landsberg had, many years earlier, bundled together various scalpels into a spring bouquet, Amanda's handwriting was once again familiarly curly. "Please don't throw this sheet away, it is one of the few souvenirs I have of Max, of whom I have not had a sign of life for two years. On that occasion he was writing to me from a prisoner-of-war camp in France—where it was exactly he obviously couldn't tell me. I think he did try to by making reference to cornfields and drawbridges but so cryptically that I didn't understand him. If I think about it, Max never had much of a talent for camouflage. It probably had something to do with his dislike of beards.

"I also, by the way, found your letter a little cryptic—this should, I beg you, be taken as a complaint not about you, but rather about things as they stand. However, I should very much have liked to know whether, on your visit to Russia, you too met that gentleman about whom I once wrote you in one of my letters from Geneva. That famous revolutionary who called himself Ulyanov in those days, and who is now celebrated as Lenin. I myself am actually moving in the most elevated revolutionary circles here. Thanks to

Sir David's kind mediation, I was able to make the acquaintance of Mr. Béla Kun, insofar as a mere interpreter can be said to make acquaintances. But before I say anything about that, I must tell you about another meeting that suddenly took me right back to that time on Lake Geneva.

"On the Tuesday after Easter, when the lobby in the Hotel Gellért was full to the brim with buffet waitresses licking vanilla ices as they listened with some boredom to a lecture on the political responsibility of serving staff, a black figure tottered through the revolving glass door. I immediately thought of a corpulent chimney sweep who, through some tragic accident, had been divested of his ladder and brooms, but on closer inspection I discovered that the man's features were familiar. It was, in fact, that knight, Lanz von Liebenfels, who scandalized everyone at Princess Urussova's with his revolting nonsense that time I described to you, and then scalded Lenin's thigh with his tea. My joy at seeing him again was not especially great, but it was outweighed by my curiosity. To my surprise, Lanz too recognized me after some squinting—he seemed about to follow his instincts for a moment and reach for my hand, but then remembered that he looked like a charcoal burner and was content to bow. The angel of death had brushed him with his wing, he confided, he had fallen among crossbreeds; and after he had cleaned himself up a little he would tell me about the whole dreadful business. Then, through a line of buffet waitresses who jumped aside in horror, he disappeared in the direction of the bathroom.

"At that moment Sir David and the children came back from a walk. In accordance with his elegant manner, my master made the two little ones stand silently beside me like two troublesome pieces of luggage which the staff had been asked to deal with. This I found extremely inopportune, because I wanted to prevent a meeting between Lanz and my charges at all costs. They both barely understand German—and would certainly not have understood the knight's Old Testament language—but I remembered that Lanz always embellished his discourses with gestures which, because of their puzzling lack of ambiguity, would tempt childish tempera-

ments to spontaneous imitation. The only way out that I could see
was to suggest that the children go on a secret mission, so I sent
them off to the hotel kitchen with the charge of observing the
patissier at work, paying special attention to whether he had set
any dainties aside for himself. Peter and Patricia love this kind of
operation—in Calcutta they once caught our cook spicing the curry
for dinner with some pipe tobacco that their father had brought
back from Smyrna. But back to Lanz, who returned, adequately
washed, from the bathroom, and now resembled a chimney sweep
only in that his suit and top hat had such a fatty sheen to them.

"I naturally assumed that Lanz had gotten into trouble because
he had been spouting his lewdness, as my father used to say, at
some meeting or other. Perhaps he had spoken too clearly, in the
presence of an only moderately tolerant audience, about his favorite
subjects—sodomy and catamites, zoophilia, and streams of sperm.
Revolutionaries can often be very prudish the minute somebody
tries to declare their epoch-making plans to be the result of sinful
emissions of semen, particularly when that somebody chooses a
language as rich in imagery as does our founder of theo-zoology.

"But nothing of the kind had happened—or at least not according to Sir Lanz. Rather, on the night of Good Friday, he had
been arrested as a black marketeer when trying to buy candles for
a nocturnal ceremony being held by the members of his order. I
was about to say something inappropriate about the blackness of
his suit when he took my hand and cried, 'They thought I was a
Jewish usurer, those crossbreed barbarians, imagine the humilia-
tion, I was a hair's breadth away from being executed, in utter
misjudgment of my historical person.' Then he raised his hands
high like a pilgrim arriving at his destination, and cried: 'Béla Kun
has given his hordes the ability to track down their adversaries,
but not the intelligence to unmask them. I shall now travel back
to Vienna immediately, and there I shall celebrate my resurrection.'

"Over the last few months I have been increasingly struck by
the number of men who seem to be under a compulsion to assume
a titanic role. Not necessarily that of Jesus Christ, like our dear
Lanz von Liebenfels; Sir David, for example, is content to present

himself to his interlocutors or business partners as Lord Disraeli. Sometimes I think the war has left behind an enormous number of spiritual costumes into which the survivors are now slipping, to satisfy an insatiable need for heroes.

"I could cite Béla Kun, whom I mentioned before, as an example of this. He looks like a cattle dealer who's been asked by a primitive artist to pose for a painting of Napoleon. When Sir David and I sought him out for the usual discussions about the delivery of howitzers, mortars, and I don't know what else, he kept throwing his head back toward the nape of his fat neck and saying, 'You are talking to a representative of the world revolution,' as if this gave him a special historical discount. I should have liked to advise him to allow at least a few curls in his pig's-bristle haircut, which would have made him look as if he at least wanted to appear less burly, but as I had no wish to get further involved in issues of revolutionary coiffure, I kept this idea to myself.

"Béla Kun did hint, by the way, that he expected world revolution in Vienna and Berlin in the near future. I am not giving away any secrets, because thanks to the poets here, this news appears verbatim in the daily press. I hope that our Sir Lanz will celebrate his rebirth in good time. Otherwise he will have to look for a new city for his new Easter.

"Should world revolution actually reach Berlin, I have given Mr. Kun your address. That may sound a little frivolous, but in the few minutes during which he dropped the pose of Napoleon reborn as Lenin, he confided to me that 'a woman comrade very devoted to him'—and my quotation marks are meant to put a distance between me and his words—is suffering from certain nervous problems, and that immediately made me think of the practice in Magdeburger Strasse. Of course my little aside that I had already met Lenin in Switzerland was not without effect. Even Sir David allowed the corner of his mouth to twitch.

"Yet again my thoughts are in Berlin. I hope you are well, after these terrible years, and in that hope I also include the children. From which you may gauge how sentimental your faithful correspondent can be."

TWENTY - FIVE

The section of the War Ministry headed by Captain Most had, in the spring of 1918, been commissioned to investigate the properties of domestic animals that might be valuable in a state of war. Captain Most, however, placed his task in a broader context: "Instinct and genius are qualities complementary to manly courage and technology," he had once remarked in conversation with Vogt, "and it is on this point that we must focus our work with animals." But genius, Most believed, had not been neglected in the operations of the general staff. If the genius that could be harnessed by the military was more or less fairly distributed among the civilized nations, then the successful mobilization of that talent, seen as latent military energy, would make all the difference between victory and defeat in battle. "War," Most stressed in a little memorandum, "must, from the perspective of military science, be seen as the ideal experimental situation for a general investigation into genius, for only in war do we find the diversity of situations that put genius unequivocally to the test." At the eastern front and near Verdun, Captain Most had gathered information on the subject, which he painstakingly evaluated in his diaries in the evening. From the Russian campaign alone he had brought back twelve closely written notebooks. *Bellum docet omnia* was his conclusion to a lengthy discussion of the conceptual and material relationship between engineers, troops of geniuses, and genius per se—war is the teacher of all things. The armistice forced the captain to broaden this thesis. Even under peacetime conditions, he now believed, the army was particularly important for the cultivation of genius. In the end, the army was, one might say, a complete construction kit including complementary types of behavior that could reveal, isolate, and thus protect genius, the most prominent quality of which, according to Vogt, was its scarcity. "If we take the recent war," wrote Most, coming to his pet subject, "as a textbook example of the wider exploitation of genius, particular shortfalls will be noted in the use made of the German military dog section and, to a lesser degree, the German pigeon post."

By the summer of 1918, representatives of the War Ministry—Captain Most among them—had established what the military cautiously called contact with the Kaiser Wilhelm Society, because, according to all available reports from the front, the use of trained dogs and messenger dogs was unscientific—and in the captain's words this meant "not getting the greatest possible savings on manpower." But this initial contact had produced no results that might have decisively altered the outcome of the war.

Most was not discouraged. "Capitulation is a means, not an end," he wrote to Vogt. "We are answerable to a power higher than those that met in Compiègne. If we establish an alliance between the two powers that have made Germany strong, the brain and the sword, then the unhappy chapters of the war will soon be expunged from the history books as trivial episodes."

Contrary to his usual habit, Vogt had not shown this letter to Cécile. She found the captain cranky, certainly, but also more than a touch too Francophobe. In addition, Most's discussion of scientific topics had seldom been precise enough for her taste. "He driveled on so romantically," she had once complained, "your Captain Mostradamus." This joke had circulated quickly and had won Cécile an entirely new reputation as a humorist.

Vogt had tried in vain to point out that for purely economic reasons their institute could not afford the luxury of taste when it came to dealing with potential sponsors. The funds that had flowed to Berlin from Krupp's foundation had long been devalued by inflation. They were chasing, hunting, crying out for new sources of finance, and what would be most welcome was a rather vaguely defined, or—best of all—even a romantic, formulation of its final purpose, because that alone would allow them to pursue their own research without interruption. That the result might later bear the title "Principles of Military Dog Training" was very much of secondary importance.

Nevertheless, Cécile had been so stubborn in her response that they had had a huge argument. Vogt stomped furiously into his study to request a meeting with Captain Most on neutral ground. Most answered promptly and suggested a discreet establishment in the Tiergarten district where he had often, he said, had discussions of an extremely confidential nature. The best place to meet would be the Grosser Stern. He, Most, would—unless Vogt said otherwise—meet him there the following day at eleven forty-five, in civilian dress.

The discreet establishment had clearly once been a kind of casino. Most led Vogt into the dining room, where the yellowish plaster on the walls was veined with broad and delicate cracks. The waiters seemed to be war veterans—one was missing a leg, another a hand, a third wore a black patch over his right eye, held in place with a pink rubber band.

"I have drafted a letter for you," said Vogt after the barley broth, "which—with your consent and your ministry's letterhead—could not fail to have an effect on the Kaiser Wilhelm Society." He drew an envelope from his flat portfolio. Most opened it and began reading.

In view of the important and wide-ranging role played by the trained dog in wartime, the planned exploitation of dogs in the reformation of the Reichswehr has become an indisputable necessity. What this requires is an in-depth scientific examination of the physical and mental capacities of dogs.

To carry out a more thorough investigation into the capabilities and the practical usefulness of dogs, a precise knowledge of the microscopic construction, the so-called architecture, of the canine brain is required, much like the extensive studies into the human brain that have already been carried out by Professor Vogt in Berlin, and likewise an examination of the capacities of the individual sections of the canine brain and the way in which they are combined in higher capacities, as revealed by recent work by the Neurobiological Institute.

It is proposed that a department of general animal psychology should be set up. Its task will be to analyze the behavior of dogs and trace it back to its mental impulses . . .

Most looked up from the letter into Vogt's eyes. "Splendidly formulated, precise, and straight to the heart of the matter."

Vogt plunged his fork into his kohlrabi.

Only the establishment of such a department, Most read on, would make it possible to differentiate, in terms of physical build and mental makeup, between individual dogs and breeds of dogs. As was well known, the dog section itself contained specimens that were variously affectionate, fearful, and distracted. Only a clear separation between the psychologies of individuals and breeds could cast light on the following question: Are particular cerebral constructions and their manifestations in mental life specific to individual *breeds* of dog, or are there only *individual* differences? And care would need to be taken to ensure that the scientific results were communicated to the dog handlers at the military kennels at Fangschleuse.

Most folded the letter in half and returned it to the light brown envelope. "I am utterly convinced that any emendations on my part could only be damaging," he said, after dabbing his lips carefully with his napkin. "The letter will leave my section this very day."

Indeed, the letter did not fail to have its effect on the president of the Kaiser Wilhelm Society. His Excellency von Harnack had allowed himself to be convinced that the study of the canine mind was not only a military matter but a major economic one as well, since it would benefit a wide range of people, particularly businessmen, and most especially dog-biscuit manufacturers. The business community would help to provide funds of which the extremely tight budget of the Kaiser Wilhelm Society was sorely in need. So von Harnack wasted little time in following up the suggestions of the War Ministry, which had in the meantime been renamed the National Defense Ministry, indeed he even consented ("despite numerous other demands on his time") to take a chair on a preliminary committee for the promotion of canine research; and when the committee was asked to deal with research into carrier pigeons as well, the president of the Kaiser Wilhelm Society was in favor of that, although he did voice the proviso that in the case of the carrier pigeon, research should be *psychological* rather than *anatomical*, to which end he requested that Privy Councillor Stumpf be brought in as a special consultant.

That the hope of acclaim from the widest circles of the population had not been unjustified was made strikingly clear on the morning of September 10, 1919, an unusually warm rainy day on which the representatives of a fairly large number of canine-related organizations from throughout the Reich met, at the invitation of the National Defense Ministry, in the former upper chamber, now the headquarters of the Kaiser Wilhelm Society.

"I bet you're off to see your doggy chums," Cécile had said mockingly when Oskar Vogt picked up his coat and umbrella. "Don't forget to take a bone along." Cécile only tolerated her husband's secrecies if she could spot romantic intrigues in them. In this area, experience had taught her to be tolerant. This dog business, on the other hand, which already had the assistants in the building gossiping, was a source of extreme irritation to her.

It was frivolous from a scientific point of view, but more important than that, Oskar was on the point of violating the hallowed rules concerning the openness of any scientific community.

Vogt had merely thrust his chin out stubbornly at his wife, and then stormed off again without locking the front door. Since his return from Petrograd he no longer even checked to see if he had his key with him or not.

A meeting between the Kaiser Wilhelm Society and various military and canine groups—which included the Wire-Haired Terrier Club, the Association of German Dachshunds, the St. Bernard Club, and the International Poodle Association—yielded few tangible results. The Prussian army command granted the Kaiser Wilhelm Society one hundred thousand marks for research on dogs and carrier pigeons. The industrial sector, on the other hand, proved reticent for the moment—with the exception of Otto Lischner of Magdeburg-Sudenburg, proprietor of Herbst Bros. (specialities: Herbst's Animal-Fiber Dog Biscuits, Herbst's Original Phosphorus Liver-Oil Puppy Food, and Herbst's Phosphorus Cod-Liver-Oil Dry Chicken Feed). Herr Lischner was donating twenty-five thousand marks in the form of a 5 percent national bond and promised to put himself at the service of future canine research, for which the president of the Kaiser Wilhelm Society thanked him in a very obliging letter.

"Captain Most," Vogt complained bitterly, "these people want me to think about the routes taken by their companies' food once it has been consumed by the animal, the duration of peristalsis, deposits of stool and urine. I would expect a more rigorous intellectual challenge. I would also expect more money to be made available by the canine associations. In short: The entire project so far has been much too modest!"

The captain remained unimpressed. On November 22, 1919, he invited Vogt to the Defense Ministry to advise him and some of his comrades from the Army Dog Institute in Fangschleuse as to what concrete form that collaboration between brain research and dog handling might take.

Vogt had attended this meeting in a very tight-fitting pea-green tweed hunting jacket, a souvenir of a lecture in Manchester before the war. Research into the mind and brain of the dog required money, he explained to the assembled military men, after establishing his sound intellectual credentials, it required dogs, and it required a suitable environment for scientific study. Dr. Klempin, he explained, who had already been introduced to the gentlemen present, had very successfully extended his previous investigations into the brain of the bear to consider comparable areas in the canine brain. In order to advance this program, the Army Dog Unit would need to deliver a dog as requested.

"Where should it be delivered?" asked Lieutenant Müller.

"We need a noise-free environment. The populace still does not understand certain sounds that an animal does not suppress if pain needs to be inflicted on it for scientific purposes."

Captain Most mentioned the possibility of carrying out the operations in question at the army's training forge in Berlin, at 23A Karlstrasse. The sounds naturally arising there would drown out any other noises that might be produced. In addition, the military security on the grounds would guarantee the necessary confidentiality of the research.

After the Reichswehr representatives had agreed to requisition ideally suitable spaces for the immediately impending *operational* measures, Vogt returned to the question of fund-raising, which continued to trouble him. He pointed out that realization of the program, which had as yet only been rapidly outlined, would swallow up decades of work and large sums of money. And, of course, dogs. "It strikes me that amassing a collection of pelts, skeletons, and possibly characteristic soft parts from the various breeds of dog as a basis for all subsequent research is the most important and also the cheapest of the tasks to be undertaken. I also think that it would be easiest to raise funds for a collection such as this, because, on the one hand, the breeders' organizations would be interested in preserving the progenitors of their breed, and, on the other, many animal lovers would certainly be glad to see a dog that they had owned for years being preserved for posterity."

"A temple to all breeds of dog," said Most, impressed, "or

rather: a museum consecrated to the diversity of breeds and the power of selection."

Vogt also encountered unanimous agreement when he suggested a similar strategy for research on carrier pigeons. Finally he invited everyone present to a lecture that he was giving on "the examination of the brain and mental life of the dog and the carrier pigeon as a central problem in the training of these animals."

"Now he's doing it with pigeons," sighed Cécile, who had found the printed invitation cards on Vogt's desk.

But unforeseen difficulties arose, involving even the project's most prominent advocates: The Army Kennel in Fangschleuse announced that it could supply no more than three dogs for scientific experiments, and, Captain Most noted in an internal report, "in working year 1920, reliably airworthy pigeons were unavailable, owing to war casualties."

Behind Vogt's back, meanwhile, Most was pursuing yet another goal, which he had encapsulated in the slogan "Revolutionize training." The dog had to become as independent of its handler as possible, while continuing to obey his will. Classic dog-training methods had traditionally observed the following premise—that the closer the connection between the dog and the human (his shape and his smell), the more reliably it carries out his commands. The relationship between dog and master was rendered problematic by their spatial separation. What was required, to encourage canine independence, was a substitute for human smell. The dog, operating alone within the test terrain, would have to follow a trail which had the same emotional ties as its master's scent, but which would not emanate from him.

"What we need," Müller wrote in his rather ponderous way to the chemist Schneise, "is an almost human-scented fluid that has every human property and yet is not produced by man."

This scent would have a simple smell, not a mixture of smells (like the herring brine they had used in the initial experiments), it should be neither poisonous nor an irritant, easily produced but impossible to imitate, not easily soluble in water, but soluble nonetheless, it should have a low freezing point, but not be too foul-smelling to humans, not inflammable, and alterable depending on use.

"So that's what a person smells like?" asked the chemist skeptically.

Most turned his attention to the next stage of his project—the creation of a universal soldier recognizable as such to the canine mind. On March 29 he called a meeting with his colleagues. The previous evening he had visited a circus with a few friends, a basically boring business that had provided him with no new insights into the subject of training—the official reason for his visit. Except for one act: an artist in his sequined leotard balanced on a high wire above the big cats' cage. At first Most's thoughts revolved around the costume. No soldier in the world, he thought, would be caught dead in an outfit like that. On the other hand: Would it be possible to walk the wire in army boots? What would happen if the artist was to fall? Could big cats be trained like working dogs? All these ideas were swimming around in his head and breaking apart into their various fragments—all the soldiers in the world, boots, rope, working dogs—and suddenly the fragments combined to form a new and coherent whole: the experimental arrangement for this new stage of inquiry toward a scientific understanding of the canine brain. Most noted:

For the dog separated from the man, the soldier exists only as the footprint that he leaves behind. This footprint has a visual and a scent-related dimension. It is shaped like the sole of a boot. The condition of the ground and the body weight of the wearer of the boot regulate the depth of the track. What we therefore require is reliable data about the average weight and average boot size of the soldiers of all the enemy armies. A mechanically adjustable leg could then be constructed, designed to wear boots variable in size. At the knee joint of the leg a can of scented material is mounted, releasing, as required, quantities of fluid into a tube leading into the heel of the boot, fluid which then seeps through a valve into the ground. The leg is suspended from a wire connected by a pulley to a metal cable running across the terrain on which the experiment is being performed. When the leg is lowered from various different heights, it is possible for it to simulate the impressions of a light-, medium- and heavy-weight soldier.

The next day he described his plan to Vogt.

"Contributes nothing to the anatomy of the brain," Vogt replied. "The crucial question is, of course: Why have you spent weeks fixated on this boot? Where is the mobilization of mass interest in our enterprise? Where are the funds?"

"The boot is a universal military phenomenon," Most answered coldly.

He refused to be distracted by Vogt's criticism. He himself bore full responsibility for the construction of the installation. Shortly after its completion the last dog passed away.

TWENTY-SIX

The gentlemen agreed unanimously that the caller had said the matter was of the greatest urgency. Any doubts, or even any hesitation, were absolutely out of the question. "You must travel tomorrow," the man with the Slavic accent had said on the telephone. "All preparations have been made. Lenin is extremely ill. My government has given me the task of asking you to come to Moscow immediately."

The gentlemen had been flattered by this. In Hamburg and Leipzig, in Munich and Stockholm, cases were being hastily packed. Professors Nonne, Bumke, and Strümpell met the very next day in Berlin, while Henschen and his son set off from Stockholm. It was March 18, 1923. It was a mild spring.

The doctors determined, to their satisfaction, that the people who had commissioned them had spared no expense in ensuring that their journey was as agreeable as possible. First-class tickets had been bought, and passports freshly issued. As soon as the delegates had crossed their respective borders into the Soviet state, special trains were laid on. The Pullman in which the Germans were traveling was fitted out with choice rococo furniture in blue, white, and gold. The care bestowed on them had been just fantastic, Max Nonne recalled; on few occasions in his life had he spent his days so comfortably and at the same time had the opportunity to converse with such clever and worldly men.

Unfortunately, once past the Russian border, a small suitcase belonging to him disappeared; along with other medications, it contained his reagents for the Wassermann test. Nonne was a specialist in diseases of the brain due to all manner of causes, but his skills in diagnosing the late stages of syphilis had made him famous. But chemicals and crucibles for flocculation tests, the professor consoled himself, would also be available in the Soviet capital.

On the platform of the Baltic Station in Moscow, the German gentlemen were greeted by a tall, very elegantly dressed man who introduced himself as Dr. Koshevnikov, Lenin's physician. For the drive to their lodgings, and for the duration of their stay in Moscow, each of the guests had a Rolls-Royce at his disposal. "The cars are gifts from English comrades," Professor Henschen reported later. "One of the People's Commissars explained it to me." Henschen was almost deaf, which is why his revelation was received with some skepticism. "The man was wearing a cowhide coat," he added defiantly.

The foreign guests were staying on the Sophia Quay, in a magnificent old palace with a view of the Kremlin. This palace, they learned, had previously belonged to the family of a sugar manufacturer who now lived in exile in Paris. The professors were astonished to see paintings from the Barbizon school, chinoiseries, baroque furniture, and Gobelins. Their meals were served on Meissen porcelain, something that had never happened to them at home. The doctors, Henschen remembered, led the life of kings. Only Strümpell from Leipzig thought it rather neglectful of them that he of all people, who for reasons of seniority felt that he was the leader of the German group, and was also acknowledged as such, could not see the Kremlin from his drawing-room window.

All his colleagues had the most wonderful cinematic panoramas of the Kremlin towers before their very eyes when their servants opened the curtains each morning, but he, Strümpell, had to look out on a gray row of houses in front of which, for reasons unknown to the professor, long lines of shabbily dressed people formed daily. As soon as the Russian hosts heard of this they moved him into a different room, but in the process he lost a Bakelite toothbrush container of which he was very fond. Strümpell complained loud and long about his loss. It was not until he was on the point of leaving that the younger Henschen found the container in the pocket of a pair of pants that his father had taken off. But, these exceptions aside, no complaints about their lodgings were heard from the delegation of doctors.

The journey to their patient, Lenin, was an arduous one. Each time they visited him, the doctors were given new passes. Before they would open a door for the doctors the guards exchanged these identity cards for new ones after subjecting them to an almost rudely ponderous examination. Making contact with the sick man was just as complicated. Without any warning as to who was to examine the patient on any particular day, the doctors were only allowed in two at a time, or three at the most. The decision as to the names and number of consultants was clearly the sole responsibility of Lenin's sister. She decided when his blood pressure should be measured or his temperature taken, or when his reflexes should be tested. She seemed most displeased by the regularity with which her brother was asked to hold a silver spoon in his hand. She responded with equanimity, however, to the fact that all the doctors were constantly running the nails of their index fingers down the bare soles of his feet. His sister categorically refused to let them take a blood sample.

Lenin sometimes spoke German, sometimes Russian—if he spoke at all. He was lying in a very sparsely furnished room, on a simple bed, with his elbows near his knees. Phases of wakefulness quickly drifted into phases of unconsciousness, and the activity of his lungs was puzzling. But as each of the doctors was only able to observe one stage of the development of the illness—Lenin spoke Russian if he was being examined by a German doctor, and the Russian doctors likewise complained of a shift in concentration on the part of the patient, which made it difficult for them to locate a precise speech disorder—diagnoses were generally impossible. From the clinical point of view the case was fairly clear-cut. After a stroke one could only recommend peace and careful treatment. A few stimulants, perhaps, or a few tranquilizers, and his blood pressure would return to normal; on its own, it was not what the art of medicine would describe as a *signum mali ominis*, or a death sentence.

As Professor Bumke said, their Russian colleagues could have found all that out for themselves. But those same Russian colleagues jeopardized any possibility of fruitful intervention with their unruly garrulousness. They went over the case again and again from the beginning, voiced various doubts, considered other methods of treatment, and seemed more enthusiastic about considering alternative treatments than they were about the straightforward treatment itself. They were even inclined to joke about their own abilities. After conversations such as these, Bumke confided much later in his memoirs, the doctors had repeatedly had to ensure that medicines which they had long since decided to administer actually found their way from the pharmacy to the sickroom, and did not remain solely an object of discussion.

These events prompted the professor to make a series of profound observations on the differences between the German temperament, which he characterized as "knuckling down to it," and the Russian character, for which he proposed the phrase "heated and romantic." His colleagues found this typology "stimulating," "trenchant," or maybe "plausible at first glance." A German polar explorer, on the other hand, who happened to be staying in Moscow and whom Bumke had very quickly befriended, assured him of the absolute accuracy of his observation.

Their evening agendas were determined by the programs at the opera and the ballet. From their VIP boxes the doctors followed

Tannhäuser and *Aïda, L'Africaine* and *Lohengrin.* After that they dined again, and the next morning—which the German doctors felt began very late—there were galleries to be visited and antique shops to be explored. People familiar with the situation, however, like the English wife of Comrade Litvinov, claimed that shopping had been considerably better before, even at the time of Lenin's first stroke in May 1922. This Mrs. Litvinov appeared surprisingly often at the various social occasions and seemed to be quite a close friend of the wife of the Commissar of Health, Semashko. But she seemed much more relaxed than the other Russian ladies. "It seems to me," she had said to Professor Henschen in English during the intermission of *Aïda*, "that you are really enjoying a doctors' picnic here in Moscow." At this they had both burst into peals of laughter, but the Englishwoman had quickly put a finger to her lips beseechingly, to ensure that Henschen kept her little impertinence a secret.

Clearly she was unusually familiar with the German doctors' field of specialization. "They should have sent for Vogt," she said at one point to a very startled Strümpell. "I don't understand why Semashko left Vogt out. He has always given me the most outstanding treatment. And as far as I have understood, this is a problem of the nerves. At least Lenin struck me as very irritable over the past year." None of the German doctors had replied to this.

From the therapeutic point of view there was really little to be done. The familiar measurements of temperature, pulse, sleep, and bowel movements barely changed. A great deal of trouble was taken in the formulation of the medical bulletins drawn up once a week in the presence of Trotsky and other dignitaries. Trotsky always acquitted himself brilliantly at these sessions, on the one hand because of the excellence of his German, and on the other because of the impressive swiftness with which he had adopted the medical style of argument. The bulletins displayed a corresponding air of confidence.

After little more than a week the first doctors set off again, since conferences or patients awaited them. The mild spring weather had kept up, and the snow, in some places six feet deep, was beginning to melt. At a farewell dinner, toasts were raised to Lenin's health and the well-being of the international medical delegation. In his after-dinner speech Strümpell made erudite connections between Russian and German music. "After all, you did hear a lot of music while you were here," Mrs. Litvinov later said to Professor Henschen. "But my hearing is so bad," he had answered. It was a very emotional farewell.

There was still the matter of remuneration to be dealt with. The next morning a clean-shaven, broad-nosed commissar of finance appeared at the palace which had previously belonged to the sugar manufacturer, and asked the gentlemen to offer a suggestion as to what their fee should be. The doctors felt that their work could be appropriately rewarded by twenty-five thousand gold marks per head. The young commissar noted down this information, disappeared, and came back two hours later with the message that, in view of the high level of competence of the assembled specialists, his government considered a figure of thirty thousand gold marks to be more appropriate. He was authorized to pay this sum immediately.

Professor Henschen later remembered that his colleague Bumke had, upon receipt of the money, set off right away to buy his wife an expensive sable fur.

A minor complication arose when Professor Henschen and his son, upon leaving, had inadvertently sat in a first-class compartment of their train rather than in the Pullman reserved for them. This delayed the departure of the train by a good hour and a half.

TWENTY-SEVEN

The two women were sitting in tall chairs by the open window through which a clear, not quite full moon was shining. The heat of the day was still drifting into the room, but Cécile had put a woolen jacket around her shoulders just to be on the safe side. She got up to offer Amanda another peach from the bowl.

"I don't quite understand your motives," she said with a little sigh after she had sat down again. "But as it's clearly a wild affection this time, I must try and empathize with my heart. My intelligence would maintain that a relationship with a man ten years younger than oneself is problematic enough if you live in the same city, which can lend you support should you for any reason separate. But your plan sounds like an expedition into the unknown, for better or for worse."

"Amos's parents are Hasidic Jews," Amanda answered after a long pause. "You'll forgive me if I don't deal with your worries straightaway, but I have to tell you a story before I get into an argument. His father is a real zaddik, a *wunderrabbi*, incredibly orthodox, with a magnificent house and an enormous congregation that runs around after him like young girls after a drawing-room tenor. The house is like a royal household, but Galician style— or perhaps not, Amos's mother wears furs from Paris, and her diamonds are cut in Amsterdam, a wild mixture of the modish and the medieval. I see Amos himself as the intellectual incarnation of that combination. He would shriek if he could hear me now, because he sees himself as a renegade, the standard-bearer of the Enlightenment, the disciple of social justice. He would shriek with laughter, though, thank the Lord. I've never met anyone who can tip so suddenly from the peak of excitement into a kind of cheerful release. On every occasion, by the way—and at the beginning of our relationship it used to worry me—I thought he was weeping with joy or shame or I don't know what. But no, it was, as you, a Frenchwoman, would say: *un éclat de rire.*"

"Not hysterical, though?" asked Cécile anxiously.

"If that kind of behavior is hysterical, then the psychologists have been chasing up the wrong tree for decades. Because I can't think of anything more liberating. Other men may experience this feeling when they finally start to sneeze after taking a pinch of snuff."

Cécile laughed at the comparison. "Beware of similes involving the nose," she said, "not in my presence, of course, but if you suspect that one of the modern psychologists or, worse, one of his supporters, might be nearby."

Amanda contentedly jabbed a fork into a peach. "Shortly before my father died—I was just sixteen—he made me promise not to read *Cyrano de Bergerac* or *Tristram Shandy* before I returned from my honeymoon. He was afraid that all the talk of noses in the two books might confuse my virginal soul. That was, by the way, one of the few promises that I have been guilty of breaking."

A privet hawkmoth fluttered through the window and disappeared into the bouquet of hollyhocks on the sideboard.

"Whenever Amos and I argue," Amanda continued, "in some miraculous way we always adopt the position that *doesn't* accord with our origins. He argues strictly rationally, and I advocate faith.

If he claims that global communism is a historical necessity that can be logically deduced, and so on, I assert instead that the movement can only be successful if everybody comes to believe in miracles again. That was something I liked so much in his shtetl, the way the rabbi was supposed to be able to jump from one side of the street to the other without the slightest effort."

"Maybe they are very narrow, the streets there," said Cécile after a moment's thought.

"Sometimes he jumps to the top of mountains in a single bound, and back down again," Amanda replied. "A good rabbi laughs at the laws of space. I also thought it very decent that all these miracles went on in secret. You shouldn't be able to see miracles or the whole thing turns into a circus." She moved her chair a little closer to the window and lit a cigarette. "On the one hand, I can quite clearly understand why Amos has dedicated himself to something that promises the supernatural in the name of reason, but, on the other hand, I'm a little worried by the vulgarity of the whole business. Miracles should not be based on electricity, pylons, or transformers. Also, as I said in one of my letters, I once met Lenin. Only very briefly, but on that occasion he struck me as being humorless in a radically petit bourgeois way, a man who only wanted to fascinate men and took women's favor for granted. In my short conversation with him I made a few frivolous observations about Ludwig van Beethoven's love life. His eyes grew cold and he said: 'Intimacies are of no interest, but the *Appassionata* is sacred to me.' You see, even Lenin is in danger of succumbing to religion."

"Maybe Beethoven's all he knows," Cécile suggested. "Maybe he's insecure and sticks to the reliability of established taste."

Amanda stubbed out her cigarette. "It seemed to me that he revered musicians more highly than music, as if he saw cultural history as a quartet played by famous minds. I only hope that whatever Amos is delegated to do in Moscow is not quite so centrally important to world history. As far as I have understood, he is to investigate the revolutionary consciousness of a few troublesome nomadic tribes in Central Asia. It sounds horrid, but my father would have described it as good solid groundwork. May God grant that it goes no further than this job. I'm less worried about him having to eat nonkosher meat than I am about them keeping him on in that circus in Moscow."

"And as his wife, have you any worries there?" asked Cécile.

Amanda's eyes followed the privet hawkmoth, which had escaped into the darkness. "Well, as for the age difference, that ten-year gap, I'm not worried at all, at least not in terms of facial wrinkles, drooping breasts, or other physical disfigurations. One falls in love with a person, not a date of birth. This is just as true for Amos as it is for me, which isn't to say that this love is immune to the constraints of time. But so long as I, to use an old-fashioned phrase, can have a taste of happiness, I shall not give so much as the slightest thought to the more distant future. And I haven't even done anything about my pension plans."

"But you describe Amos as a man who holds a powerful fascination for our sex."

"That's true, and at the same time it isn't. I've been amazed by how stubbornly Amos tries to protect himself whenever he finds himself in the company of women who are undeniably seductive, either through some spell they cast, their external attributes, or some form of erotic intelligence. He always crosses his legs and quickly buttons up an already fastened waistcoat."

"Is he afraid of women?"

"I think he's more afraid for himself. One may only be seduced by God or—the same thing, of course—by a political conviction. Of course Amos would never call this form of enticement 'seduction,' it would be too close to the horror stories about impurity that were pounded into him in his religious school."

"But you, my dear Amanda, you managed to seduce him?"

"It was all much more bizarre than that, or, if you prefer, much more conventional. In Bialystok, Sir David had been offering the usual assortment of tanks, rifles, and hand grenades to a Bolshevik arms dealer, a very elegantly dressed Jew who sometimes called himself Wallach, sometimes Litvinov, and who clearly played the role of a Lucifer in the movement, which was so conspiratorial at that time. Amos was his demon. They made some kind of deal, but to Sir David's consternation the promised deliveries did not take place at the agreed-upon time. No ship arrived as planned, teams of horses or mules had suddenly taken up pacifism or something, don't ask me to go into details. Anyway, Sir David immediately set off for Trieste, where the delivery was supposed to originate. And I stayed with the children in Bialystok, as a hostage, you might say. I think it was only because I was in his power that Amos dared to talk to me seriously. You see, I wasn't a threat to him, either in my situation or, even less, in my appearance. All that traveling around had done lasting damage to my fashions and frills. And much the same could be said about my disposition. Max Landsberg once said that my life reminded him more of a loose sequence of stories than a tightly written novel. To stay with that image, my last installment simply featured too many gentlemen whose thoughts and endeavors were too exclusively devoted to annihilation. For a time I found that environment quite stimulating: such a curious mixture of secrecy and braggadocio, ivory-tower contempt and petit bourgeois sensibility. The sight of them filled me with a kind of pleasurable disgust."

"I know something about that from making my slide preparations," said Cécile. "Sometimes when I'm dissecting I happen upon a tumor, and even that malignant growth can impress me with its refinement. But let's get back to Amos. Is he, too, part of the circle that you really want to leave?"

"Amos is much more of a will-o'-the-wisp that thinks it ought to be a guiding light. Someday he'll see that himself. But I'm his wife, not his conscience. Which reminds me—will your husband come back in time for me to say adieu? I wouldn't wish to leave Berlin without having—with all due propriety—embraced him once again."

Cécile walked to the window and drew the heavy curtains. "Oskar has a meeting at the Soviet embassy. You have no idea how neglected he felt when he wasn't invited to that consultation at Lenin's bedside. His anger grew even worse when he learned of the fees that his colleagues had pocketed for doing their rounds

so quickly. He must have written a few poisonous letters to Semashko and Bechterev. And as far as I know, Bechterev was in no
way involved in the business. And this evening the Russians clearly
want to make a conciliatory gesture. I hope it's successful. As we've
lost so much money through inflation, Oskar has declared himself
willing to take part in some scurrilous projects; he promised a
military man, a former suitor of yours, by the way, to make an
elite beast out of the German shepherd. I'm exaggerating now,
but only slightly. He also tried to interest our colleagues in pigeons
that carry messages. We had a little argument about that, Oskar
was relentless and I just laughed. Then he fell in love with a circus
rider, perhaps it happened earlier but I didn't find out until then.
I wasn't jealous, but when he said that for him she embodied
genius in harmony with nature, I laughed again and said, 'But my
dear Oskar, you aren't a horse,' and he grew somewhat intransigent
once more."

Amanda lit another cigarette, but immediately stubbed it out in
the little ashtray. "On the balcony of my hotel room a pair of
pigeons were having something that might have been described
as a *grande passion*," she said. "There was too much nature in that
for my taste, but Amos couldn't tear himself away from their
displays."

"And then he started performing courtship rituals for you?"

"He saved me, however romantic that may sound, he freed me
from my dybbuk."

"A dybbuk?" asked Cécile. "Is that a man who violates women?"

"For the Jews in Galicia a dybbuk is a manifestation of the devil.
I was a little nervous because I hadn't had any news of Sir David
for days. That's probably why I spent the day smoking too many
of those Turkish cigarettes that our partners, our watchdogs as you
might say, had kindly given me. When I put the children to bed
at night, they always told me stories they'd picked up during the
day. You will notice how our roles were growing confused. The
children became particularly enamored of the son of the porter,
who was of course geared up to put a quick end to any sudden
departure. Mind you, this guard, known only as the little hammer,

was very suspicious, and so he treated the children to stories in which the torments of heaven would mingle with the joys of hell if they ever left his side. In this case they would be avenged by a dybbuk. The descriptions of this dybbuk were very impressive, even in the tales that my children would reproduce as their bedtime stories. A few hours later I would go to sleep myself, with no pills and just a drop or two of red wine, and suddenly I'm being strangled by that dybbuk. I could only have been asleep for a few minutes, I assume I had a coughing fit, and I can only remember trying, in a very Protestant way, to make the sign of the cross and babble in Latin. Then I can still remember Amos suddenly standing in front of me and taking me in his strong arms. The state of my clothes must have been such that my appearance would have made more of a sensation in heaven than in hell, but I swear the dybbuk came first, and Amos only much later."

"Perhaps it was a case of emotional incontinence?"

"My dear Cécile, if that is the psychological score to go with the plot, then fine. But I'm surprised to find myself loving a man so much that I follow him to a country and accompany him into a world where people are constantly marching and waving their caps and flags in a way that I find oppressive. That, for me, is emotional incontinence, the loss of control over one's feelings."

Amanda looked at the very unwieldy watch fastened on her wrist with a narrow velvet band. "At Silesia Station the only kind of control that matters is control over the timetable. My feelings won't be much help there." She got up to embrace Cécile. "Like the heroine in that play that we once saw together, I shall now say, 'To Moscow, to Moscow, to Moscow!' It might sound foolish, but I have never been so fond of you as now, after our conversation. If it's possible, I will send you the odd message. I ask you to be lenient about the form in which it comes."

TWENTY-EIGHT

I f Lenin had been alive to see that, he'd have turned in his grave," the little Kalmuck said. "I swear to you, on my mother's life, the chaos was indescribable. We were getting toward Gorki that same evening, the twenty-first of January, a week ago exactly, with Lenin barely four hours dead. The snow was so thick that our train had to stop about ten times. Do you know that noise when the locomotive wheels just spin? Like a saw's teeth on iron, like the screech of a heavy pig just before you stick it. The train kept trying to struggle on through. We were thrown back and forth in our compartment, the luggage, the boxes and parcels were forever leaping out of their racks. The doctors we'd been ordered to accompany were gasping for air like carp. And at one point Maxim Maximovich, the dolt, dropped the basket with the scales he'd been personally assigned to carry, which we'd fetched specially from the State Institute."

The little Kalmuck drew on his pipe. "It was cold, too, because the heating wasn't working, and your cap would have frozen to your head. Some of the comrades standing in the corridor were crying, and all they could do was shout 'Lenin is dead,' there wasn't the slightest trace of discipline left. Those comrades couldn't even hear the calls for them to come and shovel snow. It was all simply chaotic! It was amazing!"

The soldiers in the little guardroom had been listening attentively to the storyteller. They waited until he relit his pipe. "But how come Maxim Maximovich dropped a set of scales?" asked the watchman through the silence. "What do you need scales for at a funeral? Tell me that, Volodya. What do doctors want with scales if their patient's already dead?"

The little Kalmuck smiled. "They'd been summoned to Gorki to serve as engineers for Lenin's corpse. They measured and analyzed a hero, the greatest of all our heroes, cut him to bits like some uniquely high-powered apparatus."

"They weighed his corpse?"

"Everything, absolutely everything went on the scales, the stomach, the heart, the brain. They have to be able to determine the weight precisely, according to the laws of science, every organ counts, like the springs in a mighty machine. Only somebody who knows the weight can judge how much energy there was in one of those organs."

"But Maxim Maximovich dropped the parcel with the scales?"

"He dropped it, and the little pointers were bent like chicken's feet. But I got a hammer from the engine driver, and we used it to knock the pointers back into shape."

"And what else happened?"

"On the way back, the snow had been cleared. Nonetheless, we could only move ahead very slowly. People were standing along the tracks the entire way. Sometimes *on* the tracks, too, old and young, women and children. Even in the deepest snowdrifts. As we passed by, many of them dropped to their knees, made the sign of the cross, and kissed their thumbs. If Lenin had been alive to see that, he'd have turned in his grave."

"They took the corpse to the Trade Union Building in Moscow," the lady pathologist in Stockholm reported. "Obviously there were disagreements about how to proceed next. There even seem to have been furious debates about who the legal owner of the body was—his relatives, the state, or the Communist Party. Those arguments meant that the embalming work couldn't get started until irreparable decay had set in in places. By chance I witnessed the secret police—in Moscow they were always referred to as the neighbors—transporting Lenin's brain, which had been conveyed from Gorki to Moscow separately from the rest of his mortal remains. Commissar Semashko had claimed the brain for the State Brain Research Institute. On the evening of January 24, the organ was transported in an English limousine, with a patrol of nine motorcycles riding ahead, from the Trade Union Building to the Brain Research Institute. I was standing at the window of the apartment they'd assigned me when the escort drove past. Blue and red lights from the signals on the front mudguards of the motorcycles twitched across the slush in the streets. The glowworm shivered as it slid across the patches of ice. I stopped watching. I thought: another guest of state forcing the guardsmen out into the cold. It wasn't until two days later that I learned who or what had been passing by me."

"The autopsy lasted almost four and a half hours. We worked all day, without taking a break for lunch. As People's Commissar of Health I had to be there, of course. To be frank, I didn't find it all that easy. It wasn't just your average corpse lying there helplessly in front of us. To my relief, all the doctors seemed to be fully aware of the dignity the situation called for. There was hardly any discussion about the individual findings, and everybody involved signed the report without expressing the slightest deviation from the official version. I was immediately staggered by the state of the brain. I've never seen such collapsed convolutions. Both hemispheres showed unusually widespread areas of softening. The color of the brain tissue startled me, too—where it should have had a gray or a whitish sheen, it had a yellowish orange gleam like a quince. One of the doctors said, quite reasonably: 'It's amazing that such deep thoughts can go on in such a small mass.' He meant it very respectfully. I personally sealed the glass container with the brain in it. I am well aware of the treasure for which I am responsible.

"The outward appearance of the organ is really pitiful. You could never deduce the historical greatness of its owner from its condition. After serious consideration I decided to entrust the task to Oskar Vogt of Berlin. Vogt will dissect the brain into such small pieces that its appearance at the moment of death will no longer be recognizable. Furthermore, Vogt may well be the only person who can adequately identify and describe the genius that lies within these cells. After all, he always says of himself: 'I can see farther and deeper than other people.' He can use this object to prove it. In any case, it would be absolutely impossible to display the brain to the public in its present decrepit condition. Let alone in our Pantheon. I shall circulate the appropriate suggestions among the comrades. But a close eye will have to be kept on Vogt as he carries out his examination. That's a matter for the neighbors. It's basically an ironic idea: commissioning the secret service to keep an eye on a brain operation. Applied materialism, quite in line with Ilyich's sense of the term. If he was still alive, he'd have had a laugh about that."

TWENTY-NINE

I t couldn't be called a reception, or even a soirée—that would have sounded too grand and wouldn't have been in tune with the spirit of the age. But a good dozen guests had turned up at Professor Minor's cramped flat in the Tverskaya to celebrate the article that had appeared in *Pravda* that morning. Vogt was the hero, the undisputed focus of the evening, and he received everyone's compliments with the ease of a victor who is surprised only that his opponent dared to challenge him.

"In *Pravda*," the assistants, Sapir and Sarkissov, cried in chorus, "your work has been honored in *Pravda*!"

Vogt stuck his thumbs under his waistcoat with the silver stitching. "*Our* work, gentlemen," he said, then drew in his jutting chin and nodded to the throng. "I must insist, it was the work of a collective, absolutely in keeping with the ideas of the man we have had the honor of dealing with, and when I say *we*, I beg you not to forget the ladies present here this evening, who have inspired us, spurred us on, and"—in turn he looked Mrs. Sapir and Mrs.

Sarkissov in the eye—"kept alive our *joie de vivre*. I shall take the liberty of raising a glass to the health of our collective and all its happy consequences. *Na zdaroviye!*"

"*Prost!*" answered his Russian colleagues.

"An article in *Pravda*," said Idaliya Popov enthusiastically, "an article about our work on Lenin's brain isn't just any old article, it's a public, an extremely official, honor, almost a command to continue energetically onward along our chosen path of scientific research."

"Of course we are only at the beginning of our investigations," said Vogt, "but the foundations have been laid."

Somebody threw a glass into the open fireplace, where it cheerfully exploded. "He says 'at the beginning,' you hear, he says 'at the beginning'!" Assistant Sapir burst into sobs of laughter. "After over thirty thousand brain slices, immaculately preserved in paraffin, after almost two years' work, a titanic task, our Professor Vogt says: 'I'm only at the beginning!' I could kiss you." He walked up to the professor.

"Feel free, my friend," said Vogt, "but don't forget that you're kissing a man who's pushing sixty."

"I want to kiss you too," said Idaliya Popov, "and not even my husband will be able to stop me." She took Vogt's head in both her hands, tilted it slightly, and pressed her lips and her little snub nose against the German's brow. The guests applauded merrily. "You can have no idea, my dear professor, what this article means for us and our opponents. They will gnash their teeth when they read that our method, our fixed and rigid strategy, has emerged triumphant. Their poisonous slanders—that we are too old-fashioned, too costly, too unproductive—will be forced right back between their jaws. Now we shall turn the tables and accuse them of sinning against Lenin with their criticism. We shall scourge them!"

A tray of biscuits was brought from the kitchen into the living room. The silver moved through the room as swiftly as a bucket of water along a row of firemen.

"Your musical analogy struck me as excellent" said Professor

Minor, turning to Vogt. "Where you say of Lenin's thought that it must have been like a wave of notes intertwining, breaking as quickly away from one another, and then uniting once more in glorious harmony. That was so poetically put, so concrete, and so exactly in sync with the way Lenin expressed his feelings. We were familiar with his sudden changes of tempo, the staccato of his voice, and his delight in dissonances that he alone could resolve."

Vogt modestly lowered his head.

"Particularly the speed of his thought," agreed Sapir. He struck his left palm with his right fist, crying "*bystro-bystro-bystro*" with each slap of his fist. "Be off, enough, away with the enemy. You put that splendidly in your lecture. 'The speed of thought perceptions,' you said—in German, if you'll excuse me, it sounds much too slow, but I had a colleague at Göttingen University who always cried *potz Blitz* when he had ideas like that. And that's exactly how Lenin thought and acted, *potz Blitz*, always *potz Blitz*. That's the secret of his historical greatness, that's the basis of his immortality. And we can understand it in his actions and in his cerebral cortex. In every one of the thirty-one thousand slices and particularly, as you've taught us, in those incomparably beautiful pyramid cells."

"I'm the only nonscientist here," said Mrs. Sapir, "but I must admit that the words 'pyramid cells' have made a very deep impression on me. They link our Modernist aesthetic, the rigid triangle and geometrical forms, with the wisdom of Egypt."

Everyone present drank to that. The People's Commissariat of Health had supplied two cases for the party from the representation fund, and at Vogt's suggestion the German embassy had provided four cases. The cases contained Rhine wine and sparkling wine from Baden, and vodka and cognac from Georgia. Around midnight the first songs rang out. Prosector Filimonov revealed himself to be a virtuoso accordion player whose bony fingers seldom missed their appointed buttons and keys. Vogt was sitting on the gold brocade sofa, his boots keeping time against the red silk tassels. His left arm was around Mrs. Sapir's shoulder, his right around

Mrs. Sarkissov's hip, and long past midnight he sang a song whose tune was familiar to him from his student days, but whose lyrics were his own invention:

The landlady's bosoms two pyramids are,
They hang quite perpendicular—
But if you can sample their delight
You'll never enjoy a finer night.

Prosector Filimonov tried to join in on his accordion; by Vogt's third performance of the verse he had worked out the bass accompaniment. The other guests hummed along and stamped their feet.

The gentlemen arranged to meet for a steam bath the following morning.

The steam baths were very close to the Sophia Quay, and before the revolution they had been open only to high-ranking officers in Moscow on official business. As was quite proper, the baths were more of a temple than a profane facility for the cleansing of the body. This had not changed since the revolution, and neither had the baths become any less exclusive. The graceful fountains still rose as before from the marble basins; the white wooden benches had lost none of their comfortable austerity, which kept the body in a state of alert attentiveness; the temperature of the water in the tubs, adorned with turquoise mosaics, precisely suited the needs of the sweating men.

The only thing that had changed, the only thing that had deteriorated, was the system that conveyed the steam. Some silly blunder affecting the outlet valves, perhaps nothing but the well-known indifference of the staff, said some; material wear and tear and a shortage of spare parts, said others. Either way, the steam escaped irregularly, sometimes even with a dangerous lack of control. Sometimes it fogged up the whole room, sometimes the pipes emitted only thin little clouds, as if announcing the happy outcome of a papal election from faraway Rome.

When Vogt and his group came into the tub room it was filled with thick fog. This was why Vogt didn't recognize the thin man sitting upright by a plaster Aphrodite, with his bath towel wrapped around his head like a prayer shawl. This man had quickly raised a hand in greeting, and let it fall again to massage his right knee.

Sapir and Sarkissov were eager to continue the conversation from the previous night and morning.

"I may have a terrible head," said Sapir, laughing, "but thinking's like drinking, you should always pick up where you left off. So I'd like to ask: If you can still think as quickly as Lenin despite severely collapsed cerebral convolutions, might it not be the case that the secret of genius lies in speed itself? So that any kind of acceleration, in man's physical or intellectual activity, represents a further thrust of genius? In other words: If we are to turn out geniuses, if we are to breed elites, we must devote the greatest attention to the idea of speed. I'm thinking of courses in speed-calculating, speed-writing—"

"Speed-sleeping," Vogt butted in. "Some of what you're saying makes sense, but you shouldn't forget that the brain can only work at its best if it obeys the law of vital harmony. A man who is a genius as a lover, for example, must pay for his talent by forfeiting some other ability. Everything balances out. Only very rarely do we encounter a harmonic state at the highest level."

"We have a saying about that in Belorussia," said Sapir. " 'The more stupid the cock, the happier the hen.' "

Sarkissov moved the hand which supported his brow. "You used the word 'speed-sleeping' ironically, professor, and yet I should like to return to it. Some former fellow students of mine found themselves reunited at an Institute for Labor Physiology, and there they posed a revolutionary question. They take two initial states as their starting point, both of them maximum values." Sarkissov reached for his birch rod and drew a line across the steamed-up tiles on the floor, marking its endpoints with the letters A and B. "Extreme value A, according to our definition, represents sleep or death, while point B represents the state of maximum power—or, if you prefer, immortality. According to these gentlemen's thesis, then: The faster a task is completed, the more time is left to the worker, and ideally, therefore, speed tends toward immortality. On this scale, slowness, inefficiency, and sloppiness move toward sleep, and hence in the direction of death."

Vogt wiped his eyebrows, which could barely stem the drops of sweat running from his forehead. "Experience has sadly taught me that the swift completion of a task is always compensated for by the appearance of another task, and there seems to be a devilish amount of harmony in this one, too. But I'll give it some thought in the tub."

He pulled the white linen closer around his body and stood up. "If I can find my way in all this fog," he added, before setting off.

As he passed the man with the bath towel around his head, he suddenly stopped. "Captain Most," he cried, "what a small world it is indeed. What carrier pigeon has brought you here?"

Most bared his head and leapt to his feet. "Respectfully request your discretion," he said abruptly, and extended his right hand toward Vogt. With his left hand he held his loincloth in place. "Invited here with some comrades to pursue certain military operations. Everything below maneuver level, of course."

"Understood," answered Vogt, and sat down beside the captain. "But I don't really understand. We're all quite public here."

Most brought his lips close to Vogt's ear. "Versailles," he whispered. "The victorious Western powers are interpreting the agreement very restrictively as far as our further training is concerned. But to put it as briefly as possible, I have worse fears."

"Tell me," invited Vogt, and put his bath towel to his ear like a father confessor.

"I suspect a pincer movement"—Most's voice grew more excited—"wherever we appear; I was with my colleagues in Georgia when the Red Army fired off their grapeshot and brought down the republic—officially invited, of course, although very discreetly, yet we had our photographs taken wherever we went. Secretly, of course, but I noticed it nonetheless, and I'm convinced that the comrades here are passing those pictures of our visit straight into the hands of the Western allies. Pictures like that make us vulnerable to blackmail. That will intensify the pressure on our Western borders. The Russians are hugging us to their chest and leaving our back exposed to everyone else."

"You think you're being spied on?"

"Every minute of the day! And I would also advise you to exercise the greatest care. The place is crawling with informers, Party go-betweens, and neighbors, the secret service. You can generally tell these fellows immediately by the inadequacy of their knowledge as specialists and their excessively hearty manner. Once more, I should counsel you to be very much on your guard!"

Vogt slid thoughtfully into the tub.

Upon his return, he found that the group with which he had visited the bathhouse had been joined by a pink man of medium size with remarkably flat ears, whose accent identified him beyond a doubt as a Viennese.

"You will forgive me for sitting down with you," this man said to Vogt and moved along the bench to make room for the professor, "but as I passed I heard German being spoken, and I was so delighted that I simply had to discommode these gentlemen with my society. Things are pretty dull here in Moscow. And then when I heard that you were talking about my hobbyhorse, genius, there was no stopping me. Excuse me, but for years I have been wandering through the most famous portrait collections in Europe in search of a prototype of the outstanding personality. Do you know, if you don't mind my asking, the collection of Archduke Ferdinand von Tirol? It is kept in the Hofmuseum in Vienna, not all of it, of course, the collection contains no fewer than nine hundred fifty-four individual pieces." The Austrian reached for his birch rod and ran it almost tenderly along his calf. "Do you want to know what I have discovered?" The stranger looked very quickly and very triumphantly into the faces of his listeners. "There is but one type of genius, gentlemen, and it is characterized as follows: first"— the Austrian held up his thumb—"by a fair appearance, I call it the blond phenotype, second"—and here his forefinger shot up —"with a pink complexion, bright eyes, sometimes bluish and sometimes brownish according to hair color, and"—now all five fingers were held in the air—"an expressive nose. Please note that I said expressive and not hooked. But wherever these physical characteristics appear in combination, genius is indisputably present."

The stranger slapped his left thigh. "Excuse me, I should have introduced myself before. My name is Engineer Senkowitsch."

"We must get back to our work," said Vogt gruffly. "At least that's what I intend to do this minute." He reached for his towel.

"Take the Popes," continued Engineer Senkowitsch, undaunted. "Take Calixtus III and Pius II: light blue eyes, pink complexions, excuse me, all the Medici were blond, and the poets and painters. I could name Dante, I could name Petrarch or Titian, the founders of the religious orders, for example, Ignatius Loyola, all Nordic types."

"How do you claim to know what Loyola looked like?" Prosector Filimonov asked to everyone's astonishment. "His portrait was never painted, at least not in his lifetime."

"You are an expert, I can see," said the engineer. "No, in fact, no painting of the great Jesuit was ever made in his lifetime. He forbade it. We are obliged to fall back on reconstructions. But there's nothing unusual about that, art delights in veiling the truth. How often does a painter conceal the true hair color with a cap or a scarf, how often are the objects of our admiration so old that by the time the artist comes to immortalize them, he can put only an icy gray on their heads? And of course, at an advanced age it is not always easy to diagnose the characteristic facial color. I'm thinking of Molière, of Shakespeare, of Vasco da Gama. As I've said, nature, particularly beyond the middle years, is often closed to view, it conceals its traces. But of course we also have our ways of creeping up on it."

"So do we," said Sarkissov morosely. He rested his head in his hand again.

"Given that you're brain researchers—"

"Who told you that?" asked Vogt sharply.

"I only heard something about series of slices, and my ears pricked up. I had the honor of assisting the Viennese brain researcher Professor von Economo in the manufacture of some small apparatus for a number of years. I am sure you know his name. In science, everyone is somehow connected to everyone else."

A sudden spasm in the outlet pipes filled the whole bathhouse with hot, gray fog. The gentlemen began to cough.

Vogt was the first to regain control of his voice. "Then you are also an advocate of the block method?" he asked scornfully. "So von Economo sent you here to keep an eye on me?" He rose to his feet and stood with his arms akimbo. "To which I say to you, and you can report it back in Vienna as you wish: Yes, I, or others under me, sliced Lenin's brain into frontal series because that's the only way to achieve reasonable results. To carve up this noble organ into blocks, as your master tirelessly recommends—the very man who clearly wants to spy on me even here—would be nothing less than a criminal act, a crime against science. Your master prattles on about the supposed losses that would result from my method, should it be used on an irreplaceable individual specimen. You can tell him from me"—Vogt's voice grew quieter and more intense —"that my method has the support of all the very best authorities. Your lord and master simply cannot see. If you are at all capable of understanding what seeing means in our field. Your von Economo looks at blocks, we look at details. I shall give you the benefit of the doubt and assume that you have a layman's knowledge of the details of our research, and yet I should go about my work with greater peace of mind if I could feel that I had made it plain, even to your layman's intelligence, that the slice-by-slice method guarantees scientific precision, and that as far as I'm concerned, the block method of your Herr von Economo is, in contrast, a typically sloppy piece of Viennese hackwork. In the journals that exist for that purpose alone, you may stand up for it, and it will certainly contribute to the ephemeral fame of its author, but *we* are unfortunately obliged to adhere to the much stricter standards of our medical art. Blocks or fine slices—as far as I'm concerned, it's the difference between playacting and real knowledge. I have opted for the only method for which I can and must assume responsibility. You can tell that to your employer."

Engineer Senkowitsch leapt to his feet and began to stammer an apology, but he slipped on the floor, and before he could regain his balance or the loincloth that he had dropped in his terror, Vogt had already vanished. "Back to work" were the last words that Senkowitsch heard from him.

Captain Most was still sitting motionless on his bench. As Vogt walked past him, he jumped swiftly to his feet, bowed to him, and said brusquely: "I just wanted to tell you that there are provocateurs hidden even in your own ranks. I wish you the best of luck with your task." He then disappeared in the mist.

On the way back to the hotel Vogt caught himself looking out the rear window of the car a number of times, to establish whether he was being followed by another car. There were a lot of cars behind his, but none that particularly stood out.

The Brain Research Institute was on the second floor of a neo-Gothic palace at 43 Bolshaya Yakimanka. The building had been erected at the end of the nineteenth century by a rich businessman whose architect promised to help him bring the Yaroslav style into a new golden age. When the businessman saw the result—the high, pointed gables, the little towers, the columns, and the little arches—he decided to stay in his old home.

After the revolution the building was called Bogdanov House, after the doctor and philosopher whose name adorned an institute for blood transfusion research. This institute was on the first floor, and the brain of its patron one story up.

Vogt had convened a meeting that afternoon. The only matter on the agenda was the structure of his future work: detailed examinations of particular slices, broad comparisons with other brains, consequences for research policy. The colleagues had turned out in force, and two gentlemen from the ministry had arrived, along with a younger woman who introduced herself as Olga Yakovleva, a representative from the medical faculty of the university.

Vogt requested that the lights be dimmed, and showed slides taken from individual slices on the wall with the big projector. He talked briefly about a few unexpected features that needed to be explored, and tried to keep his eye on his audience throughout the lecture. He watched as Sarkissov brought a peculiarity to his colleague Sapir's attention, as the gentlemen from the ministry briefly whispered to one another, as Olga Yakovleva took notes. None of these activities was at all unusual.

After a lab technician had opened the curtains again, Vogt came to his new favorite subject, the investigation of the brains of different races. The examination of an elite brain would open up entirely new perspectives for racial research, he explained. This was the only way of settling the question of whether the "cultural backwardness of some races" should be interpreted in relation to their social milieu or to the constitution of their cogitative organs. At this point in his exposition Olga Yakovleva raised her brown eyes from her little notebook and looked attentively at the lecturer. "In this way we will also be able to establish," Vogt concluded, "which brain functions are best developed in these races. I certainly do not need to go any further into the educational consequences of the resolution of this question. The analysis of the elite brain and its genesis, however, will provide the most important basis for the selective breeding of the brain."

The members of the audience knocked courteously on their desks.

Back at his desk in the hotel suite, Vogt thought back to what it might have been that irritated him during the lecture. No, it hadn't been the auditorium. Toward the end of his discourse Sarkissov had looked rather skeptical, that was true, but ever since his last visit to Berlin, Sarkissov had looked skeptical much of the time. He probably envied Vogt his excellent relationship with the Party heads and the state apparatus. Even that was nothing unusual. On the other hand, sparks had flown from time to time between the German and the Russian over matters of detail at various stages of the work's development. They had had discussions about this. But the two scientists were in perfect agreement about the essentials of the project. Sarkissov—there could be no doubt about this—marched at his side.

Had he been distracted by the woman from the medical faculty? Vogt searched for a vague memory; he must have met her somewhere before, two or three years ago. But he had met so many people. If it really had been the same person, would she not have reminded him of that earlier encounter? Presumably she was Jewish, in her mid-thirties or thereabouts, and her red hair also looked real. The questions she had asked toward the end of the event showed a profound knowledge of the subject. She did not, however, seem particularly familiar with pyramid cells.

Vogt removed his silver cuff links. He would put on a pullover, the hotel was not properly heated. Perhaps the room only seemed particularly cold today because Vogt had already had his bags packed. He was looking forward to Berlin. This time there was even a present for Cécile: Sapir's wife had helped him buy a samovar.

The slides of the pyramid cells had been wrong! That was it! He had talked about those cells so often that he no longer looked at the projections very closely when he came to the subject. And today he had been concentrating almost entirely on his audience. But these pyramids were quite definitely taken from a series of slices other than Lenin's. From the Armenian composer Spendiarov, perhaps, whose brain his colleagues had worked on for purposes of comparative racial research, or possibly from Lenin's friend Zurupa's right hemisphere. Zurupa's brain enjoyed preferential treatment only, of course, because of that friendship. The researchers had worked on the assumption that Lenin's genius had recognized in Zurupa an intellectual affinity which had sadly remained hidden from the public.

But to the original slices and the slides that had been made of them, only he and Sarkissov had the key, a complicated affair with a double bit that Vogt wore around his neck on a thin gold chain during his visits to Moscow.

Somebody could have made a copy, of course.

But who was the somebody? Who would be interested in torpedoing the investigations at that particular point? Or was it a matter of impugning the Germans' scientific respectability? Was

there a plan to switch a few dozen slices from comparatively unimportant brains with Lenin's series so that he, Vogt, would later
make a fool of himself?

Vogt picked up a sheet of writing paper and drew a diagram of
the conspiratorial possibilities, like the branches of a chemical
compound. It could simply be a case of theft. But why? To use
the cells to prove something that had escaped him? Would Lenin's
brain be removed from the Pantheon so that the German could
later be accused of imagining things about the material entrusted
to him? Either way he would be left looking an idiot: a negligent
administrator or an academic fool. Of course switching the preparations was a relatively simple matter. They did not bear any
names and were marked only by a code consisting of letters and
numbers. Anyone at all familiar with the art of the neuropathologist
could copy this code and apply it to similar objects. Vogt himself
had not looked at some of the series for more than a year. There
were simply too many.

Vogt got up and walked to the wardrobe next to which his
suitcases stood in a line. He pulled out a medium-sized bag with
rough canvas stretched over it. It was here that he kept the comparative preparations that he had brought back from Berlin. He
would have to have a new handle put on when he got home. Too
often he had carted the wooden container back and forth between
the different sites of his scientific work. "You wear that case like
a loincloth"—that mocking remark by Assistant Sapir echoed in
his ears—"do you actually take it off when you, well . . . ?"

Vogt had laughed and answered: "If you separate me from that
case, you remove a part of my brain, and I need it whatever
happens."

In the second compartment he kept his collection of pyramid
cell specimens. Some of them were enlarged, some less so, and
Vogt affectionately stroked his collection. He drew a little brush
from a toothbrush container to wipe a few dust particles off the
slides, holding them up to the lamp on his desk.

So immersed was he in examining his preparations that he did
not notice Olga Yakovleva until her perfume reached his nose.

"I knocked several times," his visitor said. "There was still some light coming through the crack in the door, so I just came in. During your lecture this afternoon you looked at me with such sympathy that I was bold enough to seek you out without warning you in advance. I know you're traveling back to Berlin early in the morning."

Olga Yakovleva took off her coat, removed a white kid aviator's cap, and ran her right hand through her red hair. "You're not very well protected here," she remarked scornfully, "but maybe the neighborhood gentlemen have already abandoned their posts in anticipation of your departure tomorrow and are now struggling over their reports." She took a pack of cigarettes from her coat pocket. Vogt struck a match, she took his hand and drew it close to her face. "I have a confession to make, and a request," she said, and watched the smoke rise to the ceiling in lazy, milky coils. "And for reasons not unrelated to the big ears of the neighbors, I would like to discuss it with you in the bathroom." She stubbed out the cigarette and walked into the adjoining room. A few seconds later the pipes there were droning and knocking, and water was splashing into the tub.

For a while Vogt looked thoughtfully at the bathroom door, which had fallen to. Then he put his preparations in order, packed them carefully into the case, and clipped the clasp shut. By the wardrobe mirror there was a brush, and he rapidly ran it over the sides and back of his head. He gave himself a quick look in the mirror, straightened up, and went into the bathroom.

Olga Yakovleva had piled her clothes and underwear into a heap on a little stool. She had tied a turban around her head with a white towel, from which a handful of damp red curls protruded like a curious ornament of leaves. Her pubic hair also had a coppery gleam in the little waves produced by the stream of water emerging from the brass tap. Or was it Titian red? He was unable to determine the color of the hair growing under her arms, which were held out to him as he came in. Only tiny bits of stubble could be seen, against an alabaster ground. The doctor leaned against the washstand and considered the beautiful woman's body.

"You will hardly believe that I find our situation at the moment very peculiar," said Olga Yakovleva. "But I must admit, on the other hand, that it does give me a certain frisson." She lowered her arms.

"You have set up this situation, madame," said Vogt with a slight bow, "and I am curious to know your reasons."

"If you don't mind too much, I should be most pleased if you would undress as well," Olga Yakovleva shouted into the continuing din of crashing water and howling pipes. "I only like fully dressed men to look at my naked body if they're artists or gynecologists."

Vogt sat down on the metal ledge of the tub. "Perhaps you can explain what I can do for you—professionally, I mean." He brought his left hand to his forehead, which was beaded with sweat. "I must immediately confess that I am not feeling especially amorous."

Olga Yakovleva pulled the plug out with her toes. Her toenails, Vogt noticed, were also painted red. The polish, however, was already flaking at the edges. "While this din keeps up," she said, "I shall tell you quickly that you, like any decent human being, have enemies both on the right and the left. Your enemies on the left include myself—in all admiration and friendship, of course. But what you intend to do with Lenin's brain strikes us as an academic exercise that belongs in the nineteenth century. Like all constipated materialists, you haven't understood that what we have to do is shorten history. You and your colleagues have already spent several years preparing, staining, and photographing your series of slices. You have done it with a very solid, decent, and, if you will forgive me for saying so, a very German, conscientiousness. But throughout that time you have treated the brain as your own private monopoly. For you it was a fact, not a work of art. You insisted on your technique and never made room for our imagination. You reduced the brain to a biological phenomenon, it never stimulated you. But someday you too will understand that two- or three-dimensional thinking is simply a convention of the bourgeois age."

With her index and middle fingers Olga Yakovleva drew a deep

V along both of her thighs. The nails left a pale pink mark. "I'm only telling you that so you know who your loyal enemies are." Her right hand drew semicircles beneath her breasts. "But your political opponents are much more dangerous. The conservatives, who will never see why it should be a German who has the brain of our great revolutionary at his disposal. That is the faction that forced Semashko to set the neighbors on you. No matter how many conferences on German-Soviet scientific friendship you grace with your presence."

Vogt picked up the bath sponge that lay rolled up in the basin of the sink and passed it to his visitor. "I don't think my hosts here would have left me in the dark about anything that might endanger my mission. What you were just saying about a monopoly was, if you will forgive me, complete nonsense. Lenin's brain was dissected according to all the rules of medical art and photographed so that anyone could have access to this material. Even I have studied nothing but the series of photographs for the past few years. And as photographs clearly mean publicity," he continued somewhat excitedly, "I should very much like to know what we have to argue about. These photographs can be reproduced by anyone. They are, to put it in your terms, a gift to the masses. In all modesty I might add that this gift comes from a photographer whom I personally trained, and indeed whom I personally trained in the art of seeing. In the art of seeing and taking photographs."

The rim of the bathtub was pressing so painfully into his buttocks that Vogt stood up again.

"You have no need to hide from me," said Olga Yakovleva with a smile. "After all, you don't know what I want to ask of you. But it would appear that you don't want to share this bath with me. Just lie on the bed and wait for me there!"

Vogt followed her instructions and suddenly remembered his first sexual adventure as a schoolboy.

A slim hand slid through the half-closed door to the bathroom and switched off the overhead light.

Vogt heard the zipper of a bag being opened, heard the snapping of locks on cases, heard the rustle of paper.

His side of the mattress rose gently as Olga Yakovleva got into bed. He felt a tentative hand on his leg.

"I'm not allowed to tell you, but I'll tell you anyway." Olga's fingers were now playing along his spine. "The documents I've just put in your luggage are so explosive, so filled with revolutionary energy, that they can't even be compared with your discoveries about Lenin's brain. My friends and I have"—she took Vogt's right earlobe between her teeth and released it again—"we have found a mathematical formula for the waves that create and stabilize the process of thought transference."

Vogt sighed. Olga's hand had reached his scrotum.

"We have measured the brain waves of all the well-known Russian mediums, in secret, of course, and in the process we have identified distinct physical properties: Brain waves function as controllable impulses. They can be regulated like power stations. Everything is controllable."

She moved his foreskin between thumb and forefinger, as if to make sure it was genuine. "At least we can trust you with our calculations. Here in Moscow the documents are in danger, but no one will ever suspect you of having them."

Amidst all the groaning, shrieking, and squealing of the hour that followed, one sentence lodged quite firmly in Vogt's memory: "Impotence is only a figment of the male imagination." Then the light had gone on again, and a few minutes later a door had clicked shut.

After Olga Yakovleva had left him, Vogt lay in bed for a little while. In the corridor, the sound of feet approached and faded away again. Somewhere a gramophone was playing a polka a bit too slowly.

Vogt got up and set off for the bathroom to wash his hands. The only reminders of his visitor were the steamed-up mirror and the two damp towels, their edges smeared with lipstick, which she had thrown over the stool. He sniffed them, put them back down, and rubbed his forehead with eau de cologne. As he got dressed he hummed a tune.

Before he left the hotel room he felt quickly for the key chain

around his neck and took his overshoes and fur coat out of the
wardrobe. Then he picked up the case with the canvas cover. The
woman who guarded the floor of the building had laid her head
on her folded arms and was snoring loudly when Vogt walked past
her. Four chauffeurs were playing cards in the foyer. They did not
look up when Vogt passed their table. The German professor with
the case was a familiar sight.

Outside in the street the snow was not falling softly, there was
nothing flaky about it. It hammered into his face like the thin jets
of an ice-cold shower. Vogt felt good. There was strength in this
snow, and resolution. And anything that tried to stand in its way,
it coated with white camouflage. Who would be able to tell him,
Vogt, apart from the other pedestrians, searching for their paths
along the narrow roads between the frozen hills?

The entrance to the Brain Research Institute was guarded by
two old men in worn-out sheepskins. The only signs that they
were wearing uniforms were the caps that sat at an angle on their
broad heads. Vogt tapped on the glass with the frozen-blue knuckle
of a forefinger. There was no discernible reaction from the guards.

Only a few dozen steps from the porters' lodge the cabins of an
elevator rose and fell. Vogt allowed himself to be carried upward.
His study was not locked. He took the key with the double bit
from under the front of his shirt and pulled the chain over his
head. In the office the curtains were drawn so tightly that he dared
to switch on the main light. He placed the case with the canvas
cover on the desk. Then he walked to the cupboard containing
the preparations.

An hour and a half later he knew for certain. Two complete
series from Lenin's brain had been switched for series taken from
his friend's brain. Vogt excitedly turned off the light under the
microscope. One of his colleagues had to have made this switch.
Only an expert had the knowledge necessary to make this substi-
tution. But why would the perpetrator have been content to switch
only some of the preparations? Or were they simply waiting until
Vogt left before they concluded their mysterious activity?

Anyway, they hadn't taken him into account. Vogt opened his

case and took out the collection of samples from Berlin. To leave them here in Moscow would be a sacrifice, but it was one that he would have to make if he was to preserve his scientific integrity.

During the next hour he was busy writing out new labels and sticking them on. Four glass slides broke in the process, and he brushed the fragments, with the slices of brain affixed to them, into a little brown velvet bag.

When he had finished his work he stood up, stretched, and walked over to the little sink in the next room to wash his hands. He glanced into the mirror with satisfaction. Now nobody would be able to take him for a ride; as far as he was concerned, they could do what they liked with the photographs—enlarge them, reduce them, retouch them, black them out. He, at any rate, was in possession of the original.

Before walking to the light switch, Vogt cast a farewell glance at the dark, gleaming wheels and blades of the cutting machines, the neatly arranged rows of pots of tincture, the brains awaiting treatment in the jars on the shelf.

Following a new reflex, he looked around quickly when leaving the institute. The street was empty.

Before he got on the train the following morning, he kissed all his colleagues with equal warmth. He kept the canvas-covered case in his hand all the while. The rest of his luggage was already on the train. The customs officers would not bother him. After all, Vogt had a diplomatic passport.

THIRTY

Nobody knew who had started the denunciations. But everyone in the institute noticed that the slanders were spreading like powerful malignant cells. The Buch squadron of the Berlin SA had learned from an anonymous letter that Max Berger had spent several months working as a mechanic in the overtly Communist "Red Arrow" Cycling Club. Librarian Gerda Winrich received mail with Russian stamps, and then there was Gottfried Zizik, photographic assistant, who was bragging that he had been present at an attempt on the Führer's life in Munich, neglecting to mention the fact that he had been there on the instructions of his Socialist Party cell.

The professors phrased their reciprocal accusations in the academic jargon of their field of specialization: They accused one another of "unscrupulous theft of intellectual property," declared themselves "prepared at any time to acknowledge the mitigating factors contained in paragraph 51, section 2 (diminished intellectual responsibility)," and maintained—as did Vogt in his letter to the committee chairman of his institute, Gustav Krupp von Bohlen und Halbach—that their former colleague Korbinian Brodmann suffered from persecution mania and a paranoid personality, as his students in Tübingen would be able to confirm at any time.

In his reply, Krupp von Bohlen und Halbach did not deal with this accusation. By marrying Bertha Krupp he had not only taken over a business but also inherited the diverse scientific interests of his late father-in-law. This legacy included the research carried out by Vogt, whom Margarethe described as difficult, but a friend of the family who had performed certain services for them. "Difficult," Margarethe had repeated, "and to be treated with care." Krupp von Bohlen und Halbach took pains to dedicate himself to this task with the utmost tact.

The authorities that received the denunciatory letters learned that the entire Brain Research Institute, since it had moved into its new quarters two years earlier, in 1931, had been the site of Jewish-Bolshevik machinations. Vehicles with foreign license plates were constantly turning up. One night the swastika had even been taken down. Particularly repulsive, incidentally, was the behavior of some SA deputations, who accepted invitations from the institute's management to so-called informational visits at which beer and sandwiches were regularly served, while respectable Party members were offered nothing on such occasions. Clearly the intention was to divide the forces of national advancement. And if new positions were being assigned, fighters of outstanding merit from the movement were practically ignored, another disgraceful impertinence. When new posts were created, Jews had of course been given preference, supposedly because, as former front soldiers, they had a special claim to employment. In short, the whole thing was a huge mess, and not at all what people had expected from the seizure of power, no, not at all.

Menacing rumors reached the Buch district of Berlin from the center of the capital. Three Soviet agents armed with hand grenades were on their way, via Friedrichstrasse Station, to kill the new Chancellor. Count Arco-Valley had personally planned an attempt on Hitler's life, but had apparently been arrested in time.

The Communist International had smuggled in Béla Kun and Max Hölzl, with orders to shoot Adolf Hitler in broad daylight. But where had the Communists hidden their leaders, their weapons, their resources? The SS exposed plots to show off in front of the SA and the political police in Prinz Albrecht Strasse; the political police went in search of agents provocateurs to show off in front of the SA and the SS; the SA, which had just been declared an auxiliary police force by Hermann Göring, beat up suspects to show off in front of everybody. Everybody had to be vigilant at all times and places.

Erwin Kreutzer, precision engineer, and also part-time doorman at the Brain Research Institute, was drinking his evening beer in the Schlosskrug. The local SA squadron had formerly had its meetings there, and things had often gotten pretty lively. Now there were so many comrades that they had to move. Their new address was House No. 5. But in the Schlosskrug you still saw the old familiar faces, recalling joint actions from days past; and some of them would fill you in on current machinations. Sometimes one of them would even order a round of schnapps.

It was after one of these rounds that Party member Kreutzer first heard of the Comintern agent Béla Kun and secret missions in Berlin.

"Kuhn?" he asked. "A Jew, then?"

The man at his table nodded. "One hundred percent snipcock. But you never know with the Hungarian Communists: Are they called Béla or are they called Kun? Sometimes they put their surnames in front of their first names and sometimes they do it the other way round. It's all part of their disguise."

Erwin Kreutzer decided to make a note of both names. You had to be prepared for anything up at that institute. On the way back to his service apartment he repeated the name: "You are under arrest, Comrade Béla," he said as he passed Tischner's undertakers' institute. He had a pee in the hydrangeas outside the shop window. "Herr Bolla, take a seat," he cried, after he had zipped up his fly again. "Herr Mollar; there is no point in denying it," said Erwin Kreutzer, laughing, and turned into the Torweg. It was spring, and Kreutzer smelled the moisture and the promise of events to come.

Up there where the lights still burned, on the third floor of the main building, researchers forgotten by the world were endeavoring to establish a method of quality control for the material that had just been delivered. These were the brains of the sex offender Friedhelm Saugler from Butzbach, the murderess Elsbeth Schuschel from Glogau, and the robber and murderer Karl-Heinz Bollinger from Berlin-Wilmersdorf. These brains came from a single delivery and presented a few riddles. Why was Saugler's brain, according to the test results, "as soft as India rubber," and that of Schuschel "almost like a soft cheese," while Bollinger's was "as resistant as a defective soccer ball"? These descriptions were contained in the respective reports on the organs. Why were there no reliable terms for the sense of touch?

Should one not attempt to standardize the entire process of execution? One would merely have to ensure that, after the executioner's ax had fallen, not more than fifteen minutes passed before a start was made on the crucial operations. The rule would be: While the head is still warm and the skin easily movable, that's the time to act! Care also needed to be taken to ensure that the blood was properly drained from the brain. If a sloppy assistant failed to rinse the head properly, this could lead to distorting blood clots. In this context it would be a good idea to standardize the consistency and fluidity of the solvents.

Everything would simply have to be approached much more rationally, in a much more industrial way. The city of Berlin had supplied the institute with twelve thousand brains. Maybe that was only a start. Research needed to adapt to the rules of the machine age. That too was inevitable.

THIRTY-ONE

The American was driving a brand new eight-cylinder Ford, with two gray trunks strapped to the roof. The rain was incessant, and the trees along the badly paved road to Berlin-Buch loomed barren under the low-lying sky. Election posters still hung on some of the branches like dirty little aprons.

At a fork in the road the American stopped his car. He glanced at the road map that lay open beside him. In another three or four miles he should have reached Berlin-Buch, provided he was on the right road. He wiped the steamed-up side windows with a chamois cloth. In the distance he saw a team of horses slowly moving toward him. Maybe he should ask the way again. But would the locals understand his German? With difficulty, he assumed. He was practically in the country. And even then he wouldn't be able to understand their answers. The American drew a silver box from the glove compartment, lit a cigarette, released the brake, and drove on. It was early afternoon; the cheerless, milky clouds were growing darker.

Soon the first houses of Buch appeared. Little one- or two-story buildings, in clinker brick or dark plaster, with front gardens screened from the road by tall hedges. Some of these run-down buildings did reveal the pathetic glory of their facades, with little steps leading up to the front door, but far away from the road as if taking refuge from the mud that the American's Ford was splashing out of the potholes.

Vogt had sent his visitor directions. The American was carrying the letter in his wallet, but didn't take it out because he had learned it by heart and prided himself on his good memory. "At the sharp left bend, turn right into Lindenberger Weg," he muttered. "Drive a short way up the hill and you will be able to see the grounds of the institute."

The first building the American glimpsed behind a cluster of dark spruce trees reminded him of a country house in the American South; from its roof, like a massive mushroom, had sprouted a rotunda topped by an equally massive dome. It might only have been a tower to which a classically minded architect had later added on a colonnaded doorway.

The main building of the institute, on the other hand, was free of flourishes: six floors beneath a flat roof, unadorned windows with awnings that opened outward. In the third row of windows above the entrance, two of these awnings stuck out as though to protect the bust of a goddess—Athena? Minerva?—which protruded from the wall below. This woman's profile reminded the American of a famous film actress whose name escaped him.

"My name is Muller," said the American to the man in the porter's lodge. "Please tell Professor Vogt I'm here."

Erwin Kreutzer dialed the number of Vogt's outer office.

"There's a Herr Malla here to see the boss."

"The boss said could Mister Malla wait a moment, the boss'll be down in a second."

Kreutzer replaced the handset.

"Just a minute," he called through the glass, and pointed to a chair.

A little later Vogt greeted his guest. Erwin Kreutzer was given instructions to take the trunks to the guest house in a wheel-barrow.

"I'll give you a guided tour of the grounds later," said Vogt, "but let's go to my place now, tea is ready."

Kreutzer looked at the foreign vehicle. Another big fish, he thought. Gets straight through to the boss himself, of course. Well, with a machine like that. And probably another one of those Jewish skunks. Head like an egg and a big schnoz as well.

He watched the two men walk away. "All reds together," he said, and spat in a puddle. Suddenly he had an idea. Hadn't the foreigner introduced himself as Malla? What was the name of the guy they'd been talking about the day before? There was Kohn, of course, but what was that other name, wasn't it Malla? Or Bolla? Whatever, they were looking for a Jew from abroad! He would eat his hat if that wasn't him. Kreutzer ran excitedly into his porter's lodge and dialed the number of the local branch of the SA. He urgently demanded to speak to Sturmführer Saalfeld.

There was rhubarb tart for tea at the Vogts'. "The maid baked it," Cécile explained, dismissing the American's compliment. "I'm no housewife, as you can see." The lady next to her looked amused. She had been introduced to the visitor as Frau Wurm, "a tried and true patron of the institute," as Vogt remarked.

"She has left her brain to the institute," Cécile explained, "and the brains of a number of relations, like—"

"Tell us about America," Frau Wurm interrupted her hostess.

"Yes, tell us about your lecture at the recent eugenics conference in New York," said Vogt. "You must have caused a sensation."

Professor Muller leaned back. "It was only exciting for the reactionary forces of the Eugenics Society. What I said was basically the following: You can't study genetic factors without analyzing society. A gene's value or lack of value is determined by the structure of society as a whole, the economy, culture, and so on." He drank some tea. "What we eugenicists know about the individual is not enough to form a basis for political programs. That came as a great shock to the audience, because I, as a geneticist, was saying: Environment is stronger than heredity, and we should therefore concentrate on transforming socioeconomic relations. Only when we control those, will eugenics make any sense."

"Reorganization through parliamentary democratic means," suggested Frau Wurm.

Cécile Vogt dabbed at a cake crumb on her upper lip. "Then you don't set much store by the selective breeding of the human race?"

Vogt wagged a menacing forefinger. "Don't disappoint the women," he said, laughing.

Muller hesitated for a moment.

"Only in a socialist society, I believe, will we be able to encourage women to experiment with different kinds of semen of their own free will, and only then will we be able to make scientific inferences and, even later, draw practical conclusions."

"I'm all for that," cried Vogt cheerfully. "I could put up with that kind of socialism. I've been to the Soviet Union a few times, but I've never had a eugenic welcome."

Cécile Vogt and Frau Wurm exchanged glances.

"I'm not sure," Muller continued, undaunted, "whether the project can really be carried out if it relies entirely on women's free will. Perhaps a certain degree of social control is necessary from time to time—after an agreed-upon period of experimentation. Think of the development of Soviet agriculture as a model. The first step there, too, was voluntarism: The peasants were given the land to do with it what they would—and when that didn't work, when, scientifically speaking, it was observed that the experiment wasn't working, they had to be collectivized as a means of increasing efficiency. Translated into eugenic terms, that means strict social control in the selection of donor and recipient."

"But will the semen become more efficient, my dear Muller?" Vogt let out another droning laugh.

"Have you any idea what forced collectivization meant to the Russian peasants—the executions, the deportations, the hunger?" asked Frau Wurm skeptically.

"I'm a corresponding member of the Soviet Academy of Sciences" was Muller's simple answer.

"They were originally going to put a cemetery here," said Vogt, pointing with a sweeping gesture to the grounds of the institute. "We were given the land by the city of Berlin because the groundwater isn't deep enough. It would have destroyed the coffins and urns or whatever, or sent them floating to the surface. The only reminder of the original plan is the building with the dome, the chapel of rest. We hold functions there from time to time." He drew a letter from the pocket of his lab coat. "By the way, I've had an extremely curious letter from the former president of your university in Austin, who tells me in all friendliness that the gifted research scientist Muller had been under observation by the FBI because of his publication about rays. Since when have your police taken an interest in radiation experiments?"

The American looked at Vogt in bafflement. "Rays?"

Vogt nodded. " 'Sparks' means radiation in English, doesn't it?"

"Oh, no!" said Muller. "Not that stupid old business. No, *The Spark* was the name my students gave to their newspaper, after the journal *Iskra*, which Lenin published in exile. But I only distributed that paper, believe me, the whole thing's malicious slander."

The German took the younger man's arm and guided him toward the main building. "My dear Muller," he said. "I shall now tell you, in all friendliness, two things. First of all, as a scientist your presence is extremely welcome to me, particularly as an American scientist. Your geneticist friends think very highly of you. Second, if you will forgive me, I would suggest a little reticence where politics is concerned. The signs of the times, especially in Germany, are not difficult to interpret. Possibly there are some things, in the way we see the world, that unite us, possibly more than the things that divide us. I won't go into that now. But the moment calls for shrewdness and discretion. And as much as possible of both."

The American shook his hand. "You can rely on me absolutely," he said solemnly.

As they passed Erwin Kreutzer's porter's lodge, Muller asked, "Have you by chance heard any news of Gerd Fischer? He used to work here."

Vogt stopped short. "How on earth do you know him? No, he handed in his notice. Two weeks ago. The day of the Reichstag fire."

Erwin Kreutzer had distinctly heard both question and answer. He dialed Sturmführer Saalfeld's number again. Now things were quite clear.

On the night of Wednesday to Thursday, March 15 to 16, 1933, the temperature around midnight was just above freezing. A light mist had spread over the grounds of the Brain Research Institute. The storm troopers who had cordoned off the entrances were freezing in their thin uniforms.

So far not a great deal had happened. A few small squads had turned up and marched past with about half a dozen prisoners. Some of the prisoners were still protesting loudly, and others held handkerchiefs to the spots on their heads where they had been hit by truncheons. But that had been all. No news had filtered through about the discovery of a Communist treasure trove that was said to be hidden there. Nor, apparently, had they managed to catch that Hungarian Communist who was supposed to have been there in the afternoon. They could only hope that Sturmführer Saalfeld still had a few trump cards up his sleeve. It was damn cold.

"I was already fast asleep," Cécile wrote three days later to Bertha Krupp von Bohlen und Halbach. "It must have been about half past one in the morning. I didn't hear anyone ring the bell downstairs. One of our two housemaids ran down the stairs and looked out through the little window in the door. Those storm troopers were standing in the drive, she said, bellowing away: 'Open up, open up immediately!' Then Thekla, the maid, answered that she would have to ask the professor first. One of the men immediately shouted: 'Don't tell the professor! Open up, open up immediately!' But Thekla ran straight into my room and woke me and our daughter, Marthe.

"I got up, went into the next room, and shook Oskar awake. In the meantime Marthe asked the people at the door what they wanted and who they were. But all they did was shout, 'Open up!' Then Marthe switched off the indoor light in our hall and put on the light outside. From the window of my bedroom I saw more than ten men with guns and cudgels. It was a very frightening sight. Oskar called the police right away. But that was pointless, because the policemen who did later turn up couldn't get past the storm troopers.

"A few minutes later we heard a loud clatter coming from the ground floor. The men had smashed in one of the big panes of glass with their truncheons. Then they pushed their way into all the rooms, even the cellar, and rooted around and stole things. We were standing in Oskar's bedroom when they came upstairs. Oskar was wearing only a thin pair of pajamas. They came to the door and my husband placed himself in front of us women. The ringleader was holding a pistol. He asked: 'Where have you hidden Herr Bella from Prague?' Oskar answered that he didn't know any Herr Bella, and if he was staying in the house it was without Oskar's knowledge or consent. Then he asked the man to lower his pistol. He didn't listen, though.

"We were supposed to have had dinner with this Bella person, whoever he might be. Oskar gave his word of honor that he knew nothing of any such person, and said we had witnesses. I was in a terrible state or else I might have laughed when my husband solemnly declared, 'I offer you the testimonies of five adult women.' But the ringleader was rather impressed, at least he seemed to be, although his next question sounded utterly absurd. He wanted Oskar to show him an underground passage from our residence to the crematorium where we were supposed to have hidden our Communist valuables. Of course the passage and the treasures didn't exist, as Oskar said at once. Then the leader roared: 'You are under arrest. Come with us!'

"I begged the men to let him get dressed first and take me with him. They just shrugged. But Oskar was allowed to get dressed, although they kept their eyes on him the whole time. Suddenly a fat little man with a red face came running into our bedroom and whispered something into the leader's left ear. The leader—and to this very day we don't know his name—the leader's mouth opened like a nutcracker's when you hit it on the head. He said, 'Bella has fallen into my people's net. You are free for the time being.'

"Then Oskar started protesting loudly and threatening severe consequences. The men left very quickly. In the hall another of their comrades was sitting on the sofa eating from a can of Oskar's favorite sardines. He had obviously stolen them from the cellar. This in particular made Oskar furious again. Then he went into his office to see if they'd stolen anything from there as well. I joked about it when he came back. What treasure had the storm troopers been hoping to find among the brains? Oskar said I didn't know the first thing about it, then we had another hot chocolate and went to bed . . ."

Hermann Joseph Muller was taken from his car and arrested when he stopped in front of the row of storm troopers. The description Erwin Kreutzer had given was unmistakable. When Muller explained that he had been born not in Prague or Budapest, but in New York, on December 21, 1890, and was thus quite unarguably a citizen of the United States, a uniformed man hit him in the face, laughed, and said, "Tonight we'll believe anything." His comrades joined in the laughter. They handcuffed the American and brought him to House No. 5. He was kept under guard there for an hour and a half. In the meantime a motorcycle dispatch rider drove to the headquarters of the East Berlin SA, where there was a party member on duty who knew how to read foreign passports. Sturmführer Saalfeld wanted to be completely sure.

His subordinates followed suit. In the guardroom they forced Muller to undress and show them his genitals. Then he had to turn around, kneel, and crawl along the tiled floor. "Hop, rabbit, hop!" yelled the storm troopers. All in all it promised to be a fun evening.

All the more sobering, then, was the news with which the dispatch rider returned. For one thing, headquarters had no concrete information to suggest that the Communist Béla Kun had entered Germany, and for another, this American's passport was indubitably authentic. At least on first examination.

Muller had to be set free again. Sturmführer Saalfeld declared the evening's operation over.

THIRTY-TWO

Bureaucratic reaction to the night's events was conscientious in the extreme. In the offices of the city commissioner, Dr. Klein, in Berlin's main Public Health Department, a file was immediately opened concerning the situation in Buch, and others were opened in the Ministry of the Interior, the Ministry of Education and the Arts, Police Headquarters, the National Socialist Party district offices, the Buch-Karow branch of the SA, the headquarters of the Kaiser Wilhelm Society, and the office of committee chairman Gustav Krupp von Bohlen und Halbach. Letters quoting from provisional and definitive records, memoranda, minutes, and circulars were drawn up, dispatched, noted, embellished with little marginal notes, and initialed. The Brain Research Institute had become the subject of an inquiry. But what had it all really been about? What had provoked this spectacular deployment of storm troopers? It couldn't have been the handful of Jews that Vogt employed in his institute. Other institutes were much worse in that respect. Or registered Communists. Indeed, Vogt had had that fellow Fischer, who was clearly an activist, but overall, the numbers weren't enormous. Presumably he'd taken off—no matter, one less for the new order to worry about. And what about the other malicious slander circulating at the institute? Nothing out of the ordinary, unfortunately. And that was precisely the problem with denunciations. If well directed, they were capable of moving mountains, sinking warships, but as a general form of communication they threatened, if they came into fashion, to clog the entire apparatus very quickly. If everybody was denouncing everybody else, each piece of information would be devalued as quickly as a bank note during the worst period of inflation.

Perhaps the SA knew something that they didn't want to tell anybody at this point. Perhaps the SA only wanted to stay in control of the whole business and were feeding the relevant authorities information that they could do nothing but play with at the moment. Like a cat teaching its kittens to play with dead mice. And as no one dared to predict whether the SA was the real power in the new national movement, it was important that caution should prevail for the time being, whatever the circumstances. Caution and conscientiousness.

The Buch-Karow section of the SA waited more than three months before striking again. Action had been announced against the ultranationalist German youth movements, but there wasn't a single one in Buch. So Saalfeld launched another hunt for the "Communist treasure." If that Gerd Fischer had not taken the treasure with him—and how could an individual fugitive take anything of any size?—the loot must still be on the grounds of the institute. A number of anonymous tips prompted the suspicion that the dome, the chapel of rest, the crematorium, the hall, whatever it was called, had been used as a hiding place. "A red chapel," said Saalfeld to Party Member Schluppvogt. "That'll open their eyes. Because this time everybody'll be able to see us!"

So just after nine o'clock on the morning of June 21, the twelve storm troopers made their way up Lindenberger Weg. "Come rain or snow, on us the sun will smile," they sang, their backs rigid and their arms swinging back and forth in the required manner. Today the sun was smiling, gleaming off their belt buckles and flashing across the cobblestones.

At the entrance to the institute the group leader silenced the singing. The men ran crashing up a flight of stairs to the office of Petz, the accountant.

The ringleader tore the door open. "Heil Hitler!" he yelled curtly, and extended his forearm in the Hitler salute.

"Heil Hitler," answered the terrified accountant.

"We have received a report that you are in correspondence with the Communist Gerd Fischer. There's no point in denying it. You will now tell us where the swine is hiding."

Petz raised both hands in a defensive gesture. "But I don't know where Herr Fischer is now. You have my word of honor. As a front-line soldier. After Herr Fischer's contract had expired, at the end of March, I sent his final wage packet to his sister, Ruth Fischer, in accordance with regulations. That is what Herr Fischer had demanded in writing. I can show you the documents."

Petz walked to the rolltop desk and produced a file from the bottom drawer. He licked the tip of his right forefinger in a businesslike manner, and then began to flick through the pages hectically. "Here, you see, everything carried out according to regulations."

The group leader ripped the file from his hand: a letter on the institute's writing paper, Fischer's sister's bank account reference, yours sincerely—no room for loopholes.

The storm troopers left the office in silence. They would now go straight to the chapel. Animal keeper Schopf, it had been established, kept the keys in question. Animal keeper Schopf would hand over the keys without resistance, they would make sure of that.

The search went on for more than two hours. The men broke a few chairs and tapped at the columns with the legs. They found a ladder, climbed into the dome, and shone their flashlights into the corners of the supporting beams. They tapped the floor at six-inch intervals and listened excitedly for a hollow sound. Finally

they descended into the foul-smelling mains of the state waterworks. Everything sounded hollow there. But of a secret storeroom,
a hiding place, let alone treasures, there was not a trace.

The mood among the men was sinking. Their uniforms were
filthy, and some of the comrades had skinned their knees when
their flashlights had failed. In their fury, they pissed into the mains
of the state waterworks.

Clearly only tested methods worked. Two days later animal
keeper Schopf filed the following report:

. . . some hours later I was ordered to House No. 5 for questioning. I complied without resistance. We were led into the
big meeting room in House No. 5, where we first of all sat
down on some chairs. As we entered the room we were forced
to shout "Heil Hitler." After some time, some storm troopers
with brooms, scrubbing brushes, and rags came in and ordered
us to sweep out and wash down the corridor and the room.
We did not contradict this order, but we did not comply immediately. When the order came a second time, the storm
troopers adopted a threatening attitude and ordered us, under
threat of violence, to pick up the brooms, sweep up, and scour.
I kicked aside the broom at my feet and remarked that I had
been called here for questioning, not to wash down the room.
Shortly before this, a storm trooper grabbed another prisoner
by the throat and ordered him to wash down the room. This
action strengthened my reluctance to carry out the task demanded of me, whereupon a storm trooper whom I did not
know, small and stocky in build, boxed me on the ear. I was
so shocked and surprised that I immediately replied with a
slap of my own. At this point some eight storm troopers fell
upon me, tried to throw me to the floor, and beat me with
belts, buckles, riding whips, and brooms, and a storm trooper
hit me twice on the head with a broom. The second time I
managed to grab the broom away from him. A storm trooper
drew his pistol—apparently, since I was defending myself, to
put me out of action. After beating me for quite a while, they

finally left me alone. But then another storm trooper—unversed in the German language, and with what sounded like a Polish accent—came up to me and gave me two right hooks to the chin, which I did not return, instead telling him to leave me alone. He demanded that I put down my hands, to which I replied that I was only using my hands to protect myself and would put them down if he stopped hitting me. I then, as ordered, fetched two buckets of water and received another two blows to the head from parties unknown, once apparently with the butt of a rifle, the second time with a thick-handled riding whip. A storm trooper followed me and kept treading on my heels. After I had wiped away the blood, I took the rag and washed down the big corridor and the big meeting room of House No. 5, first with my hands and then with the scrubbing brush. Then we were transported to Pankov. We had to divide up into two sections and spend a few hours doing "left turn, right turn, about-face." All the storm troopers watched us to see if we were really singing along. At the end we had to sign a declaration containing the following phrase: "I have been decently treated," which, under the circumstances, we did only under duress. Then each of us stepped forward in turn to receive a cup of coffee and a slice of bread and jam. This was my first meal since the previous evening. After this we had to stand in the courtyard for a few hours, until we were finally sent home.

Today, one day later, my head has swelled up considerably, as have my tongue, my upper jaw, and the roof of my mouth; I feel great fatigue as well as pain in the right armpit, so that I have been obliged to leave my work again and take to my bed. Because of the way I have been treated, which is very hurtful to me as a former front-line soldier, I have also fallen into a severe depression.

After returning home, animal keeper Schopf was examined by Dr. Helmchen, the institute's doctor. He was immediately struck by the "rather blue and red coloration" of the face. Dr. Helmchen observed:

> I noted slight swellings of the soft parts in the region of the right knee, as well as a saucer-sized lump in the region of the rear of the head. When the patient was asked how he felt, he mentioned general exhaustion, said that he could not swallow properly and that he felt a severe pain in the region of the upper thorax when he raised his right arm . . . When the patient asked why he could not eat very well, I found no particular symptoms apart from a slight swelling in the region of the gums of his lower right jaw and a sensitivity to pressure in the corner of the right jaw. Herr Schopf could eat semisolid food (carrots), and he could also walk and stand.

THIRTY-THREE

The police inspector had called Vogt in for questioning at 3:30 p.m. in Room 304. When the doctor was permitted to enter, he found the bald little man sitting at a desk thickly covered with files. The inspector's fists were pressed to his temples, and he was breathing heavily. He looked up and pointed to a chair.

"You're a doctor, aren't you?" he said after a short pause. "Could you recommend something for my headaches?"

Vogt looked at him in surprise.

"I've been working without a break since four o'clock this morning," the inspector complained, "and my head is spinning with all this questioning." He rubbed his red-rimmed eyes. "You, as a doctor, will understand that. That's nearly twelve hours already and it's been like this for weeks."

When Vogt leaned forward, the chair he had just sat down on creaked. The inspector gave a start and clapped his hands over his ears.

"Please avoid any kind of movement," he said in a tormented

voice, "and let's get down to the reason for our interrogation. The president of your society has put in a request for it, with the aim of protecting you and your institute against any further actions on the part of the SA by clearing up any grievances that we might have against you, have I understood correctly?"

Vogt nodded.

"Then let's bring in the stenographer." The inspector sighed and pressed a button. "What I need is a remedy for headaches that strengthens the nerves at the same time," he said while they waited for the stenographer.

An hour later the hearing was concluded. Vogt had put on record that he had harbored neither Béla Kun nor any other Communist agent, that Frau Litvinov visited him for purely medical reasons, and that no Communist treasures were hidden on the grounds of the institute. He had forcefully contested the notion that his wife had made disparaging remarks about Frederick the Great, and that he was involved in a relationship with an employee who had not yet delivered proof of her Aryan status. These were familiar accusations, which made the work go faster and easier. Nevertheless, the inspector's yawns grew increasingly violent.

Vogt stood up to take his leave. "I should only like to point out that I've been rather surprised by the delay in your response," he said coolly, "given that more than six months have passed since the last of these events."

The inspector yawned again. "The precise length of time that your file was missing," he growled. "We are all under strain here." He stood up to offer Vogt his hand. "You've examined Lenin's cranium, so surely you can come up with something for a German policeman's head." He took a few heavy steps and opened the door for his guest.

It could not have been said that Cécile had left him in the lurch. It was simply that she wasn't there now, when he so desperately needed her. As if there was nothing more important going on in the world than some conference in Copenhagen. He too would rather have been a long ways away from here. Not Copenhagen, he would have preferred Stockholm. Those had been great nights, back then, with his colleague's wife. But he had to hold the fort. He always had to hold the fort. He could have been experiencing all kinds of things in Stockholm!

Vogt stepped back from the window and switched on the desk lamp. He took his notebook out of the pocket of his lab coat and flicked through it until he found a blank page. At the top he wrote his name, the place, and the date, thought for a moment, and then added:

In the conviction that my wish will be fulfilled, I request that the slices of Frau Signe Henschen's brain be stored next to the slices of my own brain.

Beneath these lines he wrote his name again. When the ink had dried he tore out the sheet, put it in an envelope, and locked the message in the safe.

"Ashes to ashes," said Cécile, who opened the letter upon her return.

THIRTY-FOUR

The debates within the institute continued. The scientific vision, creativity, and curiosity that should have been focused on investigating the potential of the brain were instead being devoted to uncovering plots, establishing networks, following up suspicious clues. Who had been seen with whom? Who took his letters to the mailbox in person? Who made calls from public telephone booths? There was hardly any time left over for research. What mattered was survival, professional and political. What mattered was respect and honor.

In the kitchen of their service apartment, Dr. Kornmüller read to his wife a letter to Professor Egon Fischer which he had composed that afternoon. The letter was written in a visibly cramped hand, some passages were crossed out and others completed in the margin. Nonetheless, Dr. Kornmüller read very fluently:

> . . . at that time I felt obliged by our common Party membership to enter into a discussion with you under the chair-

manship of Sturmführer Saalfeld. This discussion clarified and resolved all the questions that remained between us. You have confirmed this in repeated assurances and we have shaken hands on it a number of times. I have visited you whenever any unclarities have arisen between us. Although you have been kind to my face, you have turned others against me. Your wife has said the most outrageous and mendacious things about me to Party Member Erna Weigelt and others. You and your wife have therefore most grievously infringed the agreements we made at that time, and for this reason they are herewith revoked and rendered invalid.

Please find enclosed the returned declaration of my honor in this matter. Heil Hitler!

Frau Kornmüller thought the letter was very accomplished. Her husband signed it.

It was going to be impossible to keep Vogt on as director of the institute. The general administration of the Kaiser Wilhelm Society saw this more and more clearly. Regardless of whether the officially voiced accusations were true or not. The man had simply ceased to show any leadership qualities. His colleagues walked all over him. That would have to be made plain to the chairman of the institute committee, Gustav Krupp von Bohlen und Halbach, who seemed to have a peculiar weakness for the professor. But that was his own private affair. The largest Kaiser Wilhelm Institute in Berlin could not give the impression that German scientists did not understand the signs of the times. These signs clearly pointed toward discipline and unity. Anyone who did not wish to respect them, or who was incapable of doing so, would simply have to go.

Drastic measures were under way at this very moment. Max Planck, the president of the Kaiser Wilhelm Society, had given instructions that the Civil Service Act, excluding Jews and former members of socialist organizations from administrative posts, should be painstakingly applied to all members of the society. There had been problems with this policy in the smaller institutes.

In the general administration, in Berlin Castle, petitions were pil-
ing up from directors who, either out of narrow-mindedness or
sentimental altruism, refused to see why they should fire drivers
and secretaries, storekeepers and cleaning ladies, just because they
had once—three, five, ten years earlier—been active in "Red
Relief," the Fichte Workers' Gymnastics Club, the Social Democratic Party, or the Communist Party. In the face of the battle
being fought out on the work front as ordained by the Führer, one
such grumbler from the circle of institutional directors wrote, he
found himself obliged to refuse to undertake the dismissals ordered
by the general administration. That was very much in the old spirit,
but it could be dealt with.

Vogt was sure to cause trouble as well. Or else he would simply
be incapable of giving the Communists and non-Aryans in his
institute the appropriate notification within the requisite period.
As late as August he had interceded on behalf of a woman who
was one-quarter Jewish, a librarian, on whose fate the welfare of
the institute really could not afford to depend. But that was Vogt
all over. Nothing but trouble for the authorities. And at this delicate
point in history.

The loss in scientific terms could also be kept within bounds if
Oskar Vogt was dropped. What had his research into genius produced, in the end? The fact that Lenin had been "a cerebral
athlete, an associational giant." He had published this nonsense
using these very words. Imagine: This man was the director of a
Kaiser Wilhelm Institute, and that was the fruit of his research.
The German taxpayer was footing the bill for the examination of
a Bolshevik's brain. It was only to be hoped that the whole affair
would be dead and buried in the very near future.

Frick, the Minister of the Interior, was said to have taken him
under his wing, a department head had recently said over coffee.
Frick was a clever devil, not somebody to mess with. Presumably
he was sticking up for Vogt because he had once treated a member
of Frick's family. But Frick wasn't important in the end, because
at some point the whole field of research would be put under the
control of the Ministry of Education and the Arts.

Of course Vogt had announced that in the future he would be paying more attention to the racial question in his research. But that was one of those typical academic promises. Max Planck had already reached quite a different decision on that particular matter. Vogt would have been amazed if he saw the letter from Planck containing the crucial sentence:

> I should like most humbly to request the honor of telling the Reich Minister of the Interior that the Kaiser Wilhelm Society is willing, in the furtherance of the sciences, to place itself systematically at the service of the Reich as regards research into racial hygiene.

This sentence clearly referred not to the Brain Research Institute, but to the Anthropological Institute. A different attitude prevailed there. No, Vogt had really become superfluous. It was to be hoped that the rumor to the effect that Krupp von Bohlen und Halbach planned to set up an independent institute for him in the Black Forest was true. He would be able to continue his research into genius there; he would be able to take his slide preparations with him, or some of them at least. Who could take the slightest interest in that dusty old stuff now that the Führer had turned his whole people into a nation of geniuses?

THIRTY - FIVE

The movers rang the doorbell at six o'clock in the morning, and began carrying the carefully marked boxes out of the house. They interrupted their work for half an hour at around midday, and then resumed stacking cardboard box on top of cardboard box, putting blankets between pieces of furniture, wrapping newspaper around crockery. It was after nine by the time they cleared away the beer bottles they had emptied during the course of the day. Now all that remained was to sweep up.

A week earlier, Vogt had had little metal plates nailed under the soles of his shoes. With every step he took through the empty rooms his heels clicked like toy frogs. One of the movers followed him. To this man's question as to whether the case with the canvas cover that the professor was holding should be put with the other items for removal, Vogt merely shook his head. "Then we'll see each other again in the Black Forest," called the mover and touched his cap.

When the moving van turned into the Lindenberger Weg it had

to maneuver past a limousine in which a couple sat smoking cigarettes. The side windows of the car were steamed up. The woman
wiped the damp surface with a glove. "Look, that must be the
boss's things being taken away," she said, then rolled down the
window and threw her glowing cigarette butt into the gutter. The
man kissed her and laughed. "Lenin's brain setting off on its travels
again." Giving the ignition button a violent push, he turned on
the engine.

THIRTY-SIX

The air here was just as agreeable as it was in Berlin-Buch. Fresher and healthier, even. And as long as the mail and the telephones worked smoothly, it made absolutely no difference where in the world one pursued one's research. What was of prime importance was that one's brain should continue to work at all times. He had, in fact, corresponded with Krupp von Bohlen und Halbach on this subject: "Activity delays the aging process," was the main thrust of his letter. Quite a number of different authorities might have been interested in this thesis. The Reich Labor Front, for example, which had been insisting since the beginning of the war that individual daily quotas be forced upward. The idea, of course, could not simply be promulgated, that would be a waste—it would have to be tested out on greater and more diverse material than was currently available. And that would require funds, slide preparations, and staff; with the appropriate support from Krupp, the Labor Front would certainly understand that.

It was also important to pursue new, progressive strategies. Chemicals could be used to prevent premature aging, such as that caused by hereditary diseases, for example. Premature aging—this much was certain—meant a disturbance in hormonal harmony, in layman's terms, the absence of specific active substances that influenced the normal formation and maintenance of certain fundamental organs. These active ingredients would have to be produced artificially. That would certainly open up an exciting new area for the chemical industry. The institute in the Black Forest would send out signals that would keep experts around the world on tenterhooks.

Knowing those chemists, though, it would take them years to complete their analyses. They would raise objections and refute them again, they would propose whole series of tests and counter-tests and control experiments. It would presumably be easier, less expensive, and less time-consuming to obtain the active substances for the fundamental organs by flushing them out of healthy organs. Time was too precious a commodity, especially now, in wartime. He would talk to Cécile about it and then send Krupp a letter on the subject.

"I only wondered if I might ask you very cordially for the stamps, professor," said the old mailman. "That is, if you're not a collector yourself. I have very few from the colonies." Vogt looked at the letter that Amanda von Alvensleben had sent from Saigon. It had been forwarded from Berlin to Neustadt. "Since we've had the institute down here, we've been seeing stamps I've never set eyes on before. We've gone cosmopolitan. That's something to be proud of." He undid the string around another pile of letters. "And I wanted to ask you something, professor. Is it true what they're saying in the pub, that you're holding on to the brain of that Lenin fellow?" He looked expectantly into the professor's eyes.

Vogt glared at him coldly. "Lenin's brain is in Moscow," he answered abruptly.

"The things people say"—the mailman turned to go—"as if they got paid for it."

"Over the past few years," Amanda had confided to a sheet of rice paper, "I have always fared best with imaginary careers. So I like to think that Amos has found nothing but shamans in Siberia, who preserved his faith in miracles and dissuaded him from any kind of postal contact. In this way I can deal with the fact that I haven't heard from him for almost four years. And he turns up very regularly in my dreams. If you were to conclude from this that I have turned toward mysticism here in my Asiatic surroundings, you would not be completely mistaken. The religious reasons for this are lamentably few; it has solely to do with practical considerations— only in an Eastern culture can a woman like myself grow old gracefully. Discipline, conventional behavior, and abstemiousness are virtues demanded of the young. I, on the other hand, can spend all day sitting in my vest on the veranda directly overlooking the street, smoking Manila cigars, without violating any rules of respectability. I'm old, after all, and can set my own standards.

"You will notice that I've been presenting the aging process in an entirely positive light. There's more to this than the desire to ignore the laws of biology. For the first time in my life I'm enjoying a certain economic independence, which, if you like, is entirely the result of aging: I have taken over an antique shop. And I can't get enough of old age. Add mysticism to all that and you have the twin pillars of my existence. They also shield me against homesickness during those months when the newspaper reports about Europe do not render the idea of returning impossible."

"No problems whatsoever," the former assistant said over tea. "I changed trains in Freiburg, all the trains are on time as usual. Even down here in the south. But down here you wouldn't notice the war at all."

"You're in the southwest," Vogt corrected him curtly.

"Excuse me," said the assistant, "of course, the southwest." He took a careful bite of an almond cookie and put it on his saucer. "On the train I remembered one of your old exercises. Do you remember introducing us to the art of self-hypnosis? You called it the state of partially waking sleep. One put oneself into a dozy state and at the same time registered the instruction to wake up at an external signal; we often practiced it on train journeys, forcing ourselves to go to sleep and then wake up one stop before our destination. For me, only the going-to-sleep part worked."

Vogt laughed. "A partial success, at least. But tell me about Berlin. What new scandals have there been at the institute? Who's conspiring against whom, and who's stumbled into what traps? What amorous intrigues are rousing people's passions?"

The assistant carefully put his teacup down. "Since I've been working in the Charité I've only had very tenuous contacts with your former colleagues. But six weeks ago I found a letter on my boss's table, and your name leapt out at me. Of course it was an unforgivable indiscretion to read it."

The assistant lowered his eyes in mock shame.

"And what did it say?"

The assistant opened a slim leather folder. "After I had committed the first breach of trust, my criminal energy seemed to know no bounds. I took the letter and copied it out by hand. Later I typed it up." He took a sheet of paper from the folder and handed it to Vogt. "What I didn't transcribe was the letterhead of your former institute. The sender, as you will see at the bottom, was your colleague Kornmüller."

Vogt adjusted his glasses and read:

Dear Professor de Crinis,

As we can now count on the taking of Moscow, I should like to remind you of the following:

The Moscow Brain Institute contains the complete series of slices of Lenin's brain. Do you not think it would be a good idea for you, professor, to ensure that this material should immediately be seized on your behalf in the event of the taking of Moscow? As M. Bielschowsky once told me, Lenin had a syphilitic brain disease—it would be useful to know if he was correct from a propagandistic point of view at least. In addition, one half of the brain is already supposed to be quite defective macroscopically. As far as I know, not a single slice could be taken from it, and even Vogt doesn't have an original slide preparation.

The Moscow Brain Institute is at 48 Bolshaya Yakimanka.
The head of the institute, to my knowledge, is Dr. Sarkissov.
Heil Hitler!
[signed] Dr. A. E. Kornmüller

Vogt folded the letter in half. He looked without expression into the distance for a while. "The address is wrong," he said suddenly. "It was 43 Bolshaya Yakimanka, not 48. And as far as I know, the institute hasn't moved in the interim."

"But otherwise it's true what it says in the letter? Was Lenin really, as Bielschowsky said, a syphilitic?"

Vogt shrugged. "I stand by the statements that I made at the time. The pyramid cells had spread significantly. That was why this brain was so important."

The assistant nodded. "But you never described the precise location of those cells. Could you be specific for me now?"

"The cells were widespread everywhere you looked."

"I see," said the assistant.

After dinner the assistant returned to Kornmüller's letter. "Still, it's a good thing you don't have any original slide preparations of it," he said, laughing, after the port had been poured. "Professor de Crinis immediately alerted Commissioner Rosenberg's headquarters. Since then, goes the joke, their heads have been filled with Lenin's brain. Rosenberg is already said to have sent appropriate instructions to General von Bock. The taking of Moscow could only be in a matter of days. A brain as booty sounds a bit like a crusade, don't you think? Or the story of the Holy Grail." The assistant stood up. "I much prefer port, especially yours. And as you don't have any original slide preparations, you can go on with your research in peace and quiet. Even if—and our stalwart Wehrmacht rules this out—the Russians suddenly went in search of you."

Vogt seemed lost in thought. Then he yawned and said, "Quite right, you're quite right!"

The assistant bowed before reaching for the door handle.

THIRTY-SEVEN

Vogt was alone in the compartment as far as Frankfurt. He rested his right arm on the case with the canvas cover. Various conductors had offered to stow it in the luggage rack, but on every occasion the professor had brusquely declined. From time to time he glanced up from a magazine and looked out the rain-drenched window. Just before Mannheim the train was shunted into a siding to let a military train through. Vogt automatically started counting the tanks and guns, but then he became distracted again and picked up a pencil to mark a passage in the magazine which had attracted his attention.

It was cold in the compartment. Vogt had turned up the collar of his coat, like the figure in the little picture on the wall who warned, in gothic script: "Careless talk costs lives!"

He had to change trains at Frankfurt. An adenoidal voice over the loudspeaker croaked that the Berlin train had been delayed by twelve minutes and was leaving from another platform. Vogt bought a couple of steamed sausages from a stand and quickly ate them standing up, without putting his case down. The voice over the loudspeaker announced a further delay. A little boy held up to him a newspaper announcing the Japanese attack on Pearl Harbor. Vogt suddenly felt very tired. Finally he found a bench on which five soldiers squeezed together like a concertina to make room for the professor.

He also held the case close to him on the journey to Berlin. He had to keep it on his lap, however, because so many people had forced themselves onto the train that all the seats were now taken. In the corridors, ill-tempered conductors cursed as they pushed their way laboriously to the front. None of them offered to take the case away from him, but the luggage racks were full up to the ceiling of the carriage anyway. The train smelled of damp clothes and cheap tobacco. Shortly after Kassel, Vogt fell asleep.

A new conductor shook him awake. Vogt felt a clawlike grip on his right shoulder, and opened his eyes; at first all he could see was the empty sleeve of a blue uniform flapping uselessly.

"Ticket," said a voice with a severe north German accent.

He had to jot down this dream. It had been remarkably colorful. The swastikas flying in front of the institute were blood-red, and Stalin's uniform had a silvery gleam like the light of a setting sun over a marsh lake. "I will teach you my strategy of brain research." Had Stalin spoken German or Russian? Either way, two eggs had then been broken into a glowing iron pan. "Look at the yolks," cried Stalin. "That's how we spot syphilitics. And it's also how we eliminate them." He, Vogt, then jumped back because hot splashes of fat had hit him on the thigh. The landlady of the Post Inn in Neustadt wrapped a grass-green apron around his genitals. He protested because it was an apron from the operating room. "The stains won't be coming from inside," said the landlady, laughing while she unbuttoned her blouse. "At your age all you spurt is hot air." And then Stalin walked into the landlady's bedroom. The tip of Vogt's tongue was on its way up her left nipple. "You're transporting Lenin without a ticket," Stalin shrieked. "You're sending a brain to me in Moscow without a ticket! But I'll refuse delivery. They'll take the brain back. Incredible—no ticket!"